REALM OF SMOKE

THEA ATKINSON

CHAPTER 1

The night my parents died, I was getting high. Our house, a small bungalow with three bedrooms and a veranda stretching the length of the front with white rattan chairs and tables aching to be laid out with pitchers of lemonade and tea cakes, also had a screen door that didn't so much as squeak if you opened it.

That door was my ticket out of the house without getting noticed. I pulled on a hooded sweatshirt so I could cover my hair and veil my face. Like any teen stealing out into the night after hours, I shoved on my running shoes once I got out onto that veranda well past ten pm. The only difference between me and most teens doing the same thing, was that I knew my parents wouldn't hear a thing.

I was fifteen. I had a crush on a boy two years older than me, and it was so ridiculously cliche I could have bought a greeting card for the occasion and pinned it to the front of the fridge. But like the difference between Ava Ashe and any other teen sneaking out to meet a crush was that I'd already acquired two sleeping pills from that boy so that I could make sure my parents were asleep when I snuck out.

I'd taken great pains to crush those tablets in to powder just the way that boy told me. And I stirred the dust into my parents' nightly tea, adding a dollop of honey to the chamomile as an extra precaution. I smiled as I brought the cups to them, watching to be sure they drank the entire contents because wild honey badgers couldn't stop me from going to that party and kissing that boy.

It took half an hour before they fell asleep in their chairs in front of the television. Kit had gone to bed with a book as usual. A peek through the crack in her door showed she'd fallen asleep with it propped on her pillow.

All I had to do was ease open the door and creep down the steps to the path and onto the sidewalk. Easy enough with the entire house asleep. I pulled the hood around my cheeks and kept my head low while I walked the three blocks to the abandoned bungalow where the older kids were partying. The night air sang with late season mosquitoes. It hummed with car engines and somewhere a few blocks down, a woman shouted at her partner.

Anxiety and excitement warred for all the space in my stomach. I kept swallowing and swallowing as I walked, ever certain I was about to do something that would change my life forever.

A single moment almost made me turn back.

It wasn't much. An almost unheard of drop of silence in the suburbs of the city. I paused, tilting my head toward the waft of scented air that came up from behind me. Nothing else in the street moved. The lights on the porches were all out. Dogs and cats were in for the night. The crisp October air was still enough that fallen leaves from the trees lining the street clung to the cement sidewalks as if they were keeping vigil there.

That fragrant movement of breeze should have had the clawed feet of those oak leaves skittering across the cement, whispering of days gone by to the partners now crushed to dust along the cracks. But they slept as soundly on the sidewalk as my parents did in their chairs.

A hush, heavy enough to weigh down my shoulders bade me pull the hood back. The air didn't just go still like that. Not in my neck of the woods. But just as I did that a renewed breeze lifted the fringes of hair that I'd left untied. I scraped back that veil of black, wrapping it into a handful of ponytail and tucked it beneath my collar. The air swirled the leaves into a cyclone at my feet, bringing with it the smell of copper and cinnamon.

I raked a gaze over my shoulder to be sure I wasn't being followed and saw nothing. And yet...I felt eyes were on me with the sure sting of a burn between my shoulder blades.

I shivered. Burrowing my hands beneath the sweatshirt, I crossed my arms over my chest and let the sleeves hang limp and empty. My destination was a block away by then, too close and too far to stop now. I swallowed down the sudden unease.

And then I pushed on.

That night a rebellious teen, at a critical moment in her development, arrested her development when she pressed on and until she jammed the end of a crack pipe to her lips to impress a boy who had already bragged to his friends that he was going to bed a virgin.

Within an hour of that moment, my parents were on the road looking for me, still foggy from the sleeping pills I'd put into their tea.

Two hours later, I stumbled home to find red and blue police car lights flashing in the driveway. Kit was sobbing. The police looked ever so concerned.

Two days later, my mother and father went to their eternal rest in a mossy plot at the cheapest area of the cemetery, while I hunkered down on a filthy mattress in that same abandoned bungalow. Middle of the afternoon, dressed in my funerary best, trying to forget it all happened with a healthy blast of crack smoke in an unkempt junkie's house.

Two years after that, a vampire cornered me at a different party. A handsome older man wearing a slouch hat and three days' growth of whiskers on his chin staked the vamp right in front of me. He saved me then. Told me about the supernatural world. Suggested I might make a good hunter. Gideon. My savior. The man I chased until he caught me. The man Kit hated. Such was the Ava Ashe I'd become. The woman who leaped before she looked. The hunter who became, because she didn't stop that night when a strange breeze caressed her skin.

Now, too many years later, in the land of Fae, I felt the same sense of importance of a single moment. Except, this time it was the sight of a copper door covered in runes and a hammered-on blacksteel handle. And the king of the realm was guiding me toward that frame with a firm pressure of his gloved hand.

Surveying the door and the fae in crowds all around me in the ballroom, the dais with a black cat curled around the feet of a fae mercenary, I thought about that moment long ago. I wondered if I I was given a chance to return to that night, would I turn around at the feel of the breeze playing with my hair and wafting fragrant air at me.

I wondered if I'd go home given the chance, and rummage in the linen closet for blankets and drape them over my sleeping parents. Would I curl into bed with a book and dance gleefully in a world of fantasy until my dreams remained the only things that possessed otherworldly creatures of every sort of horror and danger?

It was a question that had no answer. Not anymore. Because the moment I'd crushed those pills into a saucer and spilled the residue into teacups, the instant I paused on the street and considered going home but didn't, those had sealed the timeline the same as the moment I'd stepped into Fae to spite Gideon.

Now, I wasn't a crush-driven teen heading to a party. I was a full-fledged hunter striding to my battleground. An experienced killer who was much more alert and attuned to the prickling sensation on the back of my neck than I'd been skittering my way to a party that held my doom. Those years ago, my armor had been that sweatshirt. This moment, this now, it was a magnificent gown, spun of spider's gossamer by a fae sorceress. I was weaponless as a newborn, but I was heading to war.

Whatever answer might echo up from the ghosts of my past, the ornately decorated door ahead of me would keep its counsel. Beyond it was my battleground as I fought for the life of a goblin child and gods knew how many others that this king might decide to murder so he could hold onto his throne.

It was why I was here. I'd chosen this. I would not back down or turn away.

"Is that the throne room?" I asked the king in a small voice, just impressed enough to draw his revolting hand further to the small curve above my buttocks.

He had no idea I was a warrior. He didn't even realize he was guiding me to the battle field. Oblivious to his coming death at my hand, he expected a docile mortal woman given to him for his pleasure and restoration. A blood gift, apparently. Given to him by his enemy, a dark fae who'd died moments earlier during his own attempted assassination.

As the king's hand molded itself to the upper curve of my buttocks, I did everything I could not to recoil, even though the gloves he wore prevented skin on skin contact and I couldn't truly feel the pads of his fingers. I knew they were there, beneath that leather, burning into my flesh and digging into the curve of my back eagerly, possessively.

The gown and its body-hugging fit encouraged his touch, I supposed, though it wasn't given to me for that reason. I'd come to the ball wearing something completely different until I'd done the ridiculous thing and followed a strange woman and her fae captors below ground. That act had cost me in more ways than a loss of clothing. But the chaos that erupted afterward, as Terran tried to kill his king with magic from the City of the Dead, had cost others more. My friend Heuil one of them. The little trow was even now being healed of his injuries by the Dark Enforcer.

The only thing that kept me from striking out at each possessive stroke of Ferranus's fingers over my bare skin was repeating to myself over and over that Blade had gifted me the gown I wore. That it was a purchased specially for me. Blade. My mate, apparently, and that was a surprise too. While I'd loved Gideon in my own way, I'd never surrendered everything I was to him. I was still a jagged and barbed thing to hold in Gideon's bed.

But with Blade those places had a perfect fit and so in him, I was smoothed over. I became clean. I'd see him again soon.

I wasn't alone here. No matter that those leather-clad fingers prodded into places that made me want to slit the owner's throat, I could wait. I could hold it together. Weaponless as a newborn babe, I knew, but that didn't mean there was no weapon to hand.

I eyed the spelled blade Ferranus had tucked into his sash. The opposite side to the one that kept pressing up next to me, I didn't fail to notice. The Iron King was not a complete fool, it seemed. Or maybe after Terran's attack, he was just being extra careful.

I silently wondered about that blade. He'd not pulled it out when Terran had died, a victim of his son's power-grab. Instead, he'd used his own magic to create chaos and pain in the subjects who had come to offer him their magic in return for a chance to access their own.

I peered beneath my lashes at Ferranus. "Will we be alone in there?" I asked him ever so sweetly, thinking to distract him for a moment, and failing that, draw out the guise of the docile blood gift going naively to her doom. Fae didn't have to be the only ones possessing glamor.

The king didn't bother to look down at me. Just ahead to our destination. Toward that copper door. "We will be as alone as we need to be," he said in that stuffy tone. "Do you plan to offer me more than a taste, Cleopatra?"

Cleopatra. His name for me because I'd all but rolled out from a carpet in front of him when Erachne had used her magic to stuff me into Terran's collar. I'd dropped out to land in front of Ferranus when the healing was done, starting an entire chaotic kaleidoscope of events that led to Heuil getting nearly killed and a host of Fae tearing at their limbs as Ferranus's magic spilled over the room.

He'd expended a lot of energy then. I hoped it was enough to weaken him now, and I almost snuffed out my response as a snort of laughter, because more than a taste was exactly what I planned. It was just that my idea of a taste had everything to do with dipping that spelled blade into his throat.

"Maybe you should define 'taste', Your Grace," I said coyly.

"Your Iron Grace," he corrected and halted to eyeball a sea of fae who weren't speedy enough to part quick enough to let him through. In a flurry, they did their best to rectify their failure, and once a big enough chasm appeared in the crowds to give him and me plenty of berth, they fell to their knees, heads bowed.

He barely glanced at them.

"I'm sorry, Your Iron Grace," I said in a quivering voice. "I'm new to Fae."

The tips of his gloved fingers dipped into the skirt of the gown far enough that I felt them nestle between the cleft in my back cheeks.

"Indeed," he said as I held my breath so I wouldn't snap my elbow into his ribs. "There's nothing quite so delicious as a mortal new to Fae."

"But your guards," I said, fishing for more information while trying to maintain that coy composure. "Shouldn't be there too? Make sure you're protected."

He scoffed out loud at that. "I have all the power of the realm. I don't need protection."

I watched a young Fae with lovely mint-colored hair lift her gaze coquettishly, trying to catch the king's eye. He paused. His fingers stilled in their gentle kneading of the skin of my ass. He made a thoughtful sound deep in his throat and for a moment, I thought he was considering pulling her along with us.

I shot her a warning look. Back off, it said. Because I couldn't guarantee her life if she got dragged into the room with us. I couldn't risk her life when I took my strike.

She must have taken note of the glare, because she dropped her gaze, but not before I saw her eyes flit over the king's shoulder. Unless she'd moved from the spot where I'd marked her in my memory, Ruby Morvannon of the Nocturnes stood on the dais where the young fae's glance landed. I had no doubt the fae mercenary watched us as keenly as I would have in her place.

I dared a glance, following the female's gaze to where the mists swirled around the mercenary as she watched us. Her stoic expression hadn't slipped one bit as we closed several yards of Fae-clustered ballroom floor.

At the mercenary's feet, the King's cat glowered at us, and I shivered. I'd never known a creature to carry with it such weight of chill.

But it was a cat, after all, and the mercenary was not coming with us to the throne room. If Ferranus could be believed, no guards either. So for this little 'snack' he suggested, the King must have presumed he didn't need more than a few moments alone with his Blood Gift.

No doubt he had every intention of draining me dry to recover some of the magic he'd expended in his attack when he thought Terran was trying to kill him.

"You never said if we were going to the throne room or the harem," I said in a coy voice.

His hand left the small of my back as he leaned toward the young fae female. When he lifted her face upward with the crook of his finger, she kept her eyes low, demure. The perfect subject.

"And who has brought you to court, my young one?" he asked in a voice filled with honey. "Have you a gilded token, my dear? Might I grant your desire?"

For a second. Just one. Her eyes raised to meet his gaze and a flash of rage moved through them. But then she recovered and gave him a shy, almost coquettish smile.

"I have no one, Your Iron Grace. My lover is dead."

Dead. Her voice clipped over that word even as she darted her eyes in my direction. Something hard as ice and just as cold tightened the corners of her eyes.

Ferranus missed it, apparently, or didn't feel threatened because he gushed on in a breezy tone. "Then let me fill that void for you, young dove," he said, tilting his head as he peered into her face. "I see you have flight in your natal magic. A shifter, of sorts, are you?"

She swallowed. "An owl."

"Ah," he said. "Yes. That makes sense. Your green hair is not innate but glamor, is that right? I'm imagining it's the color of burnt wheat." He thumbed his chin. "I think you made a grave mistake in changing it. Your natural locks would favor you more."

At that, her glamor fell away, and I almost gasped.

She was gorgeous. But she was not High Fae. She was short, like Heuil. Her hair was indeed the color of burned wheat, as though smoke-scorched while it lay fallow on the field. Her eyes moved with amber tones, drowning in honey.

"I might like you to accompany us," he said in a deep-throated, lust-filled voice. "Come with us to the throne room. I know your kind enjoys the taste of flesh the way mine does. I would share it with you."

Sweet Jesus, I couldn't let this girl come along with us, not when I planned to be the only one leaving that room afterward.

I was about to shoot her a warning glance, but a blood-curdling scream erupted from behind us.

Chapter 2

A demon's shriek has a certain unforgettable shrillness, and while I wasn't expecting the sound of it there in the Iron Court's ballroom, I knew what it was even before the king swung me around in tandem to investigate the source of the note curdling on the air. In the back of my mind, I knew it was the changeling that had taken Kit's place when she'd portaled safely home. I still felt gut-punched, though, when I caught sight of the thing wearing the pretty dress my sister's glamor had been clad in when we'd arrived. Had to convince myself that the thing with three lines of needle-like teeth,...with white, pupil-less eyes and reedy arms too thin to hurl the globs of tar-like ooze it was throwing...that thing had never been Kit.

The dress was in tatters, shredded by the transformation. And the demon was already snarling its advance upon a small fae as it froze, quivering, in its path.

I wasn't sure what I expected of Ferranus in that moment. Attack. Magic. A swirl of his gloved fingers to poof the creature out of his sight. Any of those would have been normal for a powerful fae whose keep the demon had invaded. At least, in my mind. But Fae and its inhabitants kept surprising me. I couldn't truly know the way the king would react. I certainly didn't expect him to merely glower in the demon's direction, eyeballing the chaos it was creating with a low, rumbling, harumph. As though he'd been interrupted mid-sentence by a rude child, instead of the horrrified shrieks of his subjects, who couldn't use magic to defend themselves. Who couldn't strike out with a weapon without having the violence turn back on them.

in the space of time from when we'd pivoted in tandem to the moment the king made that annoyed sound in his throat, Kit's demon finally found sentience and full power. It broke free of Flint and blasted him with some sort of liquid fire that plastered the floor and danced with several feet of flame until it created a line of fire between itself and the fae who had secreted the demon into the keep.

As we watched, the fire grew and blazed hot enough that several Fae backed off instinctively. Flint was left alone, his magnificent suit scorched to reveal blistered skin. His gorgeous black hair had been singed back to his scalp. In the mortal realm, he would would look like a badass biker, but here, with so much of his skin resembling a boiled hunk of corned beef, he was no more than a scorched kitten.

And yet, horrible as he looked, he was still moving. Those powerful shoulders still looked capable. When he took a purposeful step toward a poor female who stood now in front of the demon, he might have been able to knock her out of the way before she got struck with a load of that burning tar. Might have. Fast as he was, the demon had already lobbed three cakes of goo. They peppered her face with an uncanny accuracy long before Flint threw himself in front of her. As he dropped her to the floor, pinning her beneath him, she flailed in a blind panic as the plaster of goo stole her breath.

The flames roared to a great wall of fire, and I lost sight of them, then. And even though it was a large wall, it wasn't broad. It hadn't yet encompassed the entire width of the chamber. There was still time to stop it and the demon before the entire room went up in flames.

I had to pull my shit together or this whole damn thing was going to go seven ways sideways. And here in Fae where magic was as available as breath, I wasn't foolish enough to think part of getting my shit together meant facing down a demon in a room be-spelled to ricochet violence back to the wielder. No. The smart thing to do was to enlist the magic of the most powerful in the realm. Someone for whom the magic fan would have no consequences.

In my haste to prod him into action, I might have tugged on Ferranus's arm a little too hard. He swung a glare on me. I lifted my chin stubbornly, defiantly.

"You have to do something," I said. "That thing is not going to stop. The magic ban is not working on it."

His gaze swiveled toward me, annoyed and shocked that I would say anything. Maybe he was surprised at my outward calm. Hell, I was too, knowing what that thing was capable of.

"It's going to kill everyone," I said, taking an involuntary step forward before I forced myself to remember I was supposed to be a pallid, insipid mortal woman.

He shrugged off my touch. "I would be foolish to use more of my magic until my subjects gift theirs to me."

"If you don't do something now, you'll have no subjects left. "

His glare could have pulled the mortar from bricked joints. "You are new to Fae so you can be excused this once for your insolence."

I faced him, my skirts whispering around me as I moved, wafting up my thighs, crooning notes I could barely hear.

I gestured toward where the demon tossed another, rather large glob of tar at a cluster of males. The substance split into three and slammed into their faces so hard it knocked them backward. They were covered in goo before they hit the floor. The way those poor victims writhed as they struggled for breath made my stomach lurch.

"Why isn't the spell-ban working?" I asked out loud and, without thinking, clutched at his sleeve. "Shouldn't the ban be rebounding on that thing?"

He did take a step then, but toward the dais where the cat had leaped onto the back of his vacated chair, and where Ruby had shifted into a large owlish looking thing and was preparing to take flight.

I had the gall to hook his elbow. He swung on me, his face white with rage. I ignored it. I had to.

"Why isn't the spell working?"

I thought he might answer, but then another high-pitched shriek crackled the air, vibrating through my solar plexus. The demon was getting stronger. It wasn't using fire anymore, but solely those black masses of living tar, and while Flint was still struggling to get to it and restrain it, the demon had felled at least a dozen Fae.

All of them writhed on the floor, covered in the substance, but their movements were growing quickly more still. I didn't know if they were high, low, or lesser Fae, but they were dying.

At the sound of the demon's victory shriek, the King cursed out loud.

Finally. Finally, he threw his arms up over his head. A crack of thunder sounded. Light split the air and shot up into the constellations of the ceiling. At the gesture, I felt the boom vibrate within my chest, and for a moment, I thought the heavens were falling from above us into the ballroom.

But then a name burst from his lips, one that snapped my attention back to him.

"Lilah," he said as he gestured at the dais. "Get ready."

Lilah. The black-magic witch who was the reason I'd been drawn into Fae in the first place. Lilah, the witch whose lair I'd invaded because she was using cursed objects to kill kids. Lilah who was obviously not dead even though I'd killed her myself. I surveyed the room with a quick glance, but I couldn't find her in the crowds or on the dais. Only Ruby and the cat stood where the king's gaze fell and stopped, and I had to presume the fae sorceress was cloaking herself from view.

The shrieks were intensifying, now braised by the stink of rotting meat. The demon had to be stopped. Right then.

Everything in me wanted to streak toward it and do every-thing I could to halt the violence, but I held my ground. Though it pained me, though my hands jerked at my sides with the want to strike out, I stood there the way a normal mortal would and I let the king take the lead, let the invisible sorceress he'd hired do what they should have done without my pleading. Because he was going to do something, I real-ized. The determination that took possession of his features took away the shining facade. In its place, a brutal mask settled down, reminding me that the fae folk were not so twinkling with light as mortal stories.

I waited a heartbeat, maybe two, for him to take control and as I stood there, hands itching to curl into fists, the King reached out and hooked a small male standing beside us.

The poor thing had no doubt spent a fortune to purchase a lovely green velvet blazer and fine brown leather loafers. He had no teeth, a thatch of hair that had all the hallmarks of malnutrition that turned golden locks into straw. He'd come to the Days with hope in his eyes. That hope shifted to alarmed surprise, widening the little fae's eyes at the sudden grip on his elbow.

And then all that hope, alarm, and surprise died in one second as the King buried his teeth into the poor thing's neck so deeply, so violently, that it bent the boy so far back I could see the wine-stain birthmark on the back of his neck.

I might have shouted. I know I lunged for the king, my reaction to stop him so automatic I didn't have to think. But I knew it was too late by the way the boy's legs went out from beneath him. He jerked like a hanged man and went still.

My cheeks flooded with water as I fought back the bile. A splash of liquid on marble made me doubt that I'd held back the vomit at all until I checked my feet and floor and realized it was blood that had splashed to the floor. It was gathering in a viscous pool. The boy's blood, I realized with a sick knot in my throat. I blinked to clear the image from my vision and lifted my gaze to the king.

At the youth's last spasm, the king dropped his head back. Lips swollen and covered in blood, he shot me a sidelong glance that said more than words could, and yet I heard them as if he'd spoken them aloud.

"Your fault," it said, and I swallowed hard to get words past the tightness constricting my voicebox.

"What have you done?"

You wanted me to lift the ban?" he drawled, dropping the youth into the pool of his own blood, a heap of tattered and soiled clothes and hair. "Blood, bone, and breath," Ferranus said. "A costly price for a valuable magic." He flicked his gaze toward the dais. "One," he shouted toward it.

I staggered back at the insinuation. Three deaths. That's what it would take for Lilah to wield her magic and save the rest of the chamber. One look at the poor youth lying broken and limp at the king's feet, and realized his was probably the swiftest and less painful of the trio. By the time I even felt the hollowing out of my stomach, the caving in of my chest, he had snagged a nearby page whose face had blanched to the color of a herring's belly.

In as swift a motion, the king jabbed his fingers into the page's eyes as though he were plucking a bowling ball from a bag. He shook the page viciously. Though he was not as small as the first fae youth, he might as well have been a cracked and splintered wooden toy in the king's grip. He shrieked in pain, his eyeballs squeezing out around the flesh of Ferranus's finger and thumb, nothing but jelly running down the king's arm. Somehow, Ferranus's palm covered the boy's entire face, the fingers not jammed into his sockets splaying out into the temples.

He held fast to the youth, keeping him tight in his grasp as he then bit down on the flesh of the boy's neck. A shred of skin peeled away, leaving a landing strip of raw muscle exposed. And then he did it again and again until the muscle was gone and the bone exposed. Muffled howls of pain bled out from behind the king's palm until the boy passed out. Then the sounds went still, and for a moment, I wanted to hear them renew. I wanted it to just be a breath of pause, gathering more strength to scram anew.

But he went as limp as the flayed bits of skin mounded at his own feet. My knees threatened to give way.

By then, every Fae around us, including the young trow shifter with the green hair, had started screaming and running for their lives. By the time Ferranus crunched down on bone and shook the poor fae into a rickety pile of scraps, a wide open space had opened up in the crowd surrounding the king. Fae everywhere had darted out of range, terrified they'd be next.

It was too late for the trow shifter, though.

In a heartbeat and no more, the king's hand shot out even before he dropped the page from his other hand. She was being flung upward above his head before he even touched her throat. She gasped when his fist closed around her neck. A moment when she sucked in air. Two, and she realized all the wheezing would bring nothing fresh to her lungs.

My feet slid forward of their own mind, toward the king. I had to stop this madness. Surely, he could do more. Surely he could wield his magic and smother the defensive wall of fire the demon had erected so he could wade through victims unaccosted. Surely the king could snuff out its life with a snap of his fingers. Not this...not this horror.

And then I realized he couldn't do that at all. He was as bound by the magic ban as his subjects. And if the king of the realm couldn't wield his magic except to utter this prayer of violent magic, then what could I do? If I tried to stop him, anything I did would turn on me. I knew I couldn't help her. Sickened as my gut felt, as bowed inward as my shoulders were, I was helpless here.

I was left to watch with my heart in my throat, my stomach dancing its way up to meet it, as her eyes bulged on the strain of trying to breathe through the king's magic.

When he dropped her too, my feet finally came free of their rooted terror. Seconds later, and I felt my back butt up against something sharp and hard. Somehow I'd stumbled away until I'd met the far side of the dais without realizing I was on the move. Pulling my gaze from the king and the chaos beyond him was all but impossible and yet, just as the young female fell to the floor, a sort of sizzling and popping sound came from the dais that drew my attention.

The cat had begun to stretch and morph and the jet-colored pelt became long, flowing hair. I knew the face that looked back at me, the crystalline blue eyes that swept over me in a dismissive glance that indicated she didn't care in the least that I'd killed her weeks earlier.

At least I'd thought I'd killed her. The woman she shifted into proved she was far from dead.

"Blood, bone, and breath," Ferranus yelled at her. "I've turned the key. Now, drop the ban. My Fae need to protect themselves."

Protect themselves, I noted, not that he would lift a finger of magic to help them. But as selfish as his words showed him, he'd said something else that caught my attention. Something more important than his ego.

He wanted the ban dropped.

Without the ban, weapons could be wielded. The Fae could fight back, but so could anyone else.

My gaze sliced toward where Ferranus stood with his arms outstretched, as though he wanted to pull magic from the air. His robe moved aside as he pivoted on the soles of those expensive shoes. The knife in his sash caught the light. The gleam of it winked at me.

Two thoughts ran through my mind as my eye measured the distance between the king and me and downloaded the information to my legs. Heuil was safe. Phaedre was safe.

And on the heels of those thoughts came the most important one. The only life I'd be risking that I cared about was
mine.

The three spell victims lay puddled at Ferranus's feet and
from their bodies rose a green ether that spiraled up into the
constellations in the ceiling. A soft hiss followed its journey,
a hiss that for all the screaming from the demon and the
shouting of the fae, was as clear as the toll of a bell across a
still lake.

I didn't need to be told the magic was returning. I felt it in
the way my skin buzzed, in the sigh of the fae nearest me as
they felt some oppressive energy lift that they'd not registered
until the moment it left. The ban spread like a field of flowers
blooming as the sun rose, moving from the king outward.

The demon was still wreaking havoc, but by now, it had
grown several arms that flung that evil tar in every direction.
It had begun to lob balls of fire. Wooden chairs burned with
black smoke. Several fae lay on the flagstones, encompassed
in flames.

Flint had staggered to his feet and was trying to block
someone from another blast from the monster's open mouth.
He took the hit of ooze so hard I heard the thwack of it
landing on his shoulder. He yanked it off, flinging it at the
demon's feet. Not a weapon. Not when it wasn't aimed at
anyone or anything.

The magic continued to spread, though, and I knew that
soon he would be able to fight back. They all would. And yet
the demon pushed out from the cluster of Fae surrounding
it, felling them as easily as a breath on a mist-laden cobweb.

Every other moment, it plucked someone from his path and
tore through chest and stomach to pull a veined and pulsing
heart from its place. My gorge rose when I saw the thing toss

hearts into the air so that a second head, a small thing on a whip-thin neck, shot out from its ribcage and gulped down the heart like a dog catching a treat mid-air.

By the way it shoved every obstacle in its path aside or cut it down like weeds, it became very clear that the demon planned to kill and eat its way to maturity. That with each death, bloody or not, it was gaining strength.

Ferranus knew it too, I could tell. He'd already stepped away from the three fae at his feet as though they were rubbish he'd trod into accidentally. His wild gestures at Lilah suggested he expected her to do something when he would not.

And as clear as it was to me that the demon planned to feast until it had reached some sort of heinous strength and size that would end in dozens if not hundreds of dead fae before the liberation reached them, all I could think was that this was it. This was the moment I needed.

It would take one strike at the king and that was all. Quick. Clean. He was distracted. The knife was right there.

Ruby's mist had all but obliterated her and I wasn't sure if she was watching or was spilling into and out of her own individual realm as she tried to decide if she was supposed to attack or simply wait it out. Because the threat wasn't for Ferranus. Not yet. And I was willing to bet she had orders to protect him and only him.

Except she was out of range of the king, and the threat, the real threat to Ferranus, was me. He was distracted. I was so close.

I knew one thing right then. This could end right now. The risk to Phaedre and the untold dozens of children Ferranus might decide to sire and murder.

There was no need to consider anything else. In a move so fluid, Gideon would have been proud, my feet whispered toward the king, closing the gap between us.

I was silent as a mouse, cautious as a cat. One moment he was angled away from me, the next he turned to give me exactly the perspective I needed.

My hand whipped out. My fingers closed around the handle and it felt as good in my hand as my own karambit. I pulled it free with an ease that seemed greased. The blade spun on its own into a hold so comfortable it took me a second to realize it was spelled. The jolt ran up my arm at the same time as Ferranus spun to face me.

Our eyes met.

Some hunters will say that time pulls out like taffy in the moment before the death strike. That has never happened for me. Time always seemed to speed up with the brute force of a hammer coming down on my heart. It always felt like a slam of adrenaline straight into the muscle.

But time pulled out like strings of warm taffy right then.

Something, some movement, or some noise, or some...thing caught my attention over his shoulder. The demon had doubled in size. Fae all around it had chosen to run instead of fight, and there was a clear path from the king to the demon.

I hesitated. Just for half a heartbeat. That heartbeat was enough for the demon to lower its head in an unmistakable decision to rampage across the ballroom.

Ruby scuffled out her storm of shadow. She solidified into that half-owl, half-fae looking thing. She had seen what I did. The demon was charging.

What she didn't see was what it was charging at.

I did.

Gideon. As impossible as it was to see him there, he was. And he stepped out of a crowd of Fae into the path of the demon.

CHAPTER 3

Gideon was about to die. Somehow, for some reason, he'd followed me into the land of Fae and was now about to have his head ripped off by the demon Blade swapped for Kit. At the same moment, I prayed the liberation had reached him, and he could defend himself without the magic ban turning his defense back against him.

There was no thought after that. Instinct and muscle memory took over.

My wrist flicked back over my head, angling the knife for a throw.

From the corner of my vision, I noted that the king had raised his hand as well. His brow had furrowed into a rage of wrinkles. He realized I was going to attack him, and he was going to bring his magic to bear against me.

I had a second, maybe less.

The blade left my hand with a flick powered by biceps well and truly trained over long, hard hours. I knew it would meet its mark even before it left my fingers.

At the sound of the demon's enraged and pained howl, the king dropped his hand, surprise releasing the tension in his face. My mind registered it the way it registered Gideon's shock at realizing he'd been rescued at the last second. His shoulder sagged, and he fell over onto his thighs, planting relieved palms on his legs as his head dropped between them.

My arms fell to my sides. Exhaustion and adrenaline swamping me. I felt sick inside.

I'd had a choice. The king or Gideon. I was as surprised as anyone else at the decision my body made.

The demon fell hard, and as the liberation spread at last toward those Fae who had been in its path, they fell on it with a savagery I'd not seen in the human world despite all the horrors I'd ever witnessed.

The blade I'd thrown blazed a brilliant steel blue before it disappeared.

I watched in fascinated horror, knowing I'd lost my chance to kill Ferranus, and realizing I wasn't sorry for it. The comforting scent of cinnamon gathered around me as I stood there. No words were needed when I felt Blade's presence beside me.

"You still love him," he said, but there was no jealousy in his tone. He knew as well as I did that the sort of emotion I felt for Gideon was nothing to the all-consuming fire of feeling between us.

"He saved me."

His hand brushed mine as it lay beside my thigh. A whisper of touch, not enough to reveal the depth of connection between us to anyone looking on, but powerful enough for me that I had to fight closing my eyes to savor it.

"You'll have to tell me about that sometime," he said in a husky voice that tore at my stomach.

I forced myself to step away from him and face him as though he were any other Fae in the room. "You're presuming there will be time."

His smile was crooked and endearing. "Time is what you make of it, Ponytail. Even so, it was an interesting choice. Clever and foolish both."

Anything I might have said to that died on my tongue as Ferranus drew up to us.

"You missed all the excitement, Blade," he said.

Blade let his gaze linger on mine for an instant before shifting his attention to the king. "Ruby would have been sufficient for any threats, Your Iron Grace while I did your bidding."

It was a gentle, careful reminder that he'd been out of commission at the king's behest while all the chaos went on. Nothing irreverent in his tone, but even so, the king harrumphed. He was piqued, it seemed. Angry at Blade for being elsewhere when he obviously thought he should be immediately available for defense.

"How is the little trow's injuries anyway?" Ferranus asked, but he didn't wait for an answer. Accusation waited in his tone the way a serpent prepares for a strike. When he turned those angry eyes to me, I understood exactly why.

"What sort of mortal are you?" he demanded with a shuttered look. "I've seen precious few fae fell a monster from this distance with a blade alone, let alone a demon." His eyes slashed across my face. "And just how in the hell was a demon able to get into my castle in the first place?"

Yup. Definitely accusatory.

I recoiled at the fury in his voice, but it was Blade who answered, his voice carefully, painfully neutral.

"My guess is the thing came through when the Morvannon opened a portal to the Stygian darkness."

The king swung his gaze to where Ruby stood with arms crossed, that mist curling around her and phasing her in and out again. She held her ground on the dais as if to say she was working to order and no more.

Her bright eyes watched us carefully.

The king's eyes narrowed. "I have given her leave to use her portal at her discretion without penalty. "

Of course he had.

"And it is not the full Darkness, merely a portal to her lands there." Those eyes hardened like glass. "It's more likely it came through on the heels of the magic that dropped this mortal woman from your father's cloak."

There it was. An even stronger accusation.

I did my best to keep my gaze shuttered and downcast at the comment. He was closer to the truth than he realized, but I wasn't about to poke the honey badger.

No movement from Blade. Not a single clenching of his hands at his side to show the comment worried him at how close it was to the truth. His expression remained as stoic as his posture. But there, right at the place where his jaw joined his earlobe, there was a feathering of muscle.

"If it please you, Your Iron Grace," he said, his nostrils flaring as he inhaled deliberately through his nose. "We can discuss that at leisure later. Right now, we must consider The Ban. You should have the Fae sorceress cast it over the room again. Not for your sake but for the others'. The demon is dead and the smell of blood is in the air. You know how some of us can get."

Some of us. Including the king and himself in that statement. My feet shuffled beneath my skirts as I remembered just how violent the realm of the Fae could be. Smoke and mirrors, really, for the innocent mortals who thought it was glitter and light.

The moment of opportunity had passed, anyway. An opportunity Gideon wouldn't have let slip by, but it was hard to feel remorse at my choice. Gideon was alive. So were countless fae. What was one king whose days were numbered?

"Of course," Ferranus muttered at Blade's observation. "Of course."

His wrist flicked toward the dais, drawing my gaze with it to where Lilah stood beside Ruby. Her glance swept over me as though she'd never seen me before. I felt like waving at her to show her I remembered her if she didn't remember me.

"Lilah. If you please," the king said.

She nodded, the curtain of her onyx hair waving with the movement.

"Fire, flesh, and fear," she said, jerking her chin toward the place where the demon was in tatters of skin and flesh. "It's almost as though it knew what was needed." Her grin was like watching a child draw a smile on a wooden puppet in red crayon.

I gathered from her comment that those were the ingredients for the spell, the same as the deaths of those fae the king had sacrificed to lift it in the first place. With gritted teeth, I waited silently as she scored her cheek with her fingernails. Blood burbled to the surface, creating ghastly streaks that ran down to her chin. I winced at how raw they looked even as she smeared her palms over them, painting her face with her own blood.

Dropping her head back, she began to whisper in a language I didn't understand, sending incantations to the air that drew themselves in smoke over her head. They looked for all the world like the runes on the copper door.

It occurred to me that this might be the last moment I had to attack the king, and yet I had no weapon to hand, nothing to strike fast enough to spill his blood before he defended himself. Even if I did, taking him out right then might draw the attention of the sorceress. It might put the rest of the assembly in danger. I simply didn't know and couldn't guarantee what might happen if I lunged for the king.

So I stood there, rigid, as the weight of magic suffused the room again, weaving its ban over the fae within it. For a moment, I couldn't breathe, the heat of it feeling like the interior of a coffin. Then it eased and Lilah sank to her bottom on the dais.

She looked distinctly wan, even shriveled, as though the magic had drained her of collagen and fluids. When she shifted back into a cat, it was slow and it looked very painful.

The king pivoted on his heel to face me. "She casts the best spells," he said. "Like a cook using whatever is in her pantry to make a fine and hearty meal."

The cat folded its paws beneath its chest and closed its eyes as Ferranus offered Blade a smile that seemed more authentic than before.

"Now," he said. "This Cleopatra of your father's..." Ferranus jerked his chin in my direction, managing to make it look regal instead of jerky. "You gave her the gown you purchased for the female you hoped would be a future mate. A wedding gown, if my eyes aren't playing tricks on me. Quite a generous sacrifice for any male let alone a hellhound from the Stygian Darkness."

A wedding dress. I almost gasped out my shock as Blade's eyes sliced over Ferranus's face, shuttering the suspicion in his gaze so swiftly I doubted the king saw it even if I did.

"It is no sacrifice to offer this gown to cover the gift's physical treasures from a court of gawking males."

"Even so." Ferranus panned me with a look that indicated he liked the way I looked in the gown. "I have some experience with hellhounds. I know how they can be. And they do not share. Not willingly. And to offer the gown you purchased for a potential mate to a mere mortal just to keep what will be for my eyes and not the court's....well..." At that, shockingly, the king offered a slight bow. "I offer you thanks."

The action left me blinking in surprise, but Blade revealed nothing in his posture that might suggest anything other than respect for the king.

"I deserve no gratitude for shielding her from view ," he said carefully, and in his words I heard the truth. He was very good at keeping lies from his comments. I suppose they all were, having lived with the rigor of avoiding untruths their entire lives.

The king swung toward his throne, striding to it with a graceful step until he brushed off the seat.

"Still," he said, settling onto the cushion. "I've seen the females follow you with their eyes." The king lowered his lashes. "The males as well. I've heard rumors over the decades that you don't want for partners, Dark Enforcer, but it can be lonely without a mate. This is something I know well." He let go a lengthy and aching sigh. "Perhaps this very occasion of Days might see you find that one you seek among the throng of females who have come to celebrate."

There was a long, heated pause where I was left to wonder what passed between the two of them in the silence, because a definite tension hummed through the air. Then Blade spoke, and I understood he had been corralling his words, finding a way to speak to me while addressing Ferranus. And his words, husky and passionate, filled me with warmth.

"It's true I've not found my life lonely in all these centuries. I've not found a match who could call to my heart, one who can echo the violence of it beat for beat. So while the dress may please your eye for the time being, it can be a token of that moment when I am able to watch my intended peel herself out of it. Imagine the moment I watch as her breasts fall free from that tight bodice as they offer themselves to my mouth. To see the fabric surrender to her thumbs and fingers as she eases it down over her stomach, her hips, her thighs. The moment will come when I catch a thief's glimpse of what waits for me between her legs as she lifts one foot then the other free of the skirts. Those are the images that sustain me now."

He looked at me finally, boldly, those eyes glazing over momentarily with barely concealed desire as they met mine. My entire body flushed, prickling with desire. Then, because we had an audience, he turned to the king, leaving me feeling cold and bare and feeling as undressed as he'd pictured me.

When he addressed his words to the king, they were a casual distance put carefully between them so the king would know the kind of fae he was.

"She should be a wildcat in bed after that and every time thereafter that we come together," he winked at the king inspirationally, almost jovially and the king, surprisingly, returned it. "But for those moments, I want her demure, surrendering to me with fear of the force I might take her."

Ferranus fanned his face. "Gods asunder, Blade," he said in a breathless voice. "You do paint an enticing image." He cast a glance my way, and I dropped my eyes to the floor, waiting out the moment until I heard him moving. Only then did I peek out from under my hair to watch him lean forward, all attention on the dark enforcer.

He slung his arm over the armrest and slumped back into his throne as he regarded Blade. "Makes me want to inspect this gift a bit more closely."

Eyeballing me with a renewed sense of wary interest, he patted his sash and the knife magiced itself back into place. "Our little Cleopatra has a strange affinity for be-spelled blades and I should like you to help me test a theory."

He pointed his elbow toward me even as Blade slid smoothly in between us, neatly separating me from the king without looking like it was intentional.

"You should not go alone," he said, and I thought he meant me until the king snuffed out a laugh.

"I have no need of bodyguards, and certainly not from a mortal woman no matter how good her aim." Fatigue dogged the corners of his eyes. Powerful he might be, but he was drained and was trying not to show it.

At the king's words, Blade shot a glowering frown in my direction that all but said he'd have preferred I not save Gideon's life now that the action had singled me out for closer inspection. Then he turned his attention toward the copper door. "You might want to have someone clean up the fallen." His voice was tight as he addressed the king. Filled with barely suppressed anger. "They're making the rest nervous."

If the king noticed, he only responded to the words, not the tone. "I've already sent word to my pages." He tapped his temple. "I have several on bond."

On bond. I guessed that meant some sort of telepathic tie, though I prayed such a magic wasn't so omnipotent or else he'd know exactly what Blade wanted to do with him. Because the dark enforcer was most definitely seething.

I cast a look over my shoulder toward where Gideon had stood, but he was gone. Heavens only knew what he was up to or why he was here, but at least for now, he was out of sight.

The only Fae I recognized in the crowds was Flint, and he leaned his black head toward another, much shorter, male wearing tight-fitting trousers and a blue-beaded jacket edged with gold thread.

A most intricate pattern swirled through the beads as though they were flames rising and falling over the material and not tiny gems and beads fixed in place by stitching. If it was magic, it was subtle magic, and I guessed it was meant to show a certain proficiency of power. As though he wanted to say without words that he had a tight rein on his magic.

There was a moment when the male's profile almost turned to three quarter view and a buzz of memory ran along my spine. I knew him, but I couldn't place him. I didn't think I'd seen him at the manse or with Terran's thugs.

Flint caught my eye as I strained to work out where the stranger had first caught my eye, and I could swear he said something to the fae because he, in turn, shot me a knowing glance, giving me a full-on look at his face as if he challenged me to react.

Usually I was very good at faces. Recognition is a critical skill for a hunter as I'd worked hard to perfect it, but there was something off about the stranger. Not that he looked any more peculiar than any other fae in the room, but more like mottled glass separated him from me, giving his features shape and size but not finite, definite sharpness.

I nudged at Blade with my elbow. "Who is that?" I asked. "Talking to your brother."

His gaze followed the jerk of my chin. "You mean talking to Flint?"

"Which other brother would I mean?" I said. "Since Stone has fled for some hiding place somewhere." The bitterness in my voice made him raise his eyebrows, and I realized I'd not had a chance to tell him the truth about his other brother.

Not here, though, I thought. And maybe not until I had torn the man's voice box from his throat and danced on his face with combat boots to the tune of his screaming. Because if I revealed that truth before the fae was dead, Blade would steal my vengeance from me.

So deflecting, I said, "I feel like I know him."

He shook his head, his gaze trailing away toward where the king had begun addressing the crowds with over-blown, flowery speech. "I don't know how you'd have met him, Ponytail," he said in a distracted tone. "He doesn't get much time topside and when he does, he's busy tutoring Mica."

I gawked openly toward the male, now. "That's Mica's tutor?"

He doffed a finger toward the male, who in turn inclined his head politely before giving his attention back to Flint.

I had so many questions about the tutor and why he'd be spending time with Flint instead of Mica, but before I could ask any of the ones fomenting in the back of my mind, something shoved me hard enough from behind that I stumbled.

Blade steadied me with a little touch of my elbow that sent all sorts of warm and zinging jolts through me.

I avoided his eye, knowing I'd see the same longing in his gaze that would be in mine if I looked at him. No chance of it, however. Before either of us could do more than shift our gazes, Ferranus flicked his arms out to each side, as though ridding his fingers of water or energy that clung to the tips.

"It's time," he said, and I found myself moving, without conscious effort, toward the copper door.

With a darting glance over my shoulder, I could see Blade's brow furrow. His eyes flashed as he regarded Ferranus.

If I tried to stop walking, the top half of me plunged forward so that I had to move my feet to keep from falling face first into the beautiful parquet floor.

Magic propelled me, I realized. The king's magic. Whether I wanted to move or not, he forced it on me. And he was urging me to toward that copper door, leaving Blade and Flint and Mica's tutor and the whole damn realm of the Iron Court behind us in that ballroom.

And I knew beyond that threshold waited something more dangerous than anything I left behind in this room.

CHAPTER 4

The throne room had a stark, cold interior that sent a shiver down my spine. Habit had me surveying the room with a calculated eye, looking for exits, for would-be weapons, for places a threat might lurk. Ferranus went ahead, two pages at either side of the door opening it for him and holding us back several paces before we were allowed through.

I felt Blade's eyes on me as I was forced to step into the room. Ahead of me, Ferranus had taken his place on a magnificent and cruel-looking throne. Constructed of wrought iron with sharp edges, each curled and hammered leaf reminded me of a tin can cut into strips and painted a glossy black to make the razored edges look more threatening.

But for the flat, hammered arm rests, every inch looked like it was designed to slice into flesh. Beneath the seat, a bowl made of black pottery rested on the floor.

I had to wonder what need he might have of it, and decided that despite the gold seams that scored its surface, creating patterns that reminded me of lines of liquid metal on a forge, he used the thing as a chamber pot. My nostrils flared, testing the air for proof of my theory, but nothing came back to infer I was right.

Under Ferranus' muscled thighs rested a velvet cushion the color of an eggplant, the only softness in the entire chair. I noted he didn't look ill at ease in the thing, but rather was watching me enter with a calculated eye.

He knew the effect the chair gave, and he was measuring my reaction to it.

My gaze dropped to the floor. I had no intention of showing him how pathetic I thought his obvious show of intimidation was.

But in the first, scouring glance, I'd taken in a room that curved into a full circle, with cold-looking wrought iron sconces that threw off an equally cold blue light. That glow crept up the grey stone walls in fingers that caught all the crystals in the granite and sparked the edges with white. Not a single tapestry covered stone and mortar to soften the effect of harsh stone.

But there was a door besides the one we'd come through. Not in the walls, but in the floor. The grooves of its outline were thinner. If there were grout lines, they were a tighter mortar than the rest of the floor, which possessed a thick, black mortar weaving the flagstones together.

An exit, I wondered, or an entrance?

The chandelier that hung over the throne, also constructed of wrought iron, cast shadows over Ferranus's face that put black hollows in places that made him look monstrous instead of the gorgeous high Fae he was.

An effect I was sure he'd practiced to perfection. Just taking in the room in that one glance gave me the sense that this was the true seat of power. That the throne in the ballroom was meant to impress in a different way from this one.

Here in the harsh and unforgiving atmosphere, it was easy to see what emotion the King wanted to evoke in whatever subject knelt or stood in front of him. Fear. Fear and awe.

The black flagstones were level everywhere except for a spot several feet from the throne, where the indentation grooved into the stone suggested thousands of feet and knees over centuries of audiences with the Iron King.

No other piece of furniture graced the space. With no idea what to do or how to act, I decided to fall back on Terran's hissed suggestion to kneel.

So, I strode to that dip in the floor, where it was smoother than the rest.

"Don't bother to kneel," the king said before I could sketch a curtsey. "We haven't time for that. Just wait there."

Wait. At least I felt more at ease on my feet. I crossed my hands over my hips and kept my eyes downcast. After the way he'd been able to force me to walk where he wanted, I decided it was best not to poke the bear and instead remain compliant.

"Now," he said to someone who must have been standing out of sight, cloaked either by magic or my own sense of distraction. "You may approach."

From beneath lowered lashes, I saw a hulk of shadow move into my peripheral vision. The currents of changing air carried a whiff of something familiar. Not cinnamon. But similar. A male, I knew, not just by the feel of space being taken up beside me, but by the pheromone, the sensation of tension, the sudden, unwanted curl of my lip as he took his place next to me, so close, I felt the whisper of his shoulder against mine.

"Stone," I said, barely keeping the rage from my voice, and only managing to bite down on it by clacking my teeth together over my teeth. Pain jolted through me, carrying with it the taste of blood.

The shuffling sound as he pivoted into place, the whisper of his clothes as he adjusted his jacket, all made the spot between my eyebrows grow tight. It was difficult to train my features to the calm exterior I'd practiced so often beneath Gideon's tutelage. My chest rose and fell in shallow breaths.

"You have control of your father's organization," Ferranus said in a flat voice, to which I surmised Stone nodded because the king shifted in his seat, hooking one arm over a crook of metal where the armrest met the back.

"Do all your brothers know this?" he asked.

Stone cleared his throat and all I could think about was how badly I wanted to punch it.

"Flint is aware," he said.

"And the Dark Enforcer?"

Silence then. No answer needed.

The king looked at his nails. "What do you think your elder brother will do when he discovers you have murdered your father?"

"I didn't—"

"Please," Ferranus said, making a slicing motion with his hand. "I knew Terran. He wouldn't let death rob him of a chance to see me suffer." He inclined his head toward the male at my side. "You took control. Bested the best at his own game. I might want to know how you managed it."

I felt Stone straighten up. "My father had one weakness."

"And you indulged it, manipulated it, exploited it." Ferranus didn't bother to ask what the weakness was. Obviously, he knew as well as Stone did. "And the others?" The King asked ever so politely that it couldn't be because he was merely interested.

"My father's men are in line with me."

More silence. This time from the king. I was dying to look up. Dying to see what was going on in those faces.

"They are my soldiers," the king enunciated the last two words as though they were the only words he'd spoken, and barked them out so viciously, I almost jumped out of the soft gown.

He must have noticed he'd startled me, because his voice projected my way with such clarity it almost sounded as if he was standing in front of me. "I forgot you were there, Cleopatra," he said. "You may sit if you like."

Sit. And just where did he expect me to do that, I wondered. With no choice but to do so cross-legged on the cold floor, I did just that. My position gave me a good view of the two fae, and with them focused on each other, neither paid attention to my surreptitious study.

The color had washed from Stone's face, making the hair he'd brushed back off his forehead and temples appear to be a shroud over cold flesh. A bead of sweat trailed a path behind his ear.

Good, I thought. He should be afraid. He should be terrified.

And yet it wasn't fear that sat on his face. I wasn't sure if the king noticed it, but it was that same grit I'd seen in him that first time I'd met him. A cold, calculated mask that I wanted to tear off.

Ferranus steepled his fingers between his knees as he leaned forward, his gaze a shard of ice as he took in the fae before him.

"Your father took those soldiers from my guard and made them his. He warped the Sentinels my grandsire created into something the royal court could not use. He turned them against me. Each and every one of them, but they are my soldiers. Make no mistake about that."

The currents of air buzzed with an electricity that made the hair stand on my arms. As a dressing down, it was mild, but I relished every word because Stone deserved it. I almost expected him to protest or try to wheedle himself an excuse. But like Terran, he held his ground, giving the king no quarter.

"The way my father tells it, those soldiers left of their own free will," he said, so mildly he might have been discussing the weather.

Oh, the balls on him. Just like his father. If he hadn't betrayed me so thoroughly, I'd admire that steel in his spine.

Ferranus, apparently, did not admire it. His hands clenched the metal armrests hard enough that the sharp metal edges should have cut into his flesh. His ringed fingers turned white. "And just what else did your father tell you?"

Stone's shoulders squared. "My father told me only that he was one of the Sentinels. That he fell out of favor with the House of Iron Hearts and that those he had served with all those centuries followed him."

"He stole my soldiers," Ferranus said. "He abandoned me." His fingers tapped the black iron beneath his hand. The click of a metronome crafted a dull beat as rings met metal over and over.

"Betrayed me," he said. "And yet still, I would have had him return to his rightful place as my bodyguard, as the Captain of the Sentinels. Now, he's gone and that chance will forever be impossible because of you."

I heard grief in his voice, and I knew it was real. For an instant, I pitied him. He'd lost a friend this day, perhaps not a friend the way they'd been in their heyday, but someone he remembered with fondness. I almost warmed to him, but the moment passed as he inhaled through his nose, taking a sharp, bracing breath.

"But he tried to kill me. Me. His king. His friend. The Fae whose body and magic he swore by blood oath to protect. We fought together, side by side to keep this realm from being swallowed by the Stygian Darkness."

My ears perked up at the words blood oath, as I was sure Stone's did.

"Is this why you chose Ruby of the Nocturnes to stand at your flank this day?"

Oh, it was impudent and daring and the king indulged it like he expected the answer.

"I chose her because she has no heart, and for the things I must do this day, I require warriors who do not feel."

Stone snorted, and the king lifted an eyebrow. "You do not believe she is heartless or you do not approve of my procurement of warriors who kill without emotion."

The way he said procurement made me squirm on the floor, adjusting my legs to ease the numbness in them. Blade was one of those he thought was heartless.

I glanced upward, almost automatically, forgetting for the moment that I was supposed to be showing reverence with downcast eyes.

The movement caught the king's attention and his gaze lingered on my face a little too long before it plunged lower. That pointed, possessive look made me feel naked. I had to run my palm over the garment covering my thighs to be sure I was still dressed.

I dropped my gaze quickly, pinning it to the way my gown spread over the black flagstones.

The king sighed. "I needed a soldier with a cold, calculated heart to defend the door to the veil. Someone who is efficient without the tedious issue of emotional attachment."

"You chose wisely then," Stone said in his throaty voice. "Ruby has cared for no one."

"And you?"

A shuffle of material. Perhaps Stone was turning to face the king. Perhaps the king had rustled his own cloak.

"I'm not sure what you are asking, Your Iron Grace," Stone said.

The king breezed out air through his nose. "I think you do."

I felt Stone stiffen beside me, drawing my gaze upward to see the king had stood. He met my gaze with deliberation, but he directed his words to Stone while he held my eyes pinned to his.

"You say your father drank of toxic magic, hoping that when the magic turned on him, it would ensnare me as well."

"You saw the results," Stone said in a cool voice. "You fought it back. You won."

"Of course I won," Ferranus said. "There is no one in this realm with as much power as I. It was foolish of him to think such a tactic would work."

One small scuffle of Stone's shoe on the flagstones. That was it. But it told me he was losing his nerve. The king knew it too because he closed the distance between us and knelt on one knee in front of me, holding my gaze.

"He does not know the centuries his father and I spent as comrades. He doesn't know I knew his father better than he." His eyes sliced up and sideways, taking Stone in with a raking motion. "He forgets his father knew me as well."

With a cant of his head, the shadows of the chandelier shifted to new hollows in his face, carving out his jowls into something that looked more fierce than a wolf's. "Terran wasn't stupid enough to think that ruse would work. And he would never give up seeing the moment of my death by sacrificing his own life to claim it."

When he stood, his knees popped. His sigh came long and breathy. "I have used much magic this day in response to 'your father's' attack."

At that, he reached out his hand, waggling his fingers at me. I had to force myself to take it, to show I was the compliant, naive gift he thought he'd been given.

He raised me up effortlessly. The gown swirled neatly around my hips and legs.

"If your father drank of the magic in an effort to bring me down, then how am I to believe his blood gift is not also tainted?"

I felt the color go out of my face then. The look of grit on his face, the way Stone went rigid beside me, whatever happened next wasn't going to be good.

"As I said," he droned on. "I expended much today. More at once than I have in decades. But I'm not drained so much that I can't protect myself should the need arise. It's the Days that worry me. The amount of magic I expended might impact my ability to accept the lesser fae's magic as they offer it to me, and thus the endowments themselves are at risk." His thumb ran over my wrist and it was all I could do not to pull my hand away.

"I'd not have the Days interrupted or put at risk." He paused, just long enough to make it seem like he really cared. "They have waited a hundred years for the chance to access their magic."

"I'm not sure what that has to do with me," Stone said. "I don't understand why you sent your pages to collect me and bring me here."

"Does it not?" Ferranus asked almost sweetly. "I should think it very clear since you escorted this human here. Since your father presented her to me, saying you were to be the one to receive the acknowledgment. Since you are the reason she stands before me."

Finally, girding myself against the rage I worried would show on my face, I swung my attention to Stone, expecting him to be watching me. He wasn't. His eyes were on the king and he'd gone more white than before. Alabaster, I thought. His skin was made of alabaster.

"Please," he said, putting a knot in my stomach.

"Please?" The king's face grew hard, and he took to pacing in front of us. "I need to be sure she is untainted by the magic that killed your father, that she isn't some magical time bomb waiting to explode. You will prove it to me. Now."

Right about then, I began to suspect the very thing that had Stone's skin turned clammy white, but I still wasn't expecting to hear the truth of it when the king halted beside his throne.

He gestured toward me. "I need you to taste her."

CHAPTER 5

Stone had once assured me that the fae didn't eat human flesh anymore. Standing there weaponless in front of the most powerful fae in the kingdom, I repeated those words in my head over and over.

Long moments stretched out between us as Stone stared at the king, as I tried to shrink out of sight, as Ferranus kept his gaze leveled on Stone.

"Taste her," he said again.

"Taste her?" As though Stone had no idea what the king meant.

"Yes. Taste her." The king strolled toward me, closing the distance that remained between us with strides that fell silently on the flagstones. His magnificent clothes went taut around his chest as he spread his arms, planting his hands on his hips, looking down at me.

"She was brought to me by your father, who tried to kill me." This in a stilted voice. "I would have you taste her first. To be sure her blood doesn't carry the same magic."

Stone's eyebrows rose even as a specific hunger stole over his face. His throat bobbed as he looked at me. "You are afraid my father is offering you a poisoned apple."

"I haven't lived all these centuries by being a trusting sort. Your father reminded me today of why."

Ferranus grabbed me by the arm and shoved me toward Stone. The skirts tangled in my legs, throwing me off balance, but I caught myself long before I fell against the traitor. With hands curled into fists at my sides, I let my lip curl as I regarded him.

"Don't touch me," I said in a rasp.

The muscles of his throat tightened as he swallowed. His eyes flicked over my shoulder. The king repeated the order as my chest heaved with suppressed anger. I shook my head in warning.

"Ava," he whispered, and I shook my head again. Don't, my eyes said. Not because I was afraid of him, but because I was afraid of what I'd do, what I'd risk, if he did.

"I am waiting," Ferranus said.

At that, I felt myself being thrust against Stone by whatever force had urged me across the ballroom floor and into the throne room. Stone's arm swept around my waist within those few seconds, the gown swirling around my thighs, gaping at the bodice as my back met his chest. My head lowered beneath a force I couldn't resist, exposing the back of my neck to Stone.

The heat from his body warmed me in places I grew chilled, but the fine hairs everywhere remained alert. My back was to an enemy, and my whole body knew it and was reacting.

For a second, I believed I could break free of the magic and slam my head backward into his nose, but I discovered I was paralyzed. A pitiable sob escaped me as I realized I was powerless to do more than the king's magic bid of me. Thwarted. My vengeance, nothing in the face of that power but an impotent bit of rage.

"Are you a poison apple, human?" the king asked. "Let's find out, shall we?"

Stone's lips touched down on the back of my neck. Paused there. His chest rose and pressed into me with each inhalation, and I could feel that they were shuddering, wracking movements.

"She's lovely, is she not?" Ferranus asked in a drunken voice. "The creaminess of that complexion. The lush black shadows of her hair. That throat." His voice caught on the last word, and I understood that the king was enjoying this in a sexual way. I was glad my gaze was on the floor and the tips of Stone's polished shoes, and not the king's face.

"She is lovely," Stone said against my skin. A shudder moved through him and into my core.

"Then why aren't you indulging yourself?" Ferranus asked. "What's holding you back, when I've placed her against your lips, ripe, like an apple for the taking."

All this as if I was nothing but a goblet of drink or a plate of cheese. Terrified as I might be, I knew I'd die before I let Stone break my skin without a fight. I had to find a way to make that battle possible.

"If you think I'm tainted, why not just ask me," I said. "Surely I would remember if Terran injected me with poison. Surely I wouldn't be alive if I had been. We mortals are far more fragile than you realize."

Ferranus chuffed out a laugh. "Oh, I know exactly how fragile you are," he said. "But you have no idea what he might have put inside you without you knowing."

A buzz of energy moved over my body, making me shiver. Then, suddenly, Stone stepped back. I was free to lift my head and despite it feeling heavy as a bowling ball, I heaved a glance behind me. Stone was swiping his mouth with the back of his hand. My lips curled in disgust.

Ferranus brushed at his cloak, pulling my attention away from Stone. "Tell me, Cleopatra, just what do remember of your time with Terran? Was there a moment when you felt magic when you shouldn't? A time when you awoke and felt watched? A feeling as if—"

"She was cared for," Stone said, daring to interject, and being rewarded with a glare from the king.

"Was she?" he asked, and then he stepped away to settle himself onto the velvet cushion. From his throne, he studied the two of us so intensely I had a hard time breathing through the nerves that tightened my throat.

Within a barely full exhale, I was pinwheeling across the room and slammed into the wall. My ribs screamed out in pain as they struck the stones. Stone hurtled along after me. My hands met his palm to palm for one second before he pulled me against his chest.

"I'm sorry," he said beneath his breath.

His eyes locked on mine, smoldering, half-shuttered. And then his fingers clawed their way around my wrist and spun me to face the wall. My body went on immediate alert, the hunter in me responding out of cell memory more than anything else. I fought him, tried to fight him, but he had a good grip on me. He was stronger. Faster. My every movement felt wooden and contrived.

He had me pushed up against the wall in seconds. I felt his knee ram in between my thighs even as he yanked my skirts up. The gown Blade had bought and brought for me, the one

I'd admired in Erachne's window, he would treat it like it was a whore's lingerie.

I tried to think of all the ways I'd make him suffer once this was over. I tried not to think of how Blade would want to fight me for revenge of this act, but even as I tried to find a way to keep this from happening, he shoved his legs between mine and parted them.

Rage hit me hard. Even as his body pressed me against the wall, my hands at my sides, flattened against the curve of stone beneath a sconce hissing its magical light above me, I did my best to resist. He laid his cheek against mine from behind and the brush of his whiskers surprised me.

"Are you as tasty as you look, Cleopatra?" Ferranus rasped from his chair. "Like honey and heated spice all at the same time, I bet. Do tell me if I'm right, Stone."

I twisted in Stone's grip and almost managed to break free until he grabbed both wrists and held them up higher over my head, unbalancing me.

"Fuck you," I said.

The king laughed from behind us. "Ah," he said. "Not quite the docile thing she and your father wanted us to believe, now is she?" The sound of his footsteps came as a brush of velvet against skin and no more, but I knew he had left that damn throne and had begun his trek across the room to meet us. Maybe he wanted to see it all up close.

His sigh moved my hair, so I knew he was lurking very closely nearby. "I suspected she was a fighter of some sort after that perfect strike at the demon. But now why do you suppose your father would gift me such a woman if he wasn't looking to use her to kill me?"

My heart stuttered. I tried not to react.

Even when Stone hooked my ankles with his shins, holding my legs spread apart so I couldn't move, I tried my best to look like a mere victim. But it wasn't easy, and I wasn't succeeding no matter how bad I tried.

Ferranus cleared his throat. "Perhaps he didn't realize the sort of woman he'd procured. Or maybe she has her own agenda. So many mortal women come to Fae hoping for beauty or gold."

I breathed deep, focusing so I wouldn't bite back at that remark, but it was difficult. So very difficult. And with Stone's hips ground into my ass, I was having an even harder time concentrating past the rage.

"Maybe I was abducted by a bastard with his own agenda," I ground out before my lips clamped closed with enough force that I barely got my tongue out of the way before my teeth clacked together.

I could almost hear the king thumbing his chin in thought as he said, "Maybe Terran wanted me to get too angry to test her. Maybe he expected her to piss me off so much I drained her without caution."

"You give my father too much credit," Stone said, and his hands loosened their grip on me just enough that the painful vise let blood pool back into my fingers.

"You don't know what your father was capable of," Ferranus snapped. "He was my personal bodyguard for centuries. I know him."

"Knew him," I said, correcting him as the image of Terran's body and the brackish smoke that leaked from his body ran through my mind. The image was enough to make me try to wrench my hands out of Stone's grip. "He died at your feet and you watched him suffer while it happened. Now let me the fuck go." I struggled again in frustration, getting nowhere.

At my words, the king huffed impatiently. "Get on with it," he said to Stone. "I'm tired of her shrewish mouth."

The command was enough for Stone to use his free hand to scoop one of my ankles back and up onto his hip. The movement shoved my chest and cheek flatter against the stones. If it wasn't for the hundreds of planks I did regularly to keep my core strength, I'd have slid right down the wall and fallen upside down.

"Try to escape now, mortal," Ferranus said, but his voice was breathless. He was enjoying this, the bastard.

I was off balance. The stones and grout were digging into my cheek. I could barely pull in a breath in the awkward posture, but one thing kept me from screaming my lungs out. I would kill Stone when this was over. I would mingle his blood with Ferranus's and I'd take all four eye teeth from each of them and make a mobile to hang over my bed so I could watch them clack together in a midnight breeze, the sweetest lullaby a hunter could ask for.

So, keeping that image in my head, I held still. And waited. Stone's hands spasmed briefly before his grip tightened again. "I'm sorry," he said. "I would not want to take you this way. I would not—"

"Enough," Ferranus said. "Hold her tight."

Stone complied so quickly, I wondered if he had already suspected Ferranus would demand it.

What I didn't expect was the roughness with which he gave in, or how forcefully he pinned me from behind. This was nothing like the passionate, heat-filled moments when Blade had bent me over the sink at the manse. Rough and needing as those moments were, they were consensual and hot as hell.

This was not Blade, and this was not consensual. I did my level best to struggle beneath Stone. Even so, my palms dug into the stonework as my arms stretched higher, aching as they did so, high enough that my breasts strained against the bodice of the gown.

"That's it," Ferranus growled beneath his breath. "Just like that. Let her neck strain for your mouth. Let the artery pulse like a terrified hare."

He was enjoying it far too much. My hands clawed at the stone facade, with my fingers scrabbling into the grout and trying desperately to find some purchase to leverage myself around, because I knew then that Stone was not in control. I wasn't in control.

All the control belonged to the king.

"The gown," the king said. "It's too full. Yank it up."

A clot of terror planted itself in my heart as Stone worked at my skirts with his free hand. I struggled then in earnest, gaining no more than an inch to the side, rolling my hip and ribs along the stone wall. But I was not in any position to do much more. With my hands held above me and one leg wrapped back around Stone's hip, I couldn't get the leverage I needed.

And the worst that I believed could happen looked like it was about to happen.

CHAPTER 6

Stone was going to bury his teeth in my neck and there was nothing I could do about it. Worse than that, I had the distinct impression that the king was going to force Stone to violate me. Worse even than that, was that I was certain he planned to watch it happen before he did the same.

The terror that clawed its way up my throat at the thought dragged a single word through my voice box and dropped it into the air with a rasp.

"Stop," I said in a tone that might have been partnered with twisting arms and donkey kicking legs, if I could move at all. Stone's power, his strength, the desire that sat beneath the surface that he'd kept in check, maybe even the hatred he felt for my rebuttal that ended in him hiring hoodlums to sell me to the auction houses of the Catacombs of Dread, all those things made him impossible to resist.

And knowing I couldn't do a damn single thing to stop him made the terror turn to panic. "Stop. Stop."

The words dragged themselves from me on a grated gust of breath.

From beside me the king made a humming sound so casual, I knew...just knew... he'd done this exact thing with countless other mortal men and women.

"He'll stop when I release his magic," he said matter-of-factly. "Right now, he's my puppet. And you are my gift. I'm tired of waiting. I want him to show me that you are clean."

"I'm clean," I gasped out as something from above me made a grating sound, as if a rake was scratching on slate.

"I'm fucking clean," I yelled in a keening voice that made my stomach sick. "Don't make him do this."

I strained to look up and saw with horror that the sconces above me had changed shape. The light within them had guttered to nothing, and the wrought iron itself had unfurled and reformed into hands with long fingers that were busying themselves clawing along the stone wall toward my wrists.

A muffled and startled scream slid free of my lips.

The king let go a dark chuckle. "I doubt the new leader of the Shadow Court will have a problem with being forced to do this. The stink of his desire is making the room rancid."

He fondled my hair even as Stone shifted aside to give him access. My stomach curdled as I started to imagine the worst.

Ferranus leaned in close. A hair's breadth away, close enough that I could see that the veins in his eyes held a slight blue tinge. "Make no mistake, Cleopatra," he whispered. "He might want you, but you are MINE. I decide how much he takes and when."

The fingers stroking my hair slid to the back of my neck and he grappled a hand of tresses into his fingers. Yanked. Tears immediately washed out my vision like a swamp of hard rain taking a vehicle off the road.

"Taste her," he said to Stone and for a second, just one, I thought Stone would resist. His body stiffened. His breath came out in a loud exhale. Some part of him was still in there, then. Maybe I could reach that part of him, try to find some tiny portion of the Fae who had once loved me.

"Stone," I said. Not pleading. Oh gods, no. Instead, I did what I could to use the same sort of tone I'd use on a dog to exert my dominance. "Stone, don't do this. Find yourself. Find your power."

As if drugged, his nose ran along the column of my neck, nuzzling into the back of my ear. The warmth of his breath moved over the lobe.

"I'm sorry, Ava," he said, and I realized by how slowly the syllables spilled out, how clumsy, as if his tongue was tied, that he was a puppet. His only master, the only alpha in the room, the king.

"Don't," I whispered this time, feeling that pleading victim rising in my chest and waving her hands in desperation. "This isn't you."

A guttural laugh from the king. "What do you know of Terran's second?" he said. "A Fae willing to kill his own father. You're wasting your breath, Cleopatra. He wants to taste you."

I knew the truth of that the same as the king did. But while Ferranus was confident of his ability to control Stone, I wasn't so sure.

And since my hands were pinned above me, my wrists in the iron hands, his were free to paw across my lower belly, hoisting me onto his hips. I was peeled free of the wall with that movement, my arms outstretched, my torso supported by his embrace.

The hardness beneath his trousers did not bode well. He'd once declared love for me. I'd nearly taken him to bed in the tavern the night I'd come to Fae with him. I'd wanted him once too, but betrayal has a way of stripping away passion, whether remembered or real. And he'd betrayed me. I knew he wanted me dead. This was his perfect chance to finalize his vengeance.

Would I bleed out after he bit down? Would the king take over once Stone stepped away?

I tried to swallow down the panic. Tried to find some strength in my voice, to remember what I was. Who I was. Why I was here. All the horrible things that would happen if I didn't claim my own power and claim it right then.

I tried to think of Phaedre. I'd chosen to stay because of her and the other nameless heirs the king had sired throughout the kingdom, heirs he'd hired Blade to find and execute. I brought her sweet but homely face to mind. I heard her voice, and I pulled myself together.

I shoved the panic into the closet that used to house my guilt and shame, and I slammed the damn door closed.

"He's not going to stop at a taste," I said, my voice a tremble that I had to make my bitch before the king noticed.

"He will stop," Ferranus said. "I have his magic coiling around mine like serpents. I have control."

"What if you're wrong?" I asked as Stone's teeth began to graze my neck. If there was no fury like a woman spurned, then what rage lay in the heart of a violent fae with a bruised ego?

"What if you're too weak to hold his power in check?" I asked, my voice steady. "Do you want to take that chance?"

"Weak?" Ferranus said in an indignant voice. "I assure you, I am not weak, girl."

Stone's hand started roaming over my breasts atop the gown while the other slid down the front of my thigh. I felt him gather the skirts. Cool air kissed my ankles.

Forcing my breath to move as normally as I could, I said, "Then perhaps this is the only way you can get laid."

It was a simple, offhand remark. One so carefully spoken that I suspected he'd fly into a rage at the sheer audacity of it, and I twisted my face to meet his gaze, feeling the scouring grit of mortar against my cheek. I let my gaze trail toward his own throat, let it linger on his pulse as though I could see the magic within his blood growing pale.

And I pressed on. Like I'd done in the catacombs with the auctioneers. Like I'd done with the kraken at Lilah's house. The way I'd done all those years ago when I'd made the fateful trek into the night to meet a boy while my parents slept a drugged sleep in their chairs.

"Do you have to have other fae—fae like your old friend, Terran—abduct mortal women from the earthen realm because you can't lure them for yourself?"

He offered a guileless grin, one that indicated I'd not managed to goad him in the least. "And men," he said. "I take mortal men too."

"Ah yes," I said, correcting myself. "You're an equal opportunity bully." I swallowed because I was risking a lot. Risking everything with these words. "I'm guessing that's because fae females are too much for you? Are they too strong and you need powerless mortals to get your rocks off?"

That got him. He inched closer, his face so close to mine I could make out the little sparks in his eyes like light coming off metal being hammered.

"There are no fae in the realm more powerful than me, so no, human, I am not afraid to bed one of my own kind. This isn't about fucking. This is about a blood gift that was given to me by the leader of a court that wishes to rival my own. I could choose to bury my cock inside every single one of your orifices right now if I wanted." He flicked his fingers toward Stone, whose roaming hands suddenly stopped. "I could grow myself five members and plunder you with wild abandon. I could drain you and think nothing of it." He drew back slightly, just enough to show me a flash of teeth. "I'm sure I would enjoy that very much. But right now, I want to know if you are clean. And the son of the bastard who tried to kill me will test that for me because only a fool accepts a gift from an enemy."

Leaning forward again, he let his lips rest against the corner of my mouth. "And if he dies in the tasting then I'll know the depth of Terran's betrayal and you shall be the one to taste my rage."

"And if he lives?" I asked as Stone's breath came harsher against my neck.

Ferranus cocked his head to the side, leaning away from me. "Are you asking if I plan to drain you to empty afterward?"

I said nothing, and he nodded subtly, his mouth making a thoughtful pout. "It's possible," he said, thumbing his chin. "You are my gift, after all. I can do as I wish."

His eye trailed to where the trunk sat open beside his throne. The way his gaze lingered on it before drawing back to me made me shiver. I felt the echo of the movement in Stone's body.

The king turned his attention to Stone. "It might indeed be exciting," he said. "The things in there..." he let the words trail off before he finished. "Terran did know me well. It would be a shame to let all that go to waste."

The last thing I wanted was for his attentions to stray in that direction. I had to find an alternative, one that would dissuade him from forcing Stone to taste test me and one that would solve his question of needing me clean. I had to find an answer that ended in me gaining control over both of those things. And I had to find it now.

"Cut me," I said and wrenched my body to the left to avoid Stone's hand spilling into the bodice.

"What's that, Cleopatra?" Ferranus asked.

"Cut me. Release Stone's magic so he will let me go, and then cut me. That way you can have him test my blood without worrying he'll go too far."

And with any luck, he'd have to pull out that knife he had stashed in his sash. The moment it appeared, I was sure I could wrest it from him. I'd disarmed Gideon many times in training. All I had to do was let my muscle memory do what it worked so many hours on.

Stone's palm stilled on my breast. He sucked in an audible breath, and I was sure his grip slackened. I exhaled through my nose. Close. I was so close.

"I do not worry he'll go too far," Ferranus drawled. "Because I am in control, but what you propose is interesting."

He took a step backward and pulled his knife from his sash. "Step away, Stone."

I was released swiftly, but gently. When my feet touched the floor, my hips groaned in relief.

"My hands," I said, peering up at the iron claws that encircled my wrists and held me against the wall. "All the blood has left my fingers. Can you let them go too?"

Ferranus made a thoughtful sound deep in his throat, but finally relented. The cuffs clicked free and scrabbled back up the stonework to become wrought iron sconces again. They bled out that soft, purple glow all the way down the wall to the floor.

My arms fell to my sides like over-starched pasta. Shaking them out took effort, and even more to work through the pins and needles to force blood back into my hands. My armpits and shoulder cuffs ached, but I pivoted sharply, not willing to stand with my back to the king for a moment longer.

No sooner had I managed to massage in enough blood to wiggle my fingers, than the king's hand shot out to grab my wrist.

He yanked so abruptly that I couldn't put my palm up to hold him off as I fell against his chest.

It was a firm chest, indicating he didn't merely sit on his throne and order deaths. He worked that body. It was well-muscled and powerful. I didn't want to think about how he kept in shape.

His hand moved to the side like a rattlesnake side winding its way home.

"You do realize," he murmured. "Whether mortal or Fae, women die for my touch."

CHAPTER 7

The king's smile slid over his face like oil on a hot griddle as he said the word. Die.

I gave him back the same sort of smile. "Not exactly Seinfeld level humor, but not a bad pun all things considered."

A genuine look of pleasure broke his face and for a second, I saw a creature who might have started out his life devoid of the malice that crested his brow in this present.

"I thought a mortal of your intelligence would appreciate the pun," he said, but then the naivete was gone and he urged me ahead of him, forcing my legs to move despite my resistance. With both of my hands in one of his surprisingly large maws, the knife hanging in his other, he led me toward the throne and the trunk that sat in front of it, lid open.

I tossed a look over my shoulder at Stone, who was standing so rigidly I thought he must be still under the king's control.

My own steps were leaden and forced. My willpower was as flimsy as wet tissue paper beneath the magic. A lot of magic, I knew. After all he'd expended, he was still pushing it, showing dominance, showing strength. I tried to make myself believe it was because he'd do anything to avoid showing weakness, even to over-using his powers.

He rounded the throne, dragging me along with him. With a rough shove, he forced me to lean awkwardly behind the backrest, barely peering over the top of the throne toward Stone, whose jaw had gone tense, his eyes rolling back as if he was trying very hard to find some control of himself.

Without wanting to, I found myself thrusting my backside up and out. A compelled movement that startled me as much as the rustle of material. I felt the brush of my garments over my ankles and I realized with horror he was trying to gather the skirts up over my hips.

I struggled beneath his ministrations, trying to twist and wrench out of his way. Nothing I did seemed to matter. Frustrated tears welled up in my eyes.

"Stop," I said, trying to quell the rising panic. "This isn't testing me."

"Isn't it?" he asked in a husky voice. "I could compel you to be still. I could compel your surrender."

His hands grappled even as his hips bucked, but the skirts cushioned most of the feeling between us. "I could even compel you to whore yourself to me with complete abandon and passion."

Another inept, impotent pawing of my dress. "Fuck," he growled. "Is there no end to these skirts?"

I thought of all the ways I'd fight my way out of a man's unwanted embrace. The hours of defense Gideon had drilled into me, that ended in panting, sweating sessions on the mats, tried to take control of my limbs but none of it worked. Those limbs, that control, belonged to him.

The only thing I had true possession over was my mouth.

"Quite a lover you must be," I mocked. "If you have to compel someone to fuck you."

His teeth touched down on my shoulder, a grazing threat without breaking skin. Careful, he was, even when angry. His entire body shuddered where it touched mine. I imagined my fingers moving toward the blade, wanting to grab for it but unable to move an inch of my own volition.

"Being a good lover doesn't interest me," he said. "What interests me is my own pleasure."

I sucked the back of my teeth. "Then it seems I've found the only honest man in either realm."

He chuckled at that. "Indeed," he said. "Now, unless Terran managed to plant a booby trap inside you before he dropped you from his collar like a spider's egg shaken from an old coat, I'd say it's time I show some pleasure in his gift." His finger trailed down my shoulder. "And what could be more pleasant than doing so while Stone watches and rages as I take what's mine and wants for himself."

Both of Ferranus's arms shot out to coral me between them as he settled his hands on the backrest. "But just because I have to teach the both of you a lesson, does not mean I haven't given consideration to your proposal."

At that, a page appeared from nowhere, popping soundlessly into place in front of the throne, holding a golden chalice.

I felt a nod of his head behind me that spurred the page into rounding the throne and tilting the chalice toward the king, his own hand trembling. When he caught my eye, a flare of crimson burst around his irises. Red, I realized, just a shade lighter than the crimson coiling around Blade's like snakes. I wondered what sort of fae he was.

The king's breath started coming in long drafts as he worked at the hem, trying to hoist it up over my hips.

"Fuck," he said. "How is it possible these skirts have grown thicker?"

The gown had been form-fitting. I'd recognized the cobweb gown from the window of Erachne's shop the moment Blade had presented it to me in the ballroom. I'd admired the thing. Erachne hadn't wanted to sell it to him.

It was mine, though. It knew my body, and it knew my body's mate. No doubt the Dark Enforcer had purchased it before we'd even returned to Terran's manse. The thought of it warmed my chest and held me still beneath the king's fumbling. Because I knew without a single doubt, even as Ferranus worked himself into a lather trying to get the fullness of the skirts up over my hips, that Erachne had spelled the material to respond for only two hands.

I smiled secretly at the thought as the king cursed and worked at the folds of material that hadn't been there moments before and wouldn't be there moments after he let go.

And then I thought of that knife—filled with magic—and I smiled ever broader, waiting for the moment I could grab for it, hoping that he'd be so busy trying to take his pleasure that he'd drop the compulsion. Just for a second.

"Blast it," he complained and let go with one hand long enough to grab me by the hair. "If I can't yank them up, you will. But first—"

He pulled my head back, so that I faced the apex of the ceiling and the cluster of eavesdroppers sitting atop wooden rafters, criss-crossing themselves high above us in forms so lifelike they must have been human at some time. The page edged closer, offering the lip of the chalice.

"Such thick hair," Ferranus said. "As bad as this damned dress."

As if he hated the thought of defeat, he made another attempt to yank the fabric up and cursed as if they'd grown weightier. Then, tired of fighting from below, he let go and pressed his hips harder into my backside while he thrust his hands beneath the bodice, burrowing in to find my nipple. He pinched.

Now was the time, I knew. I felt the release the way a blood pressure cuff let go. Instinct took over. I cracked my head backward. Pain splintered over my skull as the thwack resounded in the air. A millimeter of space found a cushion between the king's body and mine.

The page jumped back, startled. I heard his movement as the stars lit behind my eyelids. I waited for them to abate as my hands felt behind me, reaching for the king's hip, putting an image of him behind my eyelids amid the explosion of fireworks blinding me.

I almost thought I heard a dark, indulgent chuckle coming from somewhere in the shadows of the trunk. An image flashed through my mind, of Blade's face at the moment in the catacombs when he'd told the auctioneer that my hair belonged to him. That he planned to bid flesh and blood to reclaim it.

The thought of Blade in that moment steeled my spine. Whatever would come from my impudence, I'd take it gladly.

The king fell back a couple of steps and I didn't have to turn around to know he was probably holding onto his nose. I'd broken enough noses to know the cracking sound of cartilage letting go. I had to believe that while he wanted to rally his magic, the pain took too much attention.

But I did turn around. I had to. There was no way I was leaving a predator with full access to my back.

I expected a snap of magic as his rage rose. My fists curled at my sides automatically. My eyes darted to the walls, looking for something to race to, to pull down in defense. His knife. If I could just get to it before the blast of magic hit me.

But he wasn't angry. There was a sheen of blush over his features that spilled down his neck, plunging beneath that frivolous collar. And in that moment, I realized the lack of magical retaliation was intentional. Cocky, so damned cocky, this king to think that he could afford a hunter space to fight back.

"Oh my," the king said, breathless. "You are indeed a warrior. Fucking you would be such a novelty after centuries of damsels." He waved his hand and in a breath, I was in front of him again. This time in his embrace. He had backed me up to the throne. I felt a stab from one of the curlicues digging into my calf.

He hefted the pile of my hair onto the top of my head, and his fingers tightened, pulling the scalp taut. "Oh, how I'd love to feel all this trailing over my balls."

Long gone was the bid to play innocent damsel. There was no way Ferranus would believe that now. So to hell with trying to look like one.

"You'll feel more than my hair on your balls," I ground out. "When I slice your sac open like a peach and run your nuts over my teeth."

An abrupt, surprised laugh. "You think you have the balls to kill a king?" he asked, somehow making the words sound like a statement rather than a question.

"You'd be surprised how big my balls are," I told him with all sincerity.

A snort of air through his nose. "I've never been averse to a set of big balls," he drawled. "But I have the feeling I'd be disappointed to find a set between your legs."

"Not half as disappointed as I'll be to find a set between yours," I countered and thought I heard Stone choke on a gasp of breath.

The king watched me keenly. "Perhaps you'd prefer something else," he drawled. "Thanks to the gift of magic from my subjects over these last centuries—some of whom have some very interesting powers—I can make of my cock anything you'd like. The shape and size won't affect my pleasure, but it will most definitely affect yours."

The hard edge to his voice was an obvious threat, and in case I didn't get it, he gave me a meaningful look. There was a time to be snarky, and there was a time to shut yer trap. I feared I'd already gone too far. I clamped my mouth shut then.

His grunt of pleased satisfaction suggested I had made the right decision.

With a finger raised in warning to me, he raked his gaze from my face to Stone's. Then he sighed. Heavily. As though he'd come to some momentous and hard-fought decision.

"This has become tedious," he said. "Your magic is your own, Big Boy. But mind you, draw near slowly. I want your steps so slow, I can tell you ache with each movement."

Like a deer picking its way from a thicket onto an unfamiliar field, Stone came. His eyes didn't leave the king's face. Every muscle in his body looked to be straining wherever it was visible through his suit. His open collar showed the cords of his neck were taut. His forearms showed a powerfully knotted bulge where he'd rolled up his sleeves. Even the shoulders of his suit were bunched. He was taking his time, and it was painful, like agonizingly intentional eccentric exercises.

He threaded his way toward us and the whole time, all I could think of was I'd lost the chance to grab for that knife and now it was out of reach.

Even so, I measured how close the king was to me, how fast I'd have to be to launch myself across him. I even calculated the pace I might need to run at to hit the door to the ballroom before he could react if I couldn't access the blade.

But all that, all those minute pieces of strategy, were no good here. He was a fae. Powerful fae. And my fastest speed, my most daring snatch and slice, was useless in the face of his magic.

I watched Stone's turtle pace, that powerful fae who was now helpless to do more than follow Ferranus's commands to the letter, and I knew I'd been a fool to think the king might compare to the likes of Terran or Stone or even Blade.

So I stood there, praying for some miracle, some spark of inspiration, some happy happenstance that might deliver to me the opportunity to confront this bastard and end him.

And as if the heavens heard me, that moment came.

 Chapter 8

Ferranus huffed his appreciation for Stone's submission with each dainty step. There was a callous and calculated glee in the way he dragged me with him all the way to the front of the throne, the way he perched onto the cushion. Legs stretched out so that his heels rested against the flagstones, he sat there, chest heaving, sweat beading on his brow.

And it became very clear that the moment he sat down it was because he had to. He was tiring. The exertion of his magic to control Stone, to force me to his will, were expenditures he shouldn't have made after the great show of power he'd presented in the ballroom.

He'd exerted more than he'd wanted to. I could see it in his face and the way his hand trembled as it settled onto the armrest.

Ferranus leaned back in his chair. His boots were worn on the bottom, with scuff marks more to the outside edge, indicating his gait wasn't quite perfect.

As he sat, he tapped his finger on the armrest and for the first time, I realized he wore a heavy ring that clacked maddeningly against the iron. Clack. Click. Clack. Every two seconds, the sounds in tandem with Stone's footsteps. An agonizingly annoying sound that matched my heartbeat, the sluggish thing so tired from pounding in fear that I doubted a jolt of adrenaline would speed it up.

By the time Stone stood in front of the trunk, on the opposite side from where the king sat and I stood, Ferranus had already begun to slump in his seat. One stolen glance at Stone's face and I knew he saw it, too. But could I trust him if I made my move? Released from the king's control, would he use his magic to help me or harm me the moment I leaped for the knife?

Because the question remained as to just how tired the king was. I'd known Mica needed to take to his bed when he'd exerted too much magic at once, but the king, while weary-looking, was still upright. Powerful indeed. Or was he just hopped up on the magic he'd gained from the fae he'd killed in the ballroom?

I might have wanted to finish the job, but I wasn't a fool. I needed more evidence. I needed to be sure I could overpower him and make the killing blow. Anything else, anything less and I wouldn't just put myself in danger. I'd risk using up the last chance there might be in a hundred years to kill this bastard.

For Phaedre, I needed to be certain.

Even as the thoughts ran through my mind, even as I scanned the king's posture for evidence that he would fail at any moment, the ring on his finger glowed, catching my eye like a wink of light in a night-shrouded crypt. It was as if he'd received a jolt of caffeine.

And the moment it did, the page who remained where he'd popped into the chamber, dropped the chalice that was supposed to hold the taste of my blood.

It clattered onto the floor and rolled noisily in a semicircle. The page's eyes went wide, the reddish tinge flaring like brake lights.

"I think I shall not drink of my gift this moment," Ferranus said, his attention drifting to the page.

The page jerked as if someone had tugged on an invisible line. His gaze skittered over the room, his mouth dropping open like a landed fish. It almost looked like he was trying to scream, but nothing came from his throat but a strangled whimper.

When he skidded to a stop just in front of Ferranus, his steps both spastic and hesitant, his entire body bowed as though an archer had pulled him tight. Only his head came near the king, and it was clear he was doing all he could to keep the rest of his body out of reach.

The angle was so unnatural, so creepily affecting, that I felt like I was looking at a body that had been broken and put together wrong. Everything in my own body responded with revulsion. I wanted to reach out to him, to put him back into his natural shape.

Even as the thought crossed my mind, the page tilted his head to the side. He closed his eyes, resigned, a tear sliding down his cheek.

The king lashed out like a cobra then, so fast I didn't see the movement at all. Just a blur of color that took me far too long to understand he'd moved at all and by then, he was latched onto the page's neck like a goddamned vampire. Except...

Except it wasn't teeth that buried into the page's flesh. It was some sort of tuber, with an octopus's sucker. Just one. But it was purple and swollen and throbbing, a sharp, thorn-like prong jutting out from its center, as it clamped onto the skin. It was impossible to tear my eyes away as the page's skin went white and then grey, as it shriveled and he collapsed into a husk at the king's feet.

He slumped sideways before the chalice stopped spinning in place and the way it rang throughout the chamber when it finally came to a stop was the poor page's death knell. I shivered involuntarily.

Slowly, with what I was sure intended to be a display that would horrify me, Ferranus drew the tuber back. The sucker puckered and flared. A needle-like appendage pulled itself back into the flange of sucker and that tuber itself retracted back into the king's mouth.

It disappeared with a swallow, and Ferranus turned his eyes to mine.

"I can do that with my cock too," he said with a glint in his eye that made my stomach lurch.

I'd seen plenty of horrible things in my career as a monster hunter. I'd taken on beasts with claws and fangs and krakens with bogarts in their bellies. Witches conjured all sorts of things to make me think my nightmares had come to life.

But all I could think in that moment the king turned his attention to me with that image fresh in my mind, was that if I'd made my move to grab his knife, I'd have felt that suction on my neck, the needle plunging into my throat.

My knees sagged at the thought.

Stone was there to take up the slack, and I was still too traumatized to even care that his hands were on me, steadying me. I was actually glad to feel the warmth of someone else's touch on my bare arm.

Ferranus looked at us both and that grin grew even wider. I was sure I could see that sucker in the back of his throat. A shudder shook my core.

"I can tell you're moved," Ferranus said. "But don't concern yourself with my poor page. He isn't dead." A shrug, a glint of his eye. "Merely...empty. Without his magic, what you see is what's left of a fae when they've had all their magic drained."

My heart skipped a beat, and I felt myself clench Stone's arm all the tighter.

A chortle raised my gaze to the king once more when he said, "I know what you're thinking. You're presuming that's what will happen when the fae offer me their magic." He crossed one ankle over the other and stretched his legs out so far they almost touched the little page's crisp, singed hair. "But don't you worry about that, either. I have many ways of taking magic. My own natal magics giving me the power to accept what is freely given. Taking it by force..." he shrugged helplessly. "That's not a transference of power, that's assault. And as you see, it can be violent."

His grin made me cringe. "Kind of like the difference between rape and consensual sex. Both acts themselves are essentially the same, but only one does things to the psyche that might seem very similar to this dried up husk of fae."

I wanted terribly to tell him what I thought of him, but I took one look at the page and I held my tongue. My core trembled with the need to end this bastard. And I would, I told myself. As impossible as it seemed right then, I would find a way.

He blew air out his nose as if he'd just finished a lengthy and productive task.

"I've decided you will not go to the veil."

"Are you refusing the gift, then?" Stone asked, taking an abrupt step toward the king. One step. Then he was frozen in place again. Another reminder that while Ferranus was weary, he still had plenty of power to wield.

"That's far enough, Don Sidhe, is it?"

Stone hung his head, but from where I stood, I could see the scowl on his face.

"A ridiculous term that only humans would appreciate as it's ludicrously inaccurate. Why not Emir or Khan or Pharoah? Those are much more evocative of what you are in that pathetic manse your father built for himself."

"I believe it was a human who used the term first," Stone said, directing his words toward the floor. "A century ago."

Ferranus waved his hand to indicate he didn't think it mattered. "Whoever coined the term," he said, "you are now the leader, and since you are the son of the male who broke a blood oath, it is in my rights and duty to inform you that I must claim penalty."

I swore my heart stopped. Not because Stone's throat blanched as he shifted sideways just enough to block me from view of the king, but because I remembered what he'd told me about breaking such an oath.

Torture, death to family. Apparently, I'd wrongfully believed those things were just horrible consequences conjured and meted out by the Shadow Court to keep their soldiers in line.

Stone deserved all that and more, but I wanted to be the one to serve that justice. I wanted to see his face when I hurt him, when I revealed all I knew about his betrayal.

Edging my way out from behind his back, I side-stepped, the gown swishing in my ears.

"The fae who broke that oath is dead," I said to the king. "Surely that's enough penalty. That should be enough payment for breaking an oath."

"What penalty is suicide?" he asked. "What payment should be meted out for attempted regicide?" He touched his finger to his chin. "No. I am entitled to my entitlements, and while it grieves me to decline an exciting Blood Gift such as you, Cleopatra," he said, sighing theatrically. "My duty forbids it. Fae everywhere must remember just how sacred a blood oath is. They need to remember there are consequences to breaking one."

His ring glowed again and impossibly, the fallen page rose to his feet like a sheaf of ashen parchment. There was no life in his eyes, no muscle tension anywhere in the husk of flesh, and yet he moved. It was like seeing a ghost rise from a grave.

"Fetch me five lesser fae," Ferranus said to him. "Preferably, young and pretty ones." A frown creased his face for an instant before he continued. "But no trows," he said, tilting his head toward me and I inclined mine, thinking whatever he wanted them for, at least Heuil would be safe.

The page, with his paper mache expression, didn't move until Ferranus lifted his hand in front of his face, examining the ring, and I realized he wasn't done with his order. "Make sure you do not disturb the revelry of those around those whom you select. I want those comrades to be envious of the opportunity they have lost to honor their king."

The page spun like a filthy sheet in the wind to face the door. It opened for him without him needing to touch it, and his waft through the opening reminded me of ash on a breeze. The ruckus leakage of noise and celebration shut off like a pipe when the door clicked closed behind him.

Once he was gone, the king turned his attention back to Stone and me. He crossed his hands behind his head and leaned back. Comfortable. Unconcerned. Unafraid. Oh, how I wanted to change all those expressions.

"You want this woman," he said without looking my way. "Your desire for her was obvious earlier."

Stone said nothing. I did my best not to look his way.

"If I'm to believe your father wasn't foolish enough to offer me a tainted gift." His elbows drew together and spread out again. "then I presume you've not claimed her."

Stone swallowed and my throat burned with the desire to call him out. It was a struggle to remain silent, but I managed it. Right until Ferranus's gaze drifted toward me.

"She did not want your hands on her."

Again, Stone remained silent. The king continued, undeterred.

"She's no virgin, but she's not fae-taken."

Stone shook his head as I hung mine because if fae-taken meant what I thought, I was indeed tainted. I didn't want the king to see the truth of it on my face. I didn't want Stone to see it. What was between Blade and me was not their business.

"Good," the king said. "I would be offended at being given a second hand ride. A re-gift as the mortals call it." That greasy smile showed itself again as he canted his head toward me, expecting a laugh perhaps.

I did nothing. There was no way I was indulging him a moment longer.

The moments drew out uncomfortably as no one spoke. Ferranus watched us, Stone standing rigid, me with my arms crossed over my chest, waiting for some shift in the air.

When it did shift, it was because the door burst open and five laughing, cheerful fae spilled into the room. The page drifted over to the place where he'd fallen, looking far more crumbly than he had moments earlier. By the time he made it to the spot where he'd been struck by the king, his body rained down in dust and ash to the floor.

The pile he left was neat and tidy. Not a trace of ash in the surrounding air. The king's gaze dipped to it for an instant. "High fae work better as thralls," he said. "These ones have only a few test runs before they turn to ash. Pity."

He turned a bright smile on the horde of lesser fae who had entered and were already bowing so low in front of the throne that their hair, lush and black and sparkling with tiny bursts of magic, trailed ahead of them in pools on the flagstones.

Three females and two males. Their bodies nubile and perfect beneath tight fitting doublets and gowns.

"Rise now, " Ferranus said. "And come close." He gestured them forward, and they rose indeed. Then on they went, each of them in unison toward the king on silent, padding feet.

And in unison, they were struck. Not with one sucker but five at once that burst from the king's mouth with so much force and speed that he gagged as they shot out.

The pressure they exerted brought all five fae to their knees, and they were dragged across the tiles to where Ferranus sat. He leaned slightly forward, the force of the connection between him and the fae drawing him closer to them.

This time when Stone caught me, I clung to him.

"Don't watch," he said in a low whisper. "You can't do anything. Let them go."

Let them go. As if they were nothing, as if they didn't have lives and loves somewhere. I felt my belly lurch and my skin go cold, but I took his advice. I squeezed my eyes shut and blocked out the sounds of the fae's gasping breaths, their whimpers.

Because they weren't going down like the page had, quiet and calm. They hadn't been relieved of feeling or been numbed by a loss of control. I heard their struggles, the sounds of boots scuffing the floor, of groans of pain. All I could think was that page had suffered too, just been unable to show it. I remembered the way his face had blanched, and I realized he knew what was coming before the king struck.

The knowledge tightened my eyelids, but even with my eyes shut firmly enough to light color behind my eyelids, it wasn't enough. My mind supplied every image in technicolor, and I knew in seconds there would be five more piles of ash on the floor. I knew those poor fae would be gone forever, and I was doing nothing to stop it.

And that's why I clung to Stone. I knew I couldn't do a damn thing, and the grief and guilt of it bowed my knees so sharply I couldn't stand on my own.

It was clear the whole ordeal was over when the king cleared his throat. Only then did I realize I'd buried my face in Stone's chest. With a shove, I backed away from him, ashamed at my weakness. Embarrassed about using him as a shield when I wanted him so very dead.

"Well now," Ferranus said. "I'm glad to see Cleopatra isn't all piss and vinegar. It's good to see I can still wow a mortal woman."

I inhaled through my nose. Slowly. Regaining some calm. Wow wasn't the word I'd use to describe how I felt.

"Humans aren't accustomed to some things in Fae," Stone said in a tight voice.

"Indeed," Ferranus said, and I stole the first look at him since he'd attacked the youths who had entered the room. Somehow, he looked brighter. Fleshier. A rose bloomed in each cheek and his eyes were bright. He looked drunk.

"Now," he said, inclining his head toward me to acknowl-edge my notice. "Let's get you two married."

CHAPTER 9

"Married?" I echoed, shooting a look toward Stone. "The two of us?"

This had to be a joke.

The king sighed through his nose. "I must have been mistaken to think you one of the rare, intelligent mortal women," he said. "Who else would I be talking about if not the only couple standing in front of me. Now...." He pushed off his seat and waved at the five pages who were nothing but paper mache forms on the floor. "It's time to address my subjects."

At his comment, Stone took a step, not threatening but very aggressive, closer toward the king.

Ferranus shot him a warning glare. "Take care," he said. "One does not get too close to a king unbidden."

At that, the five thralls rose to a rustling stand. They pivoted on their feet in a wooden movement that was reminiscent of cardboard cutouts being spun around in place. Each of them stood in front of the king and it was so absurd to think of them as a cardboard bodyguard that an almost manic laugh slid free of my throat.

The thralls skidded apart to allow the king to move between the two females. He stood there, glowering at me.

"You find humor in all this?" His voice dripped with condescension.

I could only shake my head and do my best to strangle off the damned adrenaline-high laughter.

Ferranus's glower intensified, narrowing his eyes to mere slits, and that only seemed to prod the laughter to greater heights. I had to clamp my hand physically over my mouth to stuff the noise back in.

Stone elbowed me hard in the ribs. A whistle came through my fingers, followed by a sob.

That was when I realized Stone hadn't just elbowed me, but had grabbed me so hard that I had fallen against him and his arm was folded over my waist. I closed my eyes like a coward, thinking if this was a nest of vampires, I'd either be dead by now or walking away covered in blood and gore.

The thought made me whimper even harder.

"Shh," Stone murmured into my hair. "It's going to be alright. Just do as you're told, Ava."

"Is that so, Don Sidhe?" Ferranus asked too quietly. "Do you believe things will be alright after all?"

I felt Stone's nod against the top of my head. But it wasn't one of agreement. It possessed all the heaviness of a man bowing beneath an executioner's blade.

The king snorted at his reaction. "Well, then," he said. "Let's go see if it is, shall we?"

At that, I heard the thralls moving and looked up to see that two of them had grasped the handles of the trunk and were heading to the copper door that led back to the ballroom. The other three held fast to their spots, dead leaves trembling on the wind.

Impossibly, Ferranus bowed politely to both Stone, and I then gestured for us to go ahead of him. I inhaled through my nose, relieved the laughing fit seemed to be over.

With a peek upward, I caught Stone's eye. Inclining his head briefly, he released me, giving me a moment to smooth the gown down over my hips, to take a moment, however small, to collect myself.

I didn't need it. I was there already. Whatever moment of fear, of uncertain terror, was gone.

"I haven't forgotten," I said to him through clenched teeth. "I know what you did and I haven't forgotten." Then I shouldered past him to stride to the door, leaving them both behind.

I'd face what awaited me head on. Like a hunter.

The thralls carrying the trunk stood aside as the door swung open. It seemed they would let the three of us through before they lugged the heavy chest out into the ballroom.

The material of the gown barely felt present as I moved. Like the first gown Erachne had fitted to me, this one gave me an ease of movement that, strangely enough, seemed to feel less and less like I was wearing anything at all.

By the time I reached the dais, knowing the other two were behind me, it felt as if I was wearing my yoga pants and boots. I had to look down to assure myself they hadn't magically exchanged places with the dress.

The entire assembly of fae seemed to notice something had changed as we entered. Perhaps it was Ferranus's presence, or his magic, demanding they stop their revelry and dancing, the cavorting in the corners, but the room went as silent as a church.

I halted where Terran's body had been. It was cleared away now, showing no sign of his fall. No blood. No scuff of boot or single hair from his head. Off to the side, in a small cluster of fae I recognized as his thugs, stood Gideon.

His gaze glued itself to mine. The only thing that gave away his relief at seeing me was the way his chest sagged and his shoulders bowed inward. Both relief and anxiety warred for place in my own chest at seeing him there. He was unharmed. That much was a blessing.

But there was someone else I wanted to see more than anything. The Dark Enforcer. And no matter how deeply I scanned the crowds, I could not catch sight of him.

Blade was nowhere to be seen. Neither was Heuil.

Stone came up beside me and I stepped away, loathe to have him too near. "Get away from me," I said beneath my breath. "I had a moment. That's it. But don't think it entitles you to touch me."

I turned my face to his, ensuring he understood the deadly earnestness in my expression and knew I meant each word. "I'll kill you before I let that happen."

He flinched, but schooled his expression quickly. "You might have to fight the king for the honor," he said and jerked his chin to where Ferranus ascended the dais to face the crowds eddying in the room.

Cheers went up when he did, and in response, the king raised his hands, magnanimous. Humbly smiling into the crowds, indulging their applause. He looked all too generous, too beneficent.

"Bastard," I muttered, my gaze sliding again to the knife on his sash. Regret. So many regrets about my choices in the throne room.

Ruby bristled beside him, not three paces away. The shadows seemed to swirl ever more feverishly around her. I could barely look in her direction without feeling dizzy.

"Friends, fae, family," Ferranus intoned, though I doubt anyone else, but those closest heard it over the din. "Please. You're making me blush."

"Fucker," Stone said beneath his breath, and it surprised me enough to shoot him a look.

"I'd think you'd be happy," I said.

He sucked the back of his teeth. "Why would I be happy, Ava? There's nothing good about to happen here in case you haven't got the message."

My turn to snort. "I suppose if trying to have me killed didn't work, then being given me as a fucking slave bride might suffice to torture me until my dying day. Which, I might add, will be my last if I have to endure your attempts at claiming your nuptial rights."

"What?"

"Oh please," I said. "Don't pretend you aren't pissed at me for rejecting you."

I turned to him then, ignoring the sounds of the king chortling good-naturedly from the dais, the pandering words he offered his subjects, because I wanted to see his reaction as I put all the venom I could in my voice. "You hired some fae pricks to sell me on the auction blocks in the catacombs because your ego couldn't take it."

His face blanched, making his eyes stand out starkly against his skin. "I hired some males to take you back to the Velvet Boar. To see you home again."

"Right." The edge in my voice was enough to make him cringe. "So that's why you were so surprised when you saw me returning from the Shadow Trail with Blade." My hands curled into fists. "Because you thought I was 'home'. That's why you were so worried about my welfare. Because you thought I was 'home'."

"Of course," he whispered. "If I'd thought they'd taken you to the Catacombs of Dread, I would have come for you myself. I would have killed them with my own hands."

A laugh barked free. "Well, Blade did that for you. And if he knew it was you to blame, he'd tear you apart with his teeth." My lip curled back. "But he won't know. Because I'm the one who will kill you. Make no mistake. Your death is mine."

Something moved across his face. "That half-trow you made Blade heal—"

"Exactly," I said. "He sold you out. He's the only one of the gang you hired who lived to confess who hired him. But before he did that, he helped me. Back there." A break in my voice held me the rest of the words back until I could swallow and mobilize the muscles in my throat. "If it wasn't for him..." I shook my head, biting back the awful confession of those days of priming myself with drugs just to survive, the days of sickness and Blade's nursing me back to health. Those moments were mine. They belonged to me and I wouldn't repay this bastard's betrayal with the admission of my shame.

"Is that how you think of me?" he asked. "That I possess an ego so fragile that I would order the woman I love killed? Sold into slavery? Raped and assaulted and tortured by the creatures who frequent that horrible place?" His voice was thick and so weighed down by emotion that it cast a shade on my own truth. There was sincerity in his voice, I was certain of it.

"Interesting order you put those things in," was what I said, however. "Suggesting slavery would be the first and worst of the horrors."

He clutched at my arm then, and if it wasn't for the fae all around us, the king who watched from the dais, I would have yanked myself from his grip. Instead, his fingers warmed my wrist as his heated gaze ran over my face, searching for something I couldn't give him.

"It wasn't slavery I put first in the list," he said. "Trust me. Death would have been preferable to anything else you found in the catacombs. I would never have forced you to endure that."

My mind flashed back to the moment in the caves that I'd thought the same, but I refused to hear the niggling of my gut that told me his words held as much dread as I'd felt back then. Instead, I said. "You don't love me and you weren't trying to rescue me. You brought me here."

His head hung as several fae around us jostled for place closer to the dais. We got shoved and pushed and both of us ignored it. My whole attention was on him. "I did bring you here," he said. "I was wrong. I told you that. But I hired them to bring you home. It was the only way I could do so without breaking my oath to the Shadow Court. To my father."

"A father you murdered. A court you now rule. An oath that doesn't matter because you all will pay that price anyway."

At that, his head snapped up. "There is much you don't know, Ava," he said in a heartfelt tone and I felt my heart soften. Damn the thing. When he edged closer, enough that I could smell the ozone of magic swirling around him, felt the heat from his gaze smoldering over me, I almost gave in.

But then the king spoke, and it was a bark that commanded attention. We'd taken too much liberty with the time given to us. Both of us looked at the dais.

"Look at them," he said above our heads, and all the crowds swiveled bodies and necks and sometimes complete heads to look at us standing close, like lovers. "They can barely keep their hands off each other. What say you, kingdom?"

At the sound of agreeable applause and cheers that sounded a hell of a lot like: bind them, bind them, I realized the king had been telling the court that a wedding would take place. With his hands raised over his head, Ferranus beamed out at the crowds.

"Indeed, I shall be more than happy to create a mating bond between these two, but first, you all must know the basis for this surprise nuptial."

At that, a fissure opened in Ruby's swirling mass of shadow. Blade stepped through as though he had taken a fresh shower and was ready to greet a fresh day. Oh, the look of him. My pulse rate sped up. A sense of well-being flooded me. It would be alright now. Everything would be fine.

His visual scan of the room was swift and complete, and within a heartbeat, his gaze landed on me. The electric pull of his eyes might have dragged me forward, it was so intense. But Stone possessed such a grasp of my arm, that movement wasn't possible.

For his part, Blade raked his brother with a glare before heading toward me. He was halted by the king's upheld hand. Ruby stepped in front of him to bar the way.

"What is this?" he said, loud enough that even those in the back should be able to hear. There wasn't anger in his voice, but there was tension, low and vibrating. As powerful as I knew the king was, the Dark Enforcer had far more presence. My throat went dry.

"This," the king said, drawing Blade's eye. "Is a wedding, Dark Enforcer. I am about to join fae and mortal in a lifetime bond."

Blade blinked, but that was the only reaction that gave away how he felt. "I thought she was to be delivered to your harem," he said, and the hope that flared in his features made my heart ache.

Apparently, he believed he'd been summoned as that fae. But even as he held my gaze with that bright, hopeful one of his own, it was obvious he was wary of the information. Something was off, and he knew it.

I tried to warn him with my eyes, praying whatever bond he had with me, the blood he'd taken, the tracking he'd set upon me in the carriage on the way here, would protect him, protect all of us from what he'd do when he discovered the truth.

"I thought you had found her acceptable for your harem." The voice was even, but there was a shadow behind his gaze, a tension in his shoulders.

"Oh I did," Ferranus said. "At first. But the longer I consider it, the more I realize your father had delivered to me the most splendid puzzle piece to fit into the landscape of my revenge."

CHAPTER 10

They say revenge is a dish best served cold, but the room was swelteringly hot all of a sudden, and I had the feeling it was because Ferranus had turned up the heat somehow. Beside me, Stone went rigid. Blade paused in his advance and turned with bewilderment toward the king.

Next to Ruby, Lilah, in her cat form, stretched into an interested arch as she dug her claws into the seat of the throne. This. This was interesting enough for the fae sorceress to take note.

With my fists tightly pressed into my thighs, I watched Blade keenly as he processed Ferranus's words.

The Dark Enforcer stepped sideways, brushing Ruby aside in a motion that made her glare in his direction. Clearly, something had happened between the two of them. She made no move to step back in his way, but her shadows swirled slower, wrapping her in that black cloak of hers until she merely stood there, arms crossed over her chest. Her short cropped black hair rose in spikes all over her head. The hilt of her sword climbed into the air from a sheath on her back.

Her glowering presence cast a pall in the air around where she stood. Blade took his place between Ruby and the king. His fingers tapped against his leg, the only telltale sign of his uncertainty. I'd never seen anything but calm, collected confidence from him before, so those fingers tapping his leg made me uneasy.

"You're giving her to me?" Blade asked Ferranus quietly. There was wonder in his voice, and caution. "Out of revenge?"

Oh, the pain of those words. He was truly confused, and for a moment, Ferranus just stared at him in astonishment. Then he blinked and threw his head back in an unkind, mocking laughter that raised the hair on my arms. "Give her," he said. "To you?"

At the inflection of the words, Blade's hand curled into a fist ever so slowly. I was sure the king saw it, but didn't care. Maybe he relished the reaction. He let Blade stand there, waiting. An eternity passed before Blade spoke again, and in that silence my insides ached like nails were clawing through the tissues.

"If not me, then who?" he asked in a tight voice.

In his posture, the tilt of his head, the pure calmness of his voice, I knew there was some calculation going on behind his eyes. Measuring the words the king used, recalling the exact phrasing. The king watched it all go on until the moment when he added up the phrase, 'landscape of revenge'.

What he thought of the sum showed in the way his jaw tightened. A slight flutter of the muscle beneath his earlobe hollowed out his skin and his mouth moved into a grim line. He looked from me to Stone. Something awful flitted over his expression.

As badly as I wanted to draw away from his brother's side, I refused to look guilty or ashamed. Any show of such a thing would send the Dark Enforcer the wrong message. Instead, I lifted my chin and held my shoulders square. None of this was my doing. All the blame lay with the king, and he needed to place his righteous anger where it belonged.

He needed to remember we were a team. Mates.

The word warmed me from the inside out and I found in it the courage to hold my ground.

But the king, oh, that bastard. As cool as he was, he simply turned on his heel and shooed Lilah from his seat. She leaped down at Ruby's feet and the Morvannon toed her with her boot until the cat hissed and stalked, stiff-legged away.

Then the king settled into the vacated cushion, crossing one ankle over the other. Such a casual, cocky movement that I felt my lip curling in disdain.

"I would think you'd be more concerned about the revenge part." The king's eyes narrowed as he spoke to Blade. "Not worrying about who will bond with this..." his fingers fluttered in my direction as he finished the thought. "Hellishly impossible wildcat."

I wanted to hiss at him to show him just how wild a cat I could be, but I wrangled the response behind my teeth. Blade, though, his shoulders knotted into a steeple of tension beneath his suit jacket.

"You heard me say I purchased that gown for my mate," he said in a voice that didn't sound anything like him. "You told me you hoped I would gain my wish." He let go a breath through his nose. "I presumed you meant to honor me by gifting her as mine." He sent me a sidelong look, full of confidence and encouragement. Don't worry, his look said.

We've got this. No matter that he'd made me sound like a possession. He knew I was his already.

"Honor you?" the king said in a shrill voice. "You, who have done nothing but betray me? For sure, she might be that mate finally worthy of you, but that wouldn't fit into my landscape of vengeance, now would it. Oh, hell no."

Ferranus leaned forward, demanding attention, and at the words, Blade's eyes shuttered carefully. I was impressed by the speed with which he mastered his expression.

The king's smile took several seconds to reach its full affect, but when it did, it chilled my blood.

"Your father swore a blood oath to me centuries ago," he said, leaning forward just enough that the heels of his boots had to drag backward an inch to accommodate his movement. "Today he broke it. You think a blood oath is only binding in the Shadow Court?"

"I think a blood oath should never be taken lightly, nor should it be accepted lightly."

The king's ring tapped against the armrest as he regarded Blade. "And yet you think to break yours the same as your father did? You betray me the same as he did?"

"I have lived long without emotion to stay my hand," Blade said. "I have done unspeakable things without hesitation. Both for my father and for you. You know this."

A long, tension filled silence held us all in a single breath, after which Ferranus sighed. "Those unspeakable things you do for me save the realm, Dark Enforcer. They guard the very throne I sit upon. Are you fishing for gratitude?"

"I'm not asking for anything," Blade said. "Merely answering your question."

Except he didn't, I realized, but I didn't think the king did.

"Good," he said. "Because there are more tasks to accomplish before these Days are done. I would have need of you and your loyalty even if that loyalty is to violence."

I thought I heard him chuckle. "I've heard it said your father called you his blade. I see why and I was right to hire both you and the Morvannon. A weapon has no emotion."

Blade snorted, a risky move, I thought. "Hire isn't exactly the word I'd use," he said in a voice so low and threatening that it drew my gaze upward.

Ferranus glowered at him. "Were you not Terran's son, I might pull every ounce of magic from your body right now for such impudence."

There wasn't a single tic in his cheek or flush in his face as he made the declaration. It was a cold, stoic warning that made my skin crawl. But Blade...he merely held the king's gaze with the same implacable calm as his father before him, as Stone had. I thought of how they'd all faced the king without flinching and realized that perhaps that was the one thing Ferranus might actually respect, even if he spoke as though it was the worst of insults.

"You've used much magic this day," Blade said, not looking the least bit uncomfortable beneath the king's raging stare. "I doubt my father has anything to do with your clemency this moment."

At that, the king rose and stalked to the wall as if he intended to show a sense of power and casual confidence, but something about his pace suggested Blade had struck too close to home. How close, I wondered. Was he drained to the point that he might be vulnerable? Was Blade waiting for the right moment to strike? Should I take the chance myself?

A hiss of energy snapped through the air and the trunk that contained my luggage exploded from the throne room and careened across the floor as if it was on oiled rollers. So. Plenty of magic left, I realized when it came to rest smoothly in front of Blade and the lid flipped open.

Blade's gaze went wide as he looked inside.

"I summoned you because that blood oath carries a weight that requires your presence. That and that alone is why you are here."

I tried, oh, how I tried not to look up. It took every ounce of determination in me to keep my gaze on the soft material of the gown puddled around my legs. But when I failed to keep my eyes shuttered, they went to Blade. And the way his face paled put fear in my spine.

"I've acted on everything you asked of me," he said. "Shouldn't that be enough to pay for my father's mistakes."

"Have you?" Ferranus asked quietly.

"You know I have."

The king's jaw tensed as he jutted his chin out. His eyes went hard and black. "Bring the brothers," he said, and the fae thralls from earlier whisked themselves like brooms out of sight behind Ruby. Her shadows and mists swirled again before the thralls returned.

I recognized Flint first, being handled by three males who apparently had more strength than a few husks of skin should have, because he was as subdued and docile as a lamb. Mica came next, high-stepping primly between two females. He looked wan and weak and it took a moment to realize he was being supported into the ballroom by them, not being escorted.

If the room was hushed before that moment, it went as silent as the earth six feet down then.

The king stood as the brothers were walked to the front of the dais. I felt Stone's shudder, and I knew it echoed the tremble in my own core, a seismic thing that chattered through my teeth. Blade was rigid and unreadable as ever. I envied his calm facade.

The fact that he was so calm seemed to annoy Ferranus. He lifted his chin, throwing his voice over our heads to the crowds behind us.

"The Dark Enforcer and his family have spent the better part of centuries trying to take down my reign."

A growl from the crowd. Someone called for death. Ferranus held up his hand.

"Some of you have heard rumblings of a shadow court, one to rival my own legitimate court, where every fae is safe and lauded for their uniqueness. What other court in Fae would grant the lesser of us access to their magics, magics that they can't utilize on their own? I ask you this. What other?"

Nowhere came the shouts.

"No where," Ferranus echoed. "Ours alone is the court capable of gifting magic, of accepting it and being able to transfer and transform it so that those who are weakest in their powers can have the chance to enjoy it. Even for a season. Ours alone is the place where our subjects are willing to gift their magic to their king so that few can wield it. Ours. Ours alone."

He was ramping up like any great orator. Hitler. Stalin. Jim Jones. And his subjects were eating it up. Their cheers were enough to deafen me. And yet he wasn't done.

"Today you learn that the court that hides in the shadows must be dragged into the light and shown what it means to defy a king. Today they discover that their machinations are not to be ignored."

His hands, his body, all of him, were throwing itself into the speech as Blade glowered at him from where he stood. Behind the king, Ruby had drawn her sword.

This was it, I thought. This was the moment the whole bag of shit hit the fan. I braced myself for violence as he went on.

"Today you saw this court and its leader try to murder me and end my rule. End your chance of wielding your own magic."

The cacophony of noise at that was punctuated by the pressing forward of hundreds of bodies, all of them coming up against an invisible wall that I knew came from the king's powers. If he chose to let that barrier fall, I was sure Stone and I would be trampled. Blade too. I doubted even the king would be able to press them back once he let go of that force.

He didn't let go. He held it and he paced on the dais like an evangelical preacher, gesturing animatedly.

"You saw my reluctance to do harm earlier when their leader unleashed an unholy power into our midst. You saw how I fought it back, how it turned you on yourselves, how I healed you after and said nothing of the evil that he'd set upon us."

That wasn't how it went and he knew it, but the fae behind us cheered and agreed just the same, as if they too had forgotten what had really gone down. Demands of punishment rose over the air currents.

"You have to do something," I said to Stone. "You've got to intervene."

"I did intervene," he said. "I tried to stop this. I tried to get you out."

The king noticed us talking and slammed us with a jolt of power that made me stagger backward. Just enough that Stone had to catch me.

"Blood Oaths were sworn," the king said. "And Blood Oaths were broken. And now we shall make them pay."

At that, Blade stepped in front of me.

"Enough," he said. "Punish me if you must for my father's mistake, but spare the woman and our youngest. Neither of them have any call to be included. Neither of them hailed to this court you speak of. You have made use of me for your own ends. You've asked things of me that would make a regular fae pale. And yet I did them all, to your service, in the hopes of sparing my brother."

Brother, I noted, not brothers. Because only one was innocent of bloodshed. The other two could fend for themselves and Blade well knew it.

But the king didn't seem to care. His face grew hard. "Is that not the nature of a broken Blood Vow?" he asked. "Is not the risk of the innocent the threat inherent in breaking one?"

"I understand the consequences of such a vow," Blade said in a low voice.

Ferranus raked him with his eyes, letting his glower remain on Blade for far too long for comfort. "You say you understand the risks," he said. "You say you've done things in my name that we both know you've not completed."

One single movement of his fingers, one so subtle anyone might have missed it but for the fizz of air and the stink of ozone that rose around him. Of the long, keening sound of air being warped. Of the sudden appearance of a young goblin popping into place at his feet.

She wore chains on her feet and hands. Her hair was shorn to the roots, showing a purplish scalp and tender veins throbbing beneath her skin. Her face was ashen white. A sucking sound came from Blade, as though he'd gasped and tried to smother the noise.

The last thing anyone expected was to see Phaedre.

CHAPTER 11

The king looked smug.

Phaedre's bulging eyes sought something familiar and found me first. She blinked. My hands grew warm, the fingers feeling as if I'd dunked them in hot oil.

My stomach felt like it had turned itself inside out and the sensitive nerve endings and mucosa were abrading itself against the hardness of my abdominal muscles. Each breath was like ice.

Stone's hand reached for mine as if he wasn't the least bit surprised to see Phaedre, but was most heartily afraid I'd be. That's how I knew he'd known about her all along. That he expected this moment.

Rage lashed through me.

"Bastard," I spat out at him as I remembered her fear of being found out, of her words indicating someone was near. "It was you she was afraid of. It was you she knew was there, watching. You told him about her."

My elbow shot out so automatically, I was sure I'd take him off guard. But Stone easily wrangled it so that it looked like I'd somehow, for some unfathomable reason, offered him my arm like a debutante. He held it close, but firm, against his side, tucking it in harmlessly.

But if he thought that was going to stop me, he was a fool. I rounded on him, the gown moving smoothly. Even this, he blocked, pulling me close enough to whisper in my ear.

"Stop it, Ava. Your putting her in more danger."

It was an exercise of will to control my breathing. To look around me and see all the eyes watching us, the ears listening. Catching sight of Blade, and seeing him shooting me a warning look even as he stood there, immobile and calm when her life was on the line. I forced my breath to even out. I let go the tension in my arm.

If Blade could remain calm, so could I. I had to. For Phaedre's sake. I nodded slowly, indicating my submission, and Stone let me turn in his embrace so that I was facing the king and the dais, but he kept his arms on my wrists, crossing them over my hips to keep me immobile.

Maybe not such a fool after all.

"I'm going to let go of you," he said. "Please don't attack me when I do."

I gave a slight incline of my head to indicate my agreement. The king was watching, and Phaedre...she was calm. Maybe too calm. Whatever we did next, it needed to be smart. I needed to be cautious and cunning, and if need be, willing to work with the bastard who had betrayed me.

"Wait here," he said into my ear and then released me so he could take his place beside Blade. The two of them formed a barrier, a small phalanx that might be terrifying in any other setting. But here, in front of the most powerful fae in the kingdom, it wasn't enough, and both of them had to know it.

Blade spread his arms out from his body. Supplicating. Surrendering. "Take me," he said. "Punish me."

"Oh, I intend to, Dark Enforcer," Ferranus said, pivoting on his heel to return to his throne. He settled onto it, stretching his legs out in front of him. Casual. Callous. "You and your brothers. You will all suffer." His head inclined itself toward Stone. "All except for him," he said as he directed that magnanimous glance in Stone's direction. "Him I will leave alive to bond with this mortal." His eyes narrowed hatefully. "A woman whom I gather is quite special to you, considering you have her dressed in an Erachne wedding gown."

At that, Ferranus drew his attention to me again. "It was the gown that gave me the idea, really. At first, I was just going to kill you all, but leaving one of you alive to procreate seems so much better a solution. More satisfying." He sent Blade a long look. "And since you are so adept at killing, you will be my weapon for removing those fae."

"Like Hell, I will," Blade said, and I knew he meant he didn't plan to stand by and let either of those things happen.

My heart was pounding beneath my ribs so hard, I thought everyone in the ballroom would be able to hear it. "You can't force me to marry him," I said, taking a step forward.

I was immediately shoved backward by a force so controlled it placed me right back in the place I'd started.

"Beware, human." His face was a cloud of darkness that moved across his face like a storm before it cleared and he brightened. "You will behave or I will have you bound and gagged for your wedding."

Blade's face grew dark. I was sure I saw the hound's jaw shadow his own, like a spectre trying to come to life. "If you touch her," he ground out. "If any one of your host so much as breathes on her, I'd like to say I'll tear your throats out and wear your skin, but I won't need to come to her rescue. She will cut your throats herself, and I will dance in your blood along with her."

Ferranus threw his head back and chuckled. "An empty threat, Dark Enforcer, seeing as I've tested her mettle already. You don't think I'd trust a gift from my enemy do you? After how she handled the demon."

He looked at me with slanted eyes. "She has skill, this one. Not some innocent and naive human. Your father must have searched long to find her. And it makes me wonder what hold he has over her that she would even dare to try me on." His long glance took Blade in again. "Or is it that she's in love with you? Is that the reason she agreed to come to Fae."

"I didn't come to Fae," I said. "I was forced."

"As I suspected," he said. "Which means the late Don Sidhe of the Shadow Court knew your weakness. He was good at that. But as it stands, you had many chances to take my knife and attack me and you didn't." He sneered at me before gesturing at Ruby to come closer. She eddied to the edge of the dais, the blackness rising around her like dust. "Oh, yes," he drawled. "I hoped you'd try. You disappointed me."

Ferranus addressed both Stone and Blade with a glance, then. "The truth is you stand in a room filled with fae, powerful fae, who have been accosted and routed and robbed by the Shadow Court for centuries. No one will stand with you. No one will intervene."

"I don't need anyone," Blade said. "If she is unable to hurt you, trust me. I will take my own vengeance."

"Another empty threat," Ferranus said. "You forget who I am. What I'm capable of. But I'm not a monster. Your kin will not suffer. I'll make sure of that."

At that, he reached down to pat Phaedre's head, and she trembled so violently I could see it from where I stood. Behind her, Flint wrapped his arms around Mica.

I must have moved because Stone hissed into my ear to be still, and I was surprised to discover I stood next to him. Widening the phalanx.

"You're weakening," Blade said, taking a step toward the dais. "You can't take us all on." He swept his arm in a gesture toward all the thugs Terran had brought to the event.

I must have moved again, threateningly so, because a blast of magic came at me, blowing at me like a hurricane, drying my eyes, blowing my hair back.

Then, I realized that attack of power wasn't for me at all. It was for Blade, who had shifted so quickly to his hellhound form that the king hadn't had a chance to grapple his magic and aim it properly. The hound's head was slung low, its teeth bared.

A gasp went up through the room. I thought I heard a whoop come from a corner that sounded suspiciously like the little goat god I'd met earlier.

For a moment, I wondered why everything was so still, why Blade had not leaped for the king in the rage I knew seethed its way through him. Then I saw that he struggled to move, every inch of its flesh straining with muscle, fighting to push through the force.

With a flick of his wrist, the king shot out a wave of power that moved the air like waves of heat on pavement. I watched horrified as Blade transformed, painfully, slowly back into his fae form. By the time he was done, he was sweating and on his knees.

It was an effort not to run to him, but I knew to do so would make him look weak. And he wasn't weak. Just the way he was suffering the forced transformation without a sound proved that.

"For the love I bore your father, Blade, your brothers will not suffer," Ferranus said to him. "I won't torture them as is my right."

Blade's head looked too heavy for him as he raised his gaze to the king. "Why Stone?" Blade's voice was a croak.

Air whistled out of the king's nose. "Stone is the more biddable of you all. Powerful. Ruthless. But also emotive. He wants this woman. He will bear children." He looked me over. "He will love them."

My chest felt too tight. I was having a hard time breathing. Beside me, Stone's fingers curled into balls within his fist.

Ferranus put his fingers up as if counting down. "One a year, I should think," he said. "Until she is worn out. Maybe a dozen mortal years. Not so long a wait, after all. But plenty of time for me to find another woman he fancies. Another brood mare to birth half-breeds to shoulder the weight of my rage."

A horrified laugh burst through me. "One a year. You do know mortal women have the power to keep from conceiving."

I sensed the tension coming off Blade in waves as the king must have as well. He was still on his knees, and I guessed it was because he couldn't move, but he'd inched forward, his face hard and tense.

Ferranus had no interest in Blade for the moment, it seemed, as he addressed me, a gloating look plastered over his features.

"And did Terran ensure you packed such medicines before he took you from your world into this?"

My jaw was too tight to answer. I did some quick math and realized I would be due for my Depo shot soon. It wasn't just a birth control; it kept me mercifully free of any monthly bleeding that might get in the way of hunting monsters. Added with the stress my body had undergone over the last weeks, I hadn't given much thought to my regular menses.

Now, I was never so glad of that shot as I was now, but it would be a problem soon.

"And if I refuse?" I asked.

He swung his gaze to mine. "You are mortal and we are fae. I'm quite certain Stone can manage your submission whether you want it or not. That he hasn't already speaks volumes about how he feels about you."

I felt Stone tense up. Blade inched forward yet again, his expression empty. Seeing it made me think the king wasn't able to keep everything quite so controlled as he thought. A delay. A distraction. That's what Blade needed. What I needed.

"Good luck with that," I snorted. "I'm not the maternal type."

Blade gained another half inch.

Ferranus rolled his eyes. "What does that matter? You won't be raising them. Just enough time for Stone to hold the half-breed thing in his arms and look into its eyes. Feel pride. Feel love. Then--" He ran his thumb across his throat. "I should think the best and most effective manner would be for Stone to do the honors, but I have at least nine months to work that out, don't you agree, Cleopatra?"

"You're a monster," I said.

One shoulder lifted. "I am a king. And I am a Fae who was betrayed through the breaking of a blood oath. I am due my vengeance." He nodded at Blade. "He knows this as well as any fae. It's why he sold himself to me a century ago at the last Days. Isn't that right, Blade?"

The way Stone's head snapped to look at Blade, I knew this wasn't something he expected.

"I should have forced your oath," Blade said. "My service for my brother's life. That was the bargain."

"A bargain you believed kept him safe, but not the one I made," the king said. Then he looked past us all, dismissing us as he viewed the crowd behind, all who were transfixed by the spectacle.

"So what say you all? Is it time to punish the bastards who tried to steal your magic?"

Chapter 12

If I ever doubted Fae was a place where violence ruled, it was clarified for me in that instant. No sooner had Ferranus bellowed out his question, when magic broke out like a food fight. Angry, violent magic that blasted everywhere as a protest. Nothing rained down on the dais, however. Nothing touched us. But everywhere else, blasts of light struck into sconces, tiles, stones, and fae alike. It went on for a long time before Ferranus raised his hand.

At that moment, it all halted. Projectiles hung in the air. Balls of light fizzled. Anything that flew lost its ability to spread its wings.

All because the king stood.

"Lilah," he said over his shoulder to where the cat had already transformed into the fae sorceress. Her black hair was a tangle of mats and frizz, so unlike the sleek sorceress I thought I'd killed in the earthen realm. "Lilah, it's time to open the veil so my thralls can usher the gifts out of harm's way. It's about to get very dangerous in here and I'd like my gifts to be safely out of reach." He nodded toward me. "Except this one, of course. She stays."

At his words, a great hagstone appeared at the front of the dais. It looked for all the world like the Northern Lights had been captured and trapped inside a crystal. I'd seen Labradorite once at an artisan fair, where the carver had turned the stone into a dragon carved straight from the heart of the Aurora Borealis. It was gorgeous, and though I'd not had the money to purchase it, I'd regretted not using my credit card to do so for years.

This hagstone was made of the same crystal, except it stood at least ten feet high and six feet wide. The natural circle in the middle looked big enough for a small horse to gallop through. Blues and greens and bright yellows melded through each other in veins so thick the blackness of the stone took on the hue of starlight.

Through it, I had a perfect view of the king, Flint, Mica, and Phaedre. Even Ruby showed through clear and sound, and yet I had the feeling that the center was not a hollow opening but a film, like a two-way mirror.

A high keening note cut the air as it settled into place, humming at such a frequency that I wanted to stop my ears up with my palms.

The thralls began to herd various mortals into a cluster at the side of the dais, as though they were about to convocate from university. I saw Gideon there, his eyes round and alert as he scanned every inch of space around him, I knew he was mapping out every movement he was taking to the stone, memorizing it and storing it even as he searched the area for an escape or a weapon.

Even his slouch hat was stuffed into his pocket and his hair, bristling as though he'd just gotten out of bed, was spit-polished upwards so it couldn't get in his way.

I felt a rush of hope at seeing him, knowing he was brilliant at finding opportunity in the smallest things. He'd survive, I knew. I wouldn't have to worry about him. He moved aside to let two of the thralls push past him with the trunk Terran had sent ahead of me, the one Ferranus had been so keen to peek into.

His eye caught mine for one moment as the thralls lugged the trunk forward. A shiver passed through me as that green-eyed gaze of his flicked to Blade and back to me in warning. He obviously worried we'd attack at last.

But then the moment passed as the thralls got in the way. With a swinging movement back and forth, they stood before the hagstone on their side and at the arc's zenith. Just when they'd managed to gain the most height, they let go.

I flinched involuntarily, then braced for impact. I couldn't help it. When something that size, stuffed with books and instruments of gods knew what, flies toward you, you get anxious. I expected the damn thing to come crashing through and knock the three of us, Blade, Stone, and me on our asses.

But that didn't happen. Instead, the opening went opaque, like a film of wax paper had been pulled over it. Gone were the images of the king, Ruby, Phadre and the brothers as a blood-curdling screech rent the air, spilling over the center as the waxy surface took hold.

The belly of the hagstone swallowed the chest with a blast of energy that slammed back at the thralls and sent them pin-wheeling onto their backsides. I was sure I saw a flash of teeth before the circle shimmered to a clear opening again.

I looked sideways at Blade and Stone. Without me realizing it, the two of them had used the distraction to position themselves strategically. Ferranus obviously had as much ability to see through the hagstone as we had when it was active.

For an instant, I believed things could change for the better. If he couldn't see when the thing was active, if his magic was distracted, then the three of us could do something. We could stop the madness before it began.

But one glance to the side told me Ruby had been paying attention. She had come to the side of the hagstone. Her leash on Phaedre trailed behind her to the little goblin who looked around the room with blinking, bulging eyes.

Phaedre was terrified. My heart hurt for her. I wanted to run to her and cover her with my body, tell her everything was going to be alright.

Beyond her, Flint and Mica had been pushed forward. Mica had collapsed to his knees. His head hung down so that his hair obliterated his face.

"He's not well," Stone hissed out.

"No shit," Blade hissed back. "Were you starving him?"

"You know Mica," Stone retorted. "He won't hurt anyone even to save himself."

"Fuck," Blade muttered. "I left him on the mend. What have you done to him since then?"

I shoved at Stone, impatient as I noted Ruby swinging her sword out from over her shoulder. "Boys," I muttered under my breath. "I think we might need to stop arguing about stupid shit and get to kicking ass."

Too late, it seemed either our voices caught the king's ear or Ruby's decision to pull out her sword had caught his eye, because Ferranus lifted up on his toes to see over the hagstone and what was causing all the ruckus.

"Ruby," he said without turning to look her way. "Are the brothers behaving?"

"No, sire," she said, and her voice was so smokey sweet, it reminded me of burnt sugar. "No, sire, they are being quite naughty."

"Fuck you, Ruby," Stone said and spat on the floor.

Her lovely black eyebrows raised as she took in Stone with a playful glance. "I believe you have already, Stone," she said. "Many, many times. Pity you didn't seem to enjoy it." She ran her middle finger down her tongue. "Our daughter says hello, by the way."

I nearly choked at the comment. Stone all but vibrated with rage beside me. My hand shot out to grasp his, but he pushed me away.

"Enough," Ferranus said, waving at the crowds behind us. Their magic had ceased and left in its place a vacuum that created a pressure almost painful enough to make my ears hurt. "We need to get the gifts into the veil."

He didn't say so, but I guessed he wanted to rush because he was weakening. I tried to look past Stone to Blade, to send him a silent message, or to see if he thought the same, but his eye was glued to Phaedre. Her lip was trembling enough that I could see the vibration from where I stood.

As if his wish was a command the thralls heard in some silent chamber of their dried out ears, they trooped forward, ushering five women and one man: Gideon, toward the hag-stone. Everything in my body went rigid as Lilah lobbed a ball of light toward the opening. The Labradorite shivered again, the way it had before the trunk went through. The iridescent colors danced together, making me dizzy.

One by one, the women stepped into the opening. No one forced them. No one prodded them. They simply went, and it took a keen eye or someone who had suffered the same state to realize they didn't go under their own power. Controlled or compelled, the same as Stone and I had been earlier.

When it was Gideon's turn, my stomach dropped. I'd hoped he'd catch my eye, maybe mouth something at me so I could understand why he was there at all. But like the women, he raised his leg and slid his foot over the bottom curve of the stone. It shimmered, the same as it had for the others, and then it went waxy and he was gone.

All of them. Gone. Just like the trunk.

"Holy Hell," I said, the words choking up from my throat as I realized he might never step back through that portal. My mentor. The man who saved me from a vampire, who saved me from myself by giving me purpose. My lover. The man who had tossed me aside for a younger version. The reason I'd stormed Lilah's house and got caught up in fae politics.

I watched him go, and I realized that pain of being replaced hurt less now. He'd not tossed me aside at all, though he couldn't know that. He'd freed me.

And I'd never see him again.

My eyes squeezed shut at the thought. Never. His bristly chin, his slouch hat, the way he played Canadian rock bands when he worked out because he said Canucks partied like the world was going to end.

My eyelids felt like they were depositing sand into my tear ducts every time they blinked. It was taking everything I had in me to stand there, pretending I was fine with mortals being herded into a magical paddock. I tried not to think about what would happen to them when the shepherd walked through, and even as I gave thought to the king, I realized he was speaking.

His words weren't clear, and they weren't English. The sound and rasp of each syllable reminded me of the runes on his copper door, and it took a few more seconds to understand the phrases, the gestures he made along with it, making that ring flash, must be some sort of spell casting.

If the spell was meant to do something overt, I didn't see the result. All I saw was him striding forward. It was then that I noticed the spell had conjured a burgundy velvet robe. With ermine edging it in thick, round tufts of spotted white, it nestled against his jaw, making him look like a king from a fairy tale.

He looked breathtakingly magnificent as it sailed out behind him, the sash he wore around his waist showing that knife like a taunt.

But as he neared the hagstone, it shuddered as if something had struck it. An instant worm-holed before it swiveled to the side, a door with magnetic hinges repelling the king's energy enough that it couldn't remain in place and had to swing away to avoid his aura.

He passed by the hagstone altogether and gave a tug on the chain he gripped with his right hand. The movement jerked Phaedre from her spot on the floor and she struggled to catch up with him. She was left to lope along on all fours like Gollum, unable to keep up with his stride.

Most times that cloak masked her from view and she had to keep scraping it away so she could see where she was going. Twice, she tripped, and each time I saw Blade jerk and fight to control himself. Like me, he wanted badly to go to her, but like me, he knew it would just make things worse.

I found it difficult to watch, but I told myself I had to. If she could endure this humiliation in front of thousands of fae, hold her chin up even as she struggled to move, then

I wouldn't look away. I'd hold her eye, offering her what courage I could in a glance.

And although I kept my eye on Phaedre, I was more than aware of Ruby stalking behind the king as well. The tip of her sword ushered Flint ahead of her as it pressed into his back. If I expected him to be surly or arrogant, I wasn't rewarded. He came like a penitent, his head low, eyes focused on his brother's profile as Mica trod along beside him. He took most of the youth's weight. The scuffling of his feet no more than a bid to gain ground, inch by inch as he toed the younger brother's heels, prodding them forward as if his feet were the only thing keeping Mica moving.

Blade's reaction to seeing Mica struggling was a hiss of barely suppressed rage. Stone's breath had turned ragged.

Neither of them spoke. I imagined they were too angry to form words. It wasn't fear of the king that undulated through the currents of air, but violence. My chest felt as if it was caving in.

At last, the king halted. Phaedre cowered beside him, trying not to touch his leg. Flint and Mica stopped between Ferranus and Ruby. The younger flicked his gaze once at Phaedre, and she sent him a brief, wan smile.

Then, Ferranus spread his arms wide, making wings of the cloak that revealed beneath the velvet and ermine, scales glittering with the luster of abalone. The ring flashed on his hand as he clutched the edges, drawing my eye. It was weaker, I noticed, a paler glint than before.

"Fellow fae," he said, his voice booming into the air above us, catching in the chandeliers and ringing like bells. "Now that the gifts are safely behind the veil, it's time to finish this business. In the spirit of old, and the words of the mortal lands, it's time to fuck these traitors up."

CHAPTER 13

There was an instant where my entire body went still. A kid had run across the street in front of me once in the early days of my hunting career. Out of the corner of my eye, I'd seen a car coming. I'd known it couldn't stop. Shock froze everything in me for a full second, icing up the pathways as a slow pump of adrenaline squeezed its way out of constricted glands and dropped onto the same sort of traffic-way as that car barreled down. Gideon had saved the kid, then, while I'd just stood there processing the fear and hormones.

The juice hadn't gained saturation in the moments before the car and the kid met. The synapses hadn't caught the electricity.

Then everything exploded. Adrenaline lit the fuse. My feet burst into movement as my synapses shot commands along its wires as fast as a throttling heartbeat. Arms pumped. Breath caught. The kid was there. Right there and the car was about to strike and I wasn't sure I could do anything to change the outcome, but I had to try.

In the end, it had been Gideon who reacted faster and saved the kid. He'd punished me in the training halls then, forcing my body and my mind to work in closer tandem as he trained both to slog through that type of moment.

Shock paralysis would have left me dangling from a vampire's fangs long ago otherwise. It hadn't been fun training, that. Filled with not just horrors, but strange surprises as he worked to make my muscles leap ahead of the adrenaline, which for me always seemed to flood long after the shock came. He'd forced me through every sort of scenario he could think of, took me into the battleground, to desensitize me to the unexpected.

But he'd never known the crush of fae, the disgust of seeing an innocent girl with bulbous eyes—a monster herself in some circles—being humiliated by her own father. He'd not faced a powerful fae with rage in his eyes. Never trained me to think he himself would be gone forever.

So that moment drew itself out as I fought through confusion and indecision. And that moment of inaction, at last, brought the moment Gideon dreaded most.

It got him killed. And now it was about to get more innocents killed.

So many things happened at once, then, that I wasn't sure I'd be able to sort them into order later or even wrangle them into some sort of reason. I just knew that my mind did that automatic cataloging thing it did, the result of all Gideon's training.

First, Phaedre lifted her eyes to mine. It seemed significant enough that my brain snagged on the moment like a fishhook. In return, a blast of images climbed the line and jigged on it.

Faint echoes of a lost dream danced through my mind, of three fae sitting on thrones. Of a face I'd seen before but forgotten. Bright, shining silver hair and large eyes the color of the full moon. Of course, I'd seen her before. She was gorgeous in a way that burns itself into memory, and yet, my mind had released her image back into the pool of long-buried recollection.

I blinked. Phaedre mouthed something I didn't quite catch and before I could work it through, a movement from Ferranus snagged my attention.

In a flash too swift to register, one of those suckers tore free of his throat and struck Flint in the chest. The male staggered back, dropping his arm from Mica's shoulder as the force of it tossed him aside.

He made no sound, but the tentacle pulsed and quivered as it pulled at his magic. Behind me, the fae became a chorus of terrified and disgusted shouting. Horrified raptness, I thought. Like a medieval crowd at a hanging, they couldn't look away.

Mica sagged and staggered, putting his arms out for balance. A blip in the air wavered over him like a still pond disturbed by a finger...and for a second, his entire visage shifted.

Glamor, I thought. What I thought was the real Mica was nothing but glamor. My knees threatened to buckle in relief as I began to hope that the youth was somewhere safe. I might have convinced myself of it, except Blade started in reflex to help the youth. Stone held him back with a shake of his head. I understood what that look meant. To do anything would just draw the king's ire to the youth.

At that moment, the magic clamped down tight again and the youth I recognized shambled forward, looking for all the world like he was doing his best to reach the king. Violent intention wrote itself over his features so clearly I knew he planned to attack Ferranus with whatever magic he still possessed. And the moment he did, that magic would ricochet right back on him.

Whatever the youth planned to do, he was saved by the action as someone leaped from the sidelines, drawing his attention. It caught everyone's notice, stripping away gazes from the brother suffering beneath the tentacle slowly, painfully, it seemed, siphoning his magic.

This someone, Mica's tutor, I realized, lobbed a razor-sharp edge of light from his hands. He flicked his gaze to me, smirked through that haze of glamor that mottled his features.

Watch, that grin seemed to say, and so I did. I followed the path of the magic as it streaked the room toward the hagstone. It sizzled as it went, shooting sparks out in every direction that had other fae dodging and ducking to avoid getting struck.

The king was too absorbed in collecting the magic from Flint's body to notice. He was gulping on the energy as though the power was coming in too fast and he could barely get it down. I felt weak and sick as I watched, as the sound of guzzling and gagging filled the air, and I shifted my gaze to the magic that had by now stopped.

It hovered over Phaedre with all the import of the Bethlehem star. Just as the magic scissored through the chains that held her so neatly they might have been made of crisp paper, Blade made a sound of surprise.

A blur of movement. That was all I saw. The next thing I knew, Blade had rushed the king. He was already mid-streak and my heart had somehow found a way to yank my jaw open. I was going to yell. Like a rookie, I was going to shout his name and draw attention to him. My jaw clicked closed under the force of my determination. I heard it echo in my ears.

He was pulling a Gideon, I realized. Using the distraction as a moment of opportunity. And with that moment, he was going to stop this. He was going to make the bastard king pay. For a heartbeat, I almost sagged in relief.

Then, I realized what he was going to do was the wrong thing. His movements might have been too fast for me to see but Ferranus was fae. Powerful fae. And though he'd expended much energy already, he had a direct line of power to Flint.

He noticed Blade's movement, swift as it was. And another sucker discharged from his throat, widening his mouth like a snake's, ripping a gag from him at the velocity at which it shot free. Clearly, it was about to strike into the Dark Enforcer. My dark enforcer. My mate.

I charged for it without thinking. Not sure what I could even do, but instinct and muscle memory taking me along like flotsam on a wave. As fast as I sped, I was still far, far too slow to reach it in time. My body knew it. My brain was slow to catch up, and so in that same instant my feet moved, my mind considered my pathetic timing between thought and movement, and a sob of frustration tore free. Then a shout, loud and barely discernable as words.

A warning come too late. The sucker collided into flesh with a sickening, wet thunk. A grunt, of someone realizing they've been struck but haven't had time for their synapses to register the pain long enough to form a scream.

From my peripheral vision, I caught sight of a body sinking to its knees at the impact.

Someone was yelling, sobbing. I only realized it was me when I felt my palms land on the marble floor and slid, wet with tears several inches. This time when I screamed, I knew the fullness of it. It scraped my voicebox on its way by. It dragged with it tissue from my throat.

Because Blade was down. That monstrous tuber had caught him in the stomach. It had started to pulse with that undulating movement that suggested it was tearing the magic from his tissues. I dragged myself two raw feet before I noticed the shape and size of the shoulders, though powerful and broad, were not Blade's. That the jerking, spastic way that back was arching in pain and letting go in surrender could not be from the proud Dark Enforcer's body. He would never submit. Never give in. He might suffer and he might lose, but he would never surrender like that.

And if I wasn't sure it was someone else who took the blunt of that trauma, I knew it for certain when Ferranus bellowed in rage from between the worms of pulsing flesh that stretched Ferranus' mouth and throat. He'd not struck his intended target at all. Something, or someone, had got in the way.

Thrown himself in the way, taking the hit meant for his brother. Sacrificing himself so that Blade could get to Phaedre.

Stone. My mind whispered the truth to me. Stone had taken the strike right in the most tender place of his belly. Every inch of my body felt like it was a teabag left to soak too long in hot water. Stone. I hated the joy and shame that razored through me as a whimper fled his lungs. Totally involuntary. The last sound a lung makes as it realizes it may not expand again.

But for Stone's faster, reaction, his closer proximity to the king, he might not have saved Blade before that tuber plunged into his stomach. But those golden moments popped out of the ether of storm-riddled clouds to let the sun's rays through.

And he lay on his back, flat except for the way his abdomen rose in an unnatural arc beneath the force of the king's draw.

The flesh of the sucker undulated with each swallow. His face turned toward me once. Just once.

And at the look on his face, the way he sought my gaze and held it, the gorge rose to my throat. After all was said and done, he was doing this for me, that gaze said. Doing it for Blade. He wasn't sorry for it, either. He let slip his stoic mask and showed me all he was in that one look. The warrior I'd not understood. The traitor who'd held tight to his blood oath. Who was giving what he had to keep it. To keep his family and anyone he loved safe. A fae of honor, not a traitor.

I had time to see the peace slacken his features as he held my eye, and I knew I should hold his gaze. I knew he needed at least some sort of visual handhold of comfort as he died. He deserved that, at least.

My knees bagged as I sank back on my heels, gasping for breath.

And then...I tore my gaze from his.

I couldn't bear to watch him shrivel to a husk the way the thralls had. I had to turn away from him in shame because I couldn't let him see the joy I felt that it wasn't Blade lying there.

My hands flew to my ears, cradling my skull in trembling palms. In over my head. That's all that streaked through my mind. I was way over my head here.

Gideon knew that. Blade knew it. Fuck, Stone knew it and it was why he'd tried to hire those damn hoodlums to bring me home. Because that was truth and I couldn't avoid it any longer. He wasn't the enemy. He had tried to save me from all this. He'd given the last of himself to do so.

Dumbfounded, I watched, feeling a stew of emotions boiling through me, joy, terror, dread, and I pushed myself to my feet. Under that taffy like pull of time, I had plenty of moments to stand, swaying, but strong. I swung my gaze to where Blade had paused, just a half a heartbeat to look at Stone, and then...

Without a further beat of hesitation, he dove for the now freed Phaedre. In a flash of movement, he gathered her from the floor and into his arms.

She was limp. Her little arms and legs hung over Blade's. The chains jangled against each other so loudly they drowned out the sounds of cat calling and whooping from the fae behind us.

His eye caught mine as he swung around. I'd not seen such nakedness in him before. It caved in my chest to see how raw his pain was. Her chains dragged along the flagstones as he swung this way and that in indecision.

I was useless there. Stone and Flint, my only powerful allies in this, were made impotent by the king's attack. I could already see that in his rage at Stone's betrayal, he had forced more magic into the tuber embedded in Stone's belly. It pulsed faster, thickened more than Flint's. How dare the fae interfere with his vengeance?

In seconds, Blade might catch the king's rage as well.

It all happened so fast and yet time continued to drag itself out to untenable strains. I knew one thing as I held his gaze in those heartbeats. I knew I had to let him think I would be alright. I had to relieve him of worry for me when she was his priority. She needed to be. She was the reason I was here. The reason I'd stayed. Doing anything but what I had to in order to maintain her safety would be a waste.

I had to let him know I could take care of myself.

Get out, I tried to tell him. Take her and go. He shook his head, made a move toward me. He was going to come for me, like he'd said he would. Through the chaos. Over the coals of hell. Dragging himself if he had to in order to see me safe.

But with me filling his gaze, taking his attention, I saw the danger about to strike from behind that he didn't. The threat that the king had made sure would be lurking in the shadows if he was too distracted to protect himself.

That threat was already storming toward him, springing into action at the same moment as he did, as though Ruby of the Nocturnes knew Blade's mind, as well as her own. Her wings had spread. The swirling mass of shadow around her dropped to her feet like a pair of shed pants.

And more frightening than those razor sharp wings was the sight of another sucker wrestling its way out from Ferranus's throat, shoving aside the two already embedded in the brothers. That quivering length of mass was headed straight for where Mica stood with head hanging, shoulders bowed inward. A terrified youth who had decided to waste rather than taking life from another.

Someone had to do something. Blade would never make it to him before that tuber struck. We were out of options.

The thought that Blade might be lying next to Stone with tubers in his stomach, suckling the life out of him...

I didn't think more. Whatever time was left to me, I couldn't waste it. Couldn't waste Stone's sacrifice or Blade's distraction.

My feet moved. Just like that. Hunter instincts, years of training, all of it kicked in at once... and I charged.

Right for Mica.

And when my body rammed into his, I was already bracing for impact, already swerving just a hair to the left, spinning us toward the hagstone because there was only one way out of there and I knew that with nothing left in this world, no Blade, no Stone, no Gideon, I would have to protect the youngest.

The best of them.

His body felt smaller than it looked. My arms struggled to wrangle him into a hard embrace, because everything felt off about him, the grope of hands on my hips, the set of his shoulders as I pulled him against me.

He was light too, thankfully. I easily hoisted him off the ground and pivoted sharply toward the hagstone.

With all the thrust I could manage from the remnants of the initial burst, I lunged for the center.

"He's weakening," Mica said, explaining even as I wondered why Ferranus wasn't holding us in place by some invisible force. "He's used too much already."

Yes. There was a price for magic, as Mica knew well. I had to believe that what Ferranus was draining from Flint and Stone wouldn't be enough to sustain him to the point he would recover and stop us.

But I knew it would. Somehow, God help me, I knew it would be enough to sustain him long enough to wreak his vengeance.

We were at least three steps away from the hagstone. A million miles, it might have been, because right then, a kraken rose from smoke that itself came from nowhere. A chorus of impressed shouts and catcalls grew to a cacophony. Oh, what a show this was. A Days to end all Days. One the fae would talk about for centuries.

"The protection is gone," Mica said. "I'm sorry. I can't hold it. I can't do it all."

I heard Lilah shout out from behind me. "I see you, hunter," she shouted with a manic laugh bubbling beneath the words. "I know you now."

"You don't know shit," I said, and I charged for the belly of the kraken. It was smoke and mirrors. It had to be. Because if she meant it as a weapon, the violence would turn on her. Because I desperately needed it to be because I was already leaping into the air and aiming for the circle.

A second. That was all it took. I sucked in a breath and I threw everything I had into the lunge, ducking so my head would collide with the kraken in its soft parts if it wasn't really an illusion. I prayed for it to be smoke.

...And then...

CHAPTER 14

I fell through the hagstone into a realm of smoke and shadows with skeletal trees that coiled corkscrew limbs upward into a dusky skyline. Dusk, I realized. Wherever I was, night was coming.

I thought I was breathing in fire at first, before I realized I wasn't breathing at all.

It took a failed attempt to suck in air to understand that the burn I felt deep in my lungs was the result of having the wind knocked out of me. I knew they would respond, eventually. Experience gave me enough comprehension to know that the shock to the tissues would recover if I gave it time.

But seconds went by before they rebounded and even then, I had to fight to take a breath. The sooty, dark blackness of a dead fire ate away at my lungs as they tried and failed to expand.

Panic raked chipped and jagged nails through my marrow then. Scrambling, scratching, searching, I fumbled to orient myself in space, to comprehend why the world looked upside down, why the tree limbs looked like roots.

I was on my back. That much I worked out. Neck arched over something hard and round. Whatever was on my chest was the thing cutting off my air, weighing me down.

It coughed, that thing. Then it moved. Just in time to give me the desperate gasp of oxygen I needed to send juice to my brain.

Then, and only then, did the panic subside enough for me to stop flailing about like a beetle on its back.

A drag of air. Hold it. Use it to lift my head level to my chest, no matter how much it hurt to do so.

"Phaedre," I whispered as I caught sight of blue hair standing out in spikes and bulging eyes blinking back at me. "What are you doing here?"

We were chest to chest, her face in mine so long as I craned my neck upward, straining to keep it level.

"You brought me here," she said as her small hands propped against my ribs. "Don't you remember, Ava?"

My head dropped back down, all the strength in my neck sapped. Whatever was digging into my back, making my spine arch, was also doing its share of cutting off my wind.

Knowing I wasn't in immediate danger, I slid sideways, hoping to find good, solid, flat earth. I expected the gown to move with me easily, the way it did with each movement I'd made back in the ballroom. But it stuck to me in places that didn't feel right. My legs tangled in the material. I worried I'd torn it to shreds, but I figured Erachne would forgive me.

For now, Phaedre eased her weight from me a bit at a time, no doubt because I groaned without meaning to, using up the scant air I'd managed to drag in.

Thankfully, what met my back when I slid off successfully was soft mossy ground. I let my muscles relax, sagging into the earth with relief. I pulled in a deep inhale. Let it go. My eyes closed in release. Just for a second. I needed that second. I couldn't bear to look around and find any renewed threats just yet. If they were there, I reasoned, they'd have swallowed us up by now, and I had to have one moment for myself. After the adrenaline dump and panic, I needed it.

And that moment let me process it all.

"We're behind the veil," I said, remembering.

"Yes."

My nod softened the moss into a cushion that in turn hollowed into a nice groove beneath my skull. It felt deliriously good after the last few moments. A sigh escaped me. A relieved one. The veil was meant to be safe. We were safe there. At least until Ferranus came through, which I didn't think would be right away. He was...God, he was busy draining Terran's sons of their life force and their magic.

I thought I heard my breath hitch at the thought.

Small hands brushed over my cheek, bidding my eyes open. I stared up into her face, dirty as it was, beautifully ugly as it was, and a tear slid down my temple to soak into the moss. I hadn't even realized I was crying, but just feeling her touch, knowing she was safe, brought out all the acuity of the moment. She was alive. Unchained and alive. Not about to get hit by one of those horrific tubers that snaked out from the king's throat.

And yet...Yet if she was here, safe with me, then that had to mean something had happened to Blade because he never would have let her go unless he had to. And what of Mica? Last I'd known, I'd hauled him with me when I'd thrown myself at the portal. That was the whole point. I couldn't understand how I'd failed to drag him with me into the veil.

Panic seized me once more as I imagined him lying on the floor of that ballroom being tubered and drained like Flint. Like Blade might be even now.

Her voice cut through the emotion like a razor. "I'm sorry," she said, drawing my attention. "I couldn't hold your protection anymore. She got you, I'm afraid, when she blasted you."

My head twisted toward her, the flatness of confusion robbing me of emotion.

Phaedre knelt beside me, leaning in, her eyebrows scuttled together. "It's not bad, I don't think," she said canting her head as if she was trying to see beneath my back without moving me. "If it was, I doubt you'd be able to move."

I felt her hand beneath my back then, testing, exploring with tentative fingers. I winced when she touched the spot between my shoulder blades. I heard the frown in her voice when she said, "No open wound, just residual bruising of some sort. It could have been worse." She pulled her hand out and dropped her elbows on her knees as she squatted in front of me.

I swallowed, my mouth feeling raw and dry. "You said I brought you here."

She nodded even as she hung her head. "I'm ashamed to say we tricked you. Mica and I. We tricked everyone." Her eyes flicked to mine beneath hooded lids. "But it wasn't malicious, I promise."

I wasn't sure because it was a bit too dark, but I thought she smiled wanly, apologetically.

"I think I better sit up," I said.

"Sure," she said. "I'll help you."

Wrestling beneath my shoulders to assist me, she grunted and groaned, indicating it was a bit of effort. I was astounded to discover I needed the help.

I was weaker than I expected. I did what I could to push myself up, but I was sore in places I shouldn't have been. My senses even seemed blunted in strange ways. Sense of smell, for one. I wiped my finger along my nose, thinking the weird smell I kept inhaling might be the result of something stuck to my face or on my nose.

When my hand came away, it struck something solid and smooth beside me. A blink brought the trunk into focus. Right. The thralls had tossed it in. It was a sort of comfort to see it squatting there, large as life and hard as petrified oak. I moved my legs apart, testing my movement, and thought I heard a tearing of fabric. The gown. I'd finally ruined it.

But if the trunk was here, then where were Gideon and the others?

A brush of her hand over the wooden top of the chest made a scuffling sound, drawing my focus. "It's what we landed on," she said.

I eyeballed the beast beside us, giving it some thought in relation to how badly I ached. I couldn't imagine how hard I'd struck it to feel the way I did.

"It's not the cause of my pains though, apparently." I rubbed at my ribs, trying and failing to get further, to the spot between my shoulder blades and lower that burned like a bastard. No simple knock on wood could make my muscles hurt that way.

She shook her head, a movement of jerky shadow in the smoky darkness.

"No, that's on account of Lilah. She lobbed a pretty nasty bit of magic at us as we leaped through." She gestured at my hands, as though the answer lay in them. "It's my fault she was able to hurt you. I just couldn't keep the protection magic going with the glamor too."

I adjusted myself so that I leaned against the trunk, but with my spine carefully braced in a way that the touch wouldn't hurt the wounded area. My head felt like someone had given it a good crack with a blunt object.

And there was a pretty acrid smell in the air that might have been burning grass, but held a note of citrus too. And sulfur, if my nose was right. I was beginning to think whatever had happened between the moment I'd grabbed for Mica and the one when I'd lunged through the hagstone had done more damage than Lilah's magic had done.

"You might have to start again," I said between wheezing gusts of careful breaths. "I'm having trouble keeping up."

Her hand sought mine and held it in my lap as she stared into my face. Her eyes were like lamps in the shadows. Behind her, an ethereal glow lit the air but made tight corkscrews of the branches that filled the sky in lacework pattern.

"If you could see as well as me," she said. "You'd know your nail polish is gone. I realized it the moment Lilah called to you in the ballroom. It was like she was surprised to see you there. She didn't know you before, did she? But she is an enemy, is she not, Ava? You know her?"

"I do and she is," I said, recalling what Phaedre had told me when she painted my nails. "Protection from my enemies," I intoned. "That's why Ferranus couldn't...why he didn't hurt me." I paused there because what Ferranus had tried to do to me wasn't simple hurt, and I didn't want to worry her. It wasn't lost on me in that second that Stone had been able to lift my skirts when the king couldn't. Not an enemy, my mind whispered.

I owed her a debt and squeezed her fingers.

"You did well," I said. "I'm very grateful, but you're right. Your magic kept me under her radar when she should have recognized me as the hunter who killed her...or tried to kill her, at least.

"You're the reason I made it this far," I said, realizing I'd not truly done my job. "If she had recognized me, she'd have tried to kill me, I'm sure. Or alerted the king that I knew the brothers better than they told him I did."

I thought of Mica's tutor and the way he'd looked so blurry every time I looked at him. I wondered if he had something similar to keep me from recognizing him from the catacombs. Maybe because I knew his name, he thought of me as an enemy. Because of his presence in the catacombs, he probably expected me to see him the same way.

I heard the smile in her voice when she responded, shy, timid, but proud, just the same. "It's not terribly powerful magic, but I couldn't keep it up and hold my own glamor at the same time."

I turned to stare at her, comprehension settling in. "You were Mica," I said, turning my hand over to squeeze her fingers. "I knew something was off about you the moment I grabbed you."

The sigh that fled her lungs had a sharpness to it, an intention. "He played his part very well, though appearing hale and healthy must have cost him. I didn't think my father would have me killed in front of the entire court. The optics just wouldn't be right. So when I heard Ruby coming for Mica and me, I made him put the Raiment on and we swapped faces."

I patted her hand. "You put yourself in danger by doing that, Phaedre, you know that don't you? You risked your life for Mica's."

She shrugged. "A life in hiding is no life, Ava," she said. "What is my worthless existence to the shining possibility of his?"

Silence descended between us as I gave some thought to that statement. I'd thought her a child when I'd met her earlier, small, innocent to the point of naivety, but that comment showed a maturity—an aching sort of experience that most children don't have to endure. It made me realize she was those hundreds of years old. And it made me realize something else.

"You love him," I said finally.

"Is that love, Ava?" she asked so sweetly my heart ached for her. "To be willing to give up a worthless life for a valuable one?" she asked .

"Don't say that," I said. "Your life matters, Phaedre. Why else would Blade have been hiding you for so long? Why would he save you from the king in the ballroom?" My own heart squeezed as I thought of what must be happening to him even now in that chamber. A knot tied itself into my stomach that wouldn't let go despite several deep breaths.

So, I ran the back of my knuckles over her shoulder, and told myself that this was what he wanted and I tried not to let my despair creep into my voice as I soothed her. "You matter. Each breath you take matters. Your willingness to risk it for the man you love is proof of that."

"How do you know it's love?"

I tilted my head so that it met hers. "There aren't many who would risk their life for someone else. Most people just aren't that selfless."

"You do it," she murmured and shifted so she could sit next to me against the chest. "I know you do. Blade said you protect the innocent in your world."

At his name, I squeezed my eyes shut. It was almost too much to think of him outside this realm, not knowing if he was dead or alive. Just knowing Stone had done what I couldn't. Taken the hit meant for him. I wasn't sure I'd ever forgive myself for that.

I drew in a long breath and my head dropped back, nostrils flaring at the acrid smell in the air. I thought of the reasons I was brought to Fae, why Stone selected me.

"No," I said flatly. "If I was as selfless as that, I wouldn't have fled the ballroom and left the man I love behind. The truth is, I'm a killer. Any innocents saved on account of those actions are pure happenstance."

"That's not true," she said. "You might think it is, but it's not. I know killers. What you do is the result of protecting the innocent, not the other way around."

She took my hand in both of hers. "You're an angel, Ava. Don't forget it. You think you left Blade behind but the truth is he would never forgive you if you didn't. You saved me even if you thought you were saving Mica. You did that to save the brother he loves instead of worrying about never seeing your mate again. That's the sort of sacrifice that is selfless."

It felt awkward, the way she held my hand so softly, so reassuringly while she spoke those words. I didn't have the heart to argue. I wasn't in denial about myself. Blade might have smoothed out many of my rough edges and taken away the trauma that made me what I was, but it didn't change the truth of the things I'd done or the reasons I'd done them. He was good...damn he was better than good as a lover, but he wasn't a miracle worker.

And the truth was, now that I was here, I would give anything to go back and do it again. I'd stay and fight for him, with him, and die at his side if I had to because I was indeed selfish. I didn't want to be safe in a realm far removed from the dangers of the court. I wanted to be with him.

So, I pulled my hand from hers gently, because I didn't want her to sense that truth in my touch. And I did the next best thing to agreeing. I changed the subject.

"You mentioned the Raiment," I said in a musing voice. "You can't possibly mean that damn itchy corset someone stole from Blade on the Shadow Trail?"

She tittered. "He never left with it in the first place," she said. "I pinched it from his saddlebags while you two were arguing over Nutkin." She sighed. "I didn't want to steal it back, but I was worried about Mica. He'd been snooping in his father's library, looking for things he shouldn't. I blame his tutor, filling his head with ideas that Terran had a past he wasn't really Terran's son, telling him there was a prophecy that would change the entire fae realm. And he couldn't let it go. He kept searching, reading, digging through old books. I didn't want him to get caught, so I thought the corset would at least disguise him when he crept around in places he shouldn't. He had a lot of fun with that. Sometimes he became his father. Once or twice, he was Blade." She chortled. "But most of the time, he was just a maid or Terran's taster."

I adjusted my back, trying to avoid the sore spot from digging into the corner as I mulled over her comments, snagging on so many threads that it was tough to decide what to hold on to the tightest.

"I'm guessing Mica wouldn't stop reading, so you spelled the books so no one could read them," I said, deciding on one.

I felt her go rigid, defensive. "He was getting obsessed," she said. "I had to do something."

"That was very smart of you."

"Well, I'd love to take all the credit, but I didn't do them all. One book was impossible to spell. I tried several times, but it just kept changing languages as if it was mocking me. Sometimes it would go invisible and I'd think I had it taken care of only to go right back to being in English. The best I could do was blur the words."

My mind fed me images of that specific book that showed a proclivity for following me around.

"I think I know the one you mean." I elbowed the trunk behind me. "It's in here, actually, unless someone rooted around inside and took everything out before they brought it here."

She sat up straighter. "It is? Why would you bring that boring thing?"

"They all are," I said, and then realized what she'd said. "I just figured any book that would follow me around like a puppy might be something I'd want to keep an eye on. Wait. What. You read it?"

She climbed onto her knees, facing the chest. "Certainly not," she said. "Nothing but boring old history."

When I realized she was trying to hoist the cover open, I flipped over onto my knees to help her. The movement made my head swim, and it took a second for the equilibrium to settle.

"Are you alright?" she asked, pausing to look at me, those eyes lamplights in the ever encroaching darkness.

"Just woozy, I guess," I said. "Now, let's get this chest open."

We both pushed, the lid far heavier than I expected, or my arms weaker than I'd realized. She ended up doing the majority of the work, strangely strong for her size. When it creaked open with a loud groan, it held itself trembling at its peak for a second before it fell back with a shudder that rocked the chest.

"Did you hear that?" she asked.

"Just the lid," I said. "It's heavy."

Her hands dropped away and she twisted around. "No," she said. "Something else. Something from behind us. Something in the woods."

Her words made my spine tingle. Hand on the lip of the chest, I craned to see over my shoulder into the trees. Their limbs spiraled shadows up into a canopy that made brush strokes like razors across a gloaming skyline.

Panning down gave my eyes time to adjust. I blinked, shuttering my gaze, drawing my hearing into the ballgame, lifting my chin so that the air could move up along the column of my throat to my nostrils.

One thing I'd learned from Gideon was that eyesight was as much the other senses as it was vision. I brought everything I had to that moment, searching the woods, listening to the sounds that had been nothing but silence just moments earlier.

At first, I thought she meant the off-kilter, keening tone of whispering coming from the trees. Not a whisper of breeze through leaves and bark that brings with it a hush of moss and insect wings, but of real voices.

Except she wasn't looking at the trees the way I was. Her head was canted to the side, the direction of her face slightly lifted, as though she was listening for something further out.

Something bid me take her hand. I was surprised at how small it felt in mine, how soft. And the moment my palm touched hers and electricity sang through my skin like a ribbon of velvet being drawn upward.

And then I heard it. Crying. Off in the distance, so far out, that it was barely audible.

"Is that a baby?" I asked, more to myself than her.

I was already getting up, my legs obeying some primal command far greater than rational thought. I swayed on my feet for all of two seconds before I felt Phaedre's hand on my wrist, holding me back. I blinked, my brow scuttling in confusion.

"Don't," she said.

"But there's something wrong with it," I said. "It needs help."

"There's something wrong with it, yes," she said in a strange, far away voice. "It's dead."

Chapter 15

Dead babies don't cry. And trees didn't whisper. Whatever was out there, it was not of any world I knew and the fact that it was making Phaedre tremble suggested I'd be foolish to think for one second that I knew better than she did how to react. Not here. Not this close to Fae.

So I immediately went on alert. And the moment I did, I heard far more because every inch of my body was attuned to the waves of danger and threat.

The crying was just one thing bathing the air with hair-raising sound. Something else, something more sinister, wafted on a nearly silent breeze. The chills that ran over my bare shoulders had more to do with whatever that whisper was than the air itself.

"Phaedre," I said in a low voice, the kind I used during those times when I'd come upon another mortal in the vicinity of a dangerous beast. I knew without a doubt she would do whatever I asked because my voice carried the weight of command. She'd do anything. No matter how peculiar.

"I think you might need to get into the trunk."

Of course, she didn't argue and to her credit, she said only one thing. "I don't think I'll fit."

I was no stranger to how others reacted to threat and danger or the demand that they do something completely unorthodox. But the way she gripped the edge of the trunk and looked down into the belly of the chest, measuring the size, that made my heart clench.

I didn't want her to have to get in, suddenly. The sensation of dread that had a hold of my chest in that moment, burrowing in like a tic, almost made me grab her by the shoulder and hold her back. But I couldn't. Whatever darkness and smothering, cloistered air that waited to enclose her, I knew was nothing to what waited for us in those woods.

She climbed in nimbly, more so than I expected for the awkwardness I knew labored most of her movements. Her head bobbed as she rearranged the things inside to make room to duck down. She peered up at me with those lamplight eyes, blinked twice.

"I'm going to close the lid," I said, planting my palm on the back of the lid. "I won't be long."

"Where are you going?" Her voice held a quiver, one I imagined was coursing through the rest of her.

"I have to see what's out there." I leveraged my hip against the side of the chest, feeling a bit weak in the knees but also a strong compulsion that was pulling them toward the noise. "I have to make sure we're—you're not in danger."

At that, she stood suddenly. "You can't, Ava," she said.

"I won't be long," I said in as soothing a voice as I could. She needed to stay calm. Calm and safe inside the trunk so I wouldn't be distracted. "You'll be fine."

"It's not about me," she said. "You shouldn't go out there alone."

"I'll be fine too. I do this for a living, remember?"

The way she shook her head suggested she was also going to climb back out of the trunk. There was no way I was going to let that happen. Without knowing what we might be facing, the safest place for her was anywhere I wasn't. I put a gentle pressure on her shoulder.

"I'll be fine. And I won't be long."

Her resistance surprised me. I didn't expect her to be so strong. Funnily enough, she seemed to be the one with the confidence, the one with the energy. Even though I was giving it my all, it took everything I had in me to keep her from climbing back out of the trunk.

She slapped my hand aside. Easily. Too easily, I thought. "I'm going with you."

"No," I said, dropping both hands down on her shoulders and bracing myself against the side of the trunk. "You're safer here."

"But are you safer without me?" she asked quietly. "You have nothing to protect you out there."

Something flared in her eyes, enough to make me do a double take. But while it surprised me, I wasn't going to be deterred.

"I have gone into vampire dens with less," I said, hitching up the skirts of the dress and working the material between my legs and pulling it out behind me in wings that I could tie in front of my hips.

"This isn't a vampire den," she said. "You don't know what this is."

"Do you?" I asked, twisting the material into a knot.

She said nothing, just squinted at me as though she wanted to argue more, but already knew it would get her nowhere. I took the pause to scan the surrounding area and caught sight of a rather large rock. I stooped to pick it up. Although it should have fit in my palm and been light enough to heft without too much trouble, it felt like it weighed a ton.

"You think this is enough?" I asked, trying to hold it out without looking like I was straining.

Her gaze dropped to the stone, and I was sure I heard her muttering, but whatever she was saying turned into a mess of syllables that had me straining to hear. Her mouth moved. Her arms were animated. She was certainly talking to me, but no sound was coming out.

"What's that?" I asked. "What are you saying? I can't hear you."

Dizziness eddied over me with a quivering wave. I swayed backward on my heels, the stone in my hand becoming heavier. Blinking, staring, swaggering on my feet, it took several seconds for her voice to cut back in.

"I'll take a stick," I heard myself saying and panned sideways with a stupefied glance. "There's one right there. I'll use it like a sword if I have to." I grinned at her, showing my teeth and feeling almost drunk when I did.

She stared at me, those eyes flaring again. I couldn't see what was in her expression, but I figured it was worry and dread, the same thing that I heard in her voice. I felt for her, but for her own good, I had to step away. If she had any inclination to argue, I didn't want to give her the chance to try.

"Duck down," I told her and my fingers went to my lips as I realized how numb my mouth was. I tapped the flesh, feeling more than a bit foolish. I wasn't cold. I hadn't ingested anything that would change the sensation.

As my fingers met flesh and sent back signals that I was, indeed, all in one piece, I pressed on, despite the way the words came out in a slur.

"I'll come back for you. I will be fine. I promise." The S trailed off a bit too long for my taste, but she made no remark on it. Maybe she was too scared to notice.

"Promise you won't go too far," she said. "Tell me you will hurry."

"Promises like that are impossible to make and keep," I said, each syllable becoming more of a struggle than the last. "But I will do my best."

I felt the worry in her, but she relented and finally settled into the trunk. Blinked twice, those lamps in her eyes going as dark as the shadows inside, stealing my sight of her. Once. Twice. When she opened them again and peered up, I could swear there was a glow around her entire body that lit the belly of the interior. For a second, a wash of sound rumbled up around me, booming through my chest. A mash of images swam inside the shadows, then were gone.

Whatever magic she was tossing out, it was distracting. I shook my head to clear it. "I'm closing the lid now," I told her.

"Promise me you won't be long."

"I can't do that," I repeated. "But I can tell you that I will crawl over hot coals in the middle of hell to get back to you, if I have to. I will come to you."

Even as the words flew from my mouth, I paused, canting my head sideways, thinking I'd heard the words before. Then a sigh fled my lungs like a death rattle, and I eased the lid down.

Once it had settled into place, I inhaled, feeling very much like I'd laid a friend to rest. But that was ridiculous. Even so, the irresistible urge to knock on the top consumed me.

My palm ran over the surface to the center as I fought the urge. Then, because I couldn't do it after all, I gave it three sharp raps. Four raps came back at me, and only then could I take a step back, my eyes on the trunk for a dozen steps before I could spin on my heel and start the picking, stumbling meander through the woods.

Making my legs move proved to be more of a challenge than I thought, but I pressed on. The surrounding smoke started to tingle on my skin. The smell of sulfur grew stronger, over-powering any scent of pine or moss. Each step was a struggle that felt punctuated by the growing stink, the burning of the smoke on my skin. Powering through became a battle of wills as I brushed aside scratching boughs of evergreens and tripped over tangles of shrubbery.

More than once, I had to pluck some thorny bit of twig from my bare arms and shoulders. A few times they left scratches that stung, leaving me with tiny rivulets of blood running down my skin. Something caught in my hair. Scrap-ing it all away from my face only sent thorns into the pads of my fingers, and I yelped. Sucked blood off my fingers.

But I pushed on, not even sure anymore why I was moving so doggedly forward. I just knew I had to. A salmon soldiering its way to the spawning grounds.

By the time I reached the treeline, I had to sit on a fallen trunk to catch my breath. It seemed like I'd been walking for miles and hours. I wasn't even sure why I'd set out in the first place. I'd be much more comfortable on my couch, binge-watching Outlander and snacking on razor thin slices of parmesan cheese.

Yet whatever drove me on seemed so damned important that I got up once more and pushed myself forward. Despite my legs quivering more with every step. Even if my breath was laboring.

And then, as if I'd stepped from one hard line of a child's drawing to another, the thorns and brambles stopped. Ahead of me, a large expanse of verdant grassland, clipped short by grass-eating fauna. Wild horses, I thought, and sheep. A goat or two. On sight of me, they bolted, leaving me to stand there, gawking, with my eyelids blinking slow as a cursed doll.

The scenery was different, but it looked familiar. The countryside around a medieval castle, I thought. In the distance, I was sure I could even make out the outline of a stone facade with massive walls and arrow-slit windows.

The rolling hills cast a pungently sweet aroma of grass and moss that was a welcome change from the sulfur that had dogged my steps. The smell of dew just laid onto the foliage wet my palate. I was thirsty, I realized. How long had it been since I'd taken a drink?

At the bar, I figured. With Gideon. I'd had a shot of tequila, hadn't I? I'd stolen something from him. I'd been pissed because Shea had dared knock on my door and told me my ex-lover, her new lover, was in trouble.

I looked down at the ground. My boots looked out of place beneath the hem of some beautiful dress that caught the moonlight just right. Like beads of dew on a spider's gossamer web. Blinking, I heeled off one, then the other so that my feet were bare. That looked better. More natural.

A sigh of contentment fled my lungs. I felt peaceful. Like I was home. I found a broad enough tree stump and I sat. Stared at my surroundings, listened to the air. I watched the night pull a blanket over the sky and the grass move on a silent breeze, and my core relaxed.

And then, even as that sense of belonging clutched at me, tugging at something in my soul, another sensation crept over me, one I knew far better than the sense of contentment and peace.

Something I knew so well that I didn't need to see the creatures coming out of the woods to know they were there.

Danger.

 Chapter 16

They came like the mist that crept through the brambles and branches. I knew them the moment they broke into the clearing.

The last time I had seen them, they had been dragging what I thought was a mortal girl out of the grand ballroom. Then, I'd not given any thought whether I should follow or not. I'd been raked over by fae just like them in the Catacombs of Dread. I wasn't going to let it happen to anyone else.

There was no young woman this time. They came for me as though they knew I was there. On silent, padding feet, they moved through the grass and foliage without moving a single frond.

I rose to my feet slowly. My eyelids took forever to lower and rise. A drunkard, I was, swaying on legs that felt like toothpicks balancing a series of bowling balls. The air brushed where they were naked, my skirts tucked up and tied around my hips to facilitate fighting and movement.

Except I couldn't marshal any movement. Not for far too many moments, and when my brain finally found liberation and shot out commands to my limbs, it was as if the megaphone was unplugged. I had a hard time coordinating. I couldn't remember how to throw a punch or sweep with my feet. When one of them grappled my wrist in his hand, I stared at it for long seconds, trying to remember if I was supposed to try to break the hold or kick or run.

I waited too long, and by the time I slid my other hand between his forearms to grab onto my hand and yank to break his hold, three others swarmed me and made the movement useless.

A sob fled my lungs, one of frustration and rage. That they'd found me here, that made me the most angry. Not that they'd overwhelmed me. Not that I'd forgotten how to defend myself.

I was pissed that they'd stolen those moments of peace.

Lashing out came easily then. I kicked, however awkwardly, however fruitlessly, but I kicked. I might have hit a shin or a nose before I lost all ability to move at all. At least six of them wrangled me into the air, one to each limb. One of them slipped something over my head, shutting out everything from my vision except for the coarse weave that somehow glowed beneath the material the way eyelids did when closed but lifted heavenward.

I didn't struggle. I couldn't. They carried me like a sac, letting my back sag beneath me. My head hung down heavily, past my shoulders, my hair dragging in the grass as they went. The hood slipped an inch, enough for me to breathe unfettered. I shook my head back and forth, dislodging it further, until, with the swaying movement of my body as it was carried, the hood finally fell free.

Above me, the sky melted. The moon dripped rivulets of light. Behind me, the corkscrew limbs of the trees unwound themselves while the trunks bowed low enough for the branches to root into the earth.

Everything bobbed even though I felt as if I was barely moving, the tread of my abductors smooth and effortless.

I watched as the entire forest, from the grass to the trees to the skyline above me and the crickets below me, turned to stone with a shudder that felt as if the entire world had gasped along with me.

And I recognized this place too. I'd tread down the stone steps to this place from inside the ballroom, seeking that young woman. I'd fought off the same creatures, somewhat human but feral. I knew the bars made of blacksteel, the inhabitants beyond them. I knew the smell of sulfur and the feel of the flagstones beneath my back.

They left me long enough to turn to those cells and the clang of gears being released, of locks liberating themselves, echoed through the small space. I tried to roll over, but my body wouldn't obey. I was left to lie there on my back while shadows moved over the ceiling, growing larger and then tightening above me into a single fist before even that was obliterated by the sight of a dozen more of those same creatures.

"What do you want?" I rasped out.

They leaned down as one, baring their teeth in those broad, whalelike mouths. Sharp canines. A flash of black tongue. Someone whimpered into the darkness and the sound came back to me in echo. Me. That someone was me and I was terrified because my mind had already flooded with the image of Ferranus and his tubers and suckers. The sight of them being stuffed into soft bellies and into choking mouths.

Now my mind was feeding those same visions to my limbs and spine because I fully expected I'd be on the other end of one of them in a few seconds. Fear swamped me long before the adrenaline tried to cough its way from my glands. It tried in vain to fire me up. The choke on my engine hacked and failed.

The moment those mouths touched down on my bare skin, arms, legs, thighs. Everywhere. That was the moment my body came alive finally. Arching up in a spasm so powerful, so fast, my throat hurt with the force of it, I kicked out.

Those mouths that had landed already like night moths on silk fell away. Bolstered, I used the thrust of that kick to twist and wrench myself sideways, dislodging yet another mouth from my arm.

Someone growled.

"Fuck you," I spat out, aiming the curse at the closest creature, even though I wasn't even sure he could hear anything except the growling and suckling as the others fought for purchase on my skin again.

He looked almost spectral, not very different from the fae in the ballroom, but different enough that I was surprised I hadn't noticed the first time that they were slightly different. They looked almost human...and yet. They weren't human. Like a clay form that hadn't baked quite right.

My fist flew out, old muscle memory coming awake.

"Get the. Fuck. Off me."

I struck a nose, I thought. The thing reared back with a howl. But as he made space, others rushed in to fill it.

I lost myself to the frenzy then, letting my training do the work, checking out my brain as the rest of me took over. Punches flew. Nails scratched. Teeth bit down wherever they could. I tasted rotten eggs. Sour milk. Rancid meat. It was enough to make me gag, but I didn't stop. I couldn't.

If all I had available to me as a weapon was my teeth, my nails, and my feet, I was going to give it.

When I'd met them before, they'd overwhelmed me. I'd run. Afraid. Beaten and bruised, I'd fled the dungeon and found my way to the ballroom. Heuil had found me. Barely saved me. It had been Erachne's magic that healed me.

No one would come for me here. No one knew where I was. And even if they did, I was sure they'd never be able to follow.

A whisper padded through my mind on soft kitten feet that Blade would come. He'd promised to find me. He had my blood. He knew the sound of my breath and the tempo of my heartbeat.

He'd come for me.

I knew it. And yet I knew it would be too late.

Like before, I was no match for them, no matter how I fought and twisted and bit down on whatever came at me. But this time, I felt as if the stakes were higher. Before, it felt like my body was at risk.

This time, I had a terrible sense that I was risking something far more precious.

I found enough space to yell at them. "What in the fuck do you want? What do you want from me?"

As unexpected as it was, an answer came back. "They want your essence, whatever magic lies in the spark of your heart that makes it fire. They want to return home."

At the sound of the female voice, the creatures recoiled. Only when they'd pulled away did I realize some had buried their teeth in my skin and as they tore free of me, I winced, feeling little stinging nettles of burn in various places.

I crab-walked backward until I felt my shoulders butt up into one of the prison cells. The hard metal bars dug into my spine. That spot between my shoulder blades burned all the way through to my solar plexus.

My eyes strained to see through the shadows for the female fae I knew would be standing there. I remembered her voice. I knew the electricity of her.

"Where are you?" I demanded. "Show yourself."

A form peeled itself from the shadows. I didn't need to see the cloud of fire-red hair to know who the voice belonged to.

And yet, when she came into the light, it wasn't the gorgeous auburn-haired fae who had lured me away from the ballroom by duping me into believing she was a mortal woman being assaulted by three fae.

What came into the light was a horror-sized canine, both magnificent and terrifying in the cut of shoulders rippling like a big cat's as it shed the darkness. The set of its jowls, boxy and square, was anything but a tame dog. Built for power and force, there should have been no way for such a rasp of smoky voice to usher forth, let alone answer me, and I expected no reply.

Instead, I waited, because when a beast that large and that predatory sullied forth from its lair, shedding its form for each step so fluidly into a new, more human one, prey froze.

And she did stalk from that darkness as though her entire being was made of it, and with each inch she lost of its cover, her form took new shape. Shedding like a snake, so that the canine peeled away in clusters of filmy shade that itself disappeared into the shadows behind her.

By the time she had come forward far enough that the stub of tail bobbed once and was gone, she had plucked from thin air the same guise as the young, red-haired woman I'd followed into the depths of Ferranus's dungeons.

As disconcerting as it was to see the wavering form move from one shape to the next, it was the sensation that beneath the flesh of a mortal looking woman, that predator still lurked beneath the skin no deeper than the fatty layer.

I felt a keen sense that a single move could turn the tide of life to death in the way she angled her body and let the woman show through despite the spectre of hound hovering, doing its best to remain hidden from view and failing.

She dressed herself in red leather with black trimmings cut and inlaid into spots on her shoulders and knees, the elbows. Places that bent and moved, I realized. To give some suppleness to her movement.

Black boots climbed her legs to mid thigh. They creaked with each step as though they needed breaking in, and I foolishly found myself wondering why she'd bother to create such an illusion and not bother to make the glamor one of comfort and quiet. In my silent question, I found my answer. This was her other form. The hellhound had been the primary one. The true one.

She came within several yards of me before stopping. She shot a grin at me then, that was both crooked and familiar. Those eyes flashed like lightning. I was sure I caught sight of a coiling movement around her irises.

"Took you long enough," I said, finding some bravado despite being curled up against the bars. My knees pulled up and trembling.

"For a trembling mortal, you have a sassy mouth."

I was trembling, I realized, but I wasn't ready to concede. "I have nothing to gain by being coy."

She didn't shrug. It seemed a movement beneath her, but she did raise her auburn eyebrows at me. Her jaw ticked sideways. Thinking.

I pushed myself up further, straighter. Waited for her to speak.

Instead, she strolled the few paces toward me. The creatures shrank back against the bars. Not afraid, strangely enough. Somehow...reverent.

She knelt on one knee in front of me. Waited. Just like I was. But hell if I was going to break the silence. She'd have to be the first to crack through the barrier and find me waiting.

It took several seconds before she smiled again, a slow movement across that gorgeous face. Her eyes sparked again. Something moved around the irises and, despite my resolve, I spoke first.

"What do you want from me?" I asked.

"What I've always wanted of you, Ava Ashe. To see what you are made of."

A gasp shredded my throat.

"You know this place?" she asked in a measured tone.

It took me several beats of breath to realize what she was asking, and for the impact of what that meant to sink in.

I wasn't in the veil at all.

CHAPTER 17

I'd fled a battle a handful of times in my years as a hunter. Every time, it was because I knew I had to run or I wouldn't survive. And survival for me was less about living and more about vengeance on the thing that wanted me dead.

But the last time I'd run from a fight it had been out of pure fear, not tactical retreat. And it had been from the same place I'd seen this fae before. That place had the same cells with dingy iron bars, the same stone walls and creeping darkness. That battle had been riven with the same unholy looking, wasted fae.

"I'm in Kumara," I said in a flat voice, not the least bit surprised to hear the name on my lips like worn velvet. My gaze flitted over her shoulder, trying to take in what might be lurking in those shadows if what was in front of me was already enough to make me tremble. "You said you were waiting to see what I was made of."

She made a thoughtful sound in the back of her throat as if she'd already decided. In that moment, I knew I had to find a way to get up. Get up or die there.

Get up or die. The phrase clanged like a bell in my head. I'd seen her another time, hadn't I? After Erachne had spun me into a cocoon so I could heal. After Heuil had found me on the fringes of Kumara in the stairwell outside the ballroom...if there even was a stairwell outside the ballroom. I wasn't sure of anything anymore.

"Sticks and stones," I said, feeling as though there was an echo in the room, one that wasn't within earshot. A strange, dizzying déjà vu.

"And puppy dog tails," she murmured. "Let's not forget those." She chuckled softly.

I had to force myself not to think about that stub of tail I'd seen peeling away into darkness. I planted an elbow and forearm on the flagstones and leveraged my torso upwards.

I gained enough height to look her straight in the knee.

"Why am I here?" I asked. "Why aren't I in the veil?"

"Is that where you intended to go?"

"You think I'd want to come here?"

"I'd think after fleeing in such a rush like a coward before, you'd have been dying to get back to prove what you are."

My legs pulled up and inward. A reflex, maybe. Or a decision to look less weak. I wasn't sure until the words tore free from my throat in a bitter flood.

"I'm no coward."

The arm draped over her knee gave a little flex before her fingers went still again. I could hardly tear my gaze from the way her hand hung so loosely, so casually toward the flagstones.

"No?" she asked. "Cowards run. Warriors retreat so they can return for a second shot."

An unspoken question clung to her comment, that was as much a taunt as the way she'd somehow pulled my own thoughts to the surface. Which are you, it asked.

"I don't need to prove who I am to you," I said.

"Certainly not," she said. "Especially when you haven't proven it to yourself."

"I know what I am," I said.

"Yes. A coward."

"I'm not a coward."

She ran a thumb over her bottom lip thoughtfully, and I watched it whisper down her chin to her throat. With a neat motion, she dragged it over her neck, then looped it around to the back before she dropped her head sideways, lolling it on her shoulders. Hanging, that motion said in a small gesture.

Who are you?" I asked. "What is Kumara?"

She rolled her gaze toward the creatures, all but vibrating beside the bars where they'd retreated to. "She doesn't understand."

She sounded as though she was pouting, but I didn't have the mental bandwidth to peer up into her face. I would be horrified to see that muzzle, all boxy and powerful, waiting to chomp down on my nose.

That image itself gave me another inch of victory in my attempt to rise. The elbow propped on the floor became a palm. The palm pushed harder into the flagstones.

"Where am I?"

She jerked a thumb over her shoulder. "You see them. You remember them from before. Same scenery. Same me. Had you stayed long enough last time you would have your answers already."

I snorted, the blood coming back to my limbs, finally. "You mean I would be dead already," I said.

She only blinked at me, her lips making a move that was very nearly a smile, as if I'd made some sort of joke I wasn't privy to.

The expression made me angry. "Your playthings attacked me last time. They were trying to kill me. I wasn't ready to die. That's why I ran. Tactical Retreat, they call it."

Another half smile, infuriating me further. I pulled my knees beneath me. The flagstones, though smooth, were cold on my bare skin. A tiny pebble embedded into my right knee and I rolled over onto my hand, shifting my weight enough to readjust.

The movement, sudden and jerky, cost me. I hung there for a half second, everything swimming. It seemed to take forever for the dizziness to abate.

But it did. And once my belly stopped its own determined rebellion and the vacuum in my ears quieted, I dragged in one long, bracing breath.

That was when I shot to my feet like a runner. The gown loosed itself from the warrior knot I'd tied into it and it cascaded down my legs to sweep my bare insteps.

I held my fists up. Defensive stance. "I'm not ready to die now either."

Her auburn brows lifted. Impressed? I had no idea and I didn't care. I just knew I felt more like myself again. Dazed, maybe, a bit weak and somewhat dizzy, but more myself.

The recollection of dozens of fights fired my muscles. I felt like I could breathe again. And for every moment of arrogant silence she granted me, I took one more furious inhale. "I'm not a coward."

"I'm here, now," I went on. "Not running. Facing you." I jerked my thumb toward the cages and the creatures moaning softly in front of them. "Facing your minions again if I have to."

That pulled a comment from her, finally. "You think they are the things to be afraid of here?" She laughed. "They only want one thing, and it's not something they can get from you, though they'll try." She pouted in their direction. "And they aren't mine," she said thoughtfully. "I only care for them here."

I snorted. "Some care, putting them behind bars."

A hand went to her chest. "Only the most dangerous are held behind bars here," she said. "For their own protection." She cast a look down my length. "And for those who come here unprepared."

"So they were in cages for me, last time?" I sniffed in disbelief. "Then why did you release them at all? Why have them attack me."

"I told you. To see what you are made of."

One more time, she grazed my entire height with a scornful glance.

"So you've measured me, then."

"I have."

My fingers curled into balls at my sides. "Then loose them again," I said with a lifted chin. "You'll see you're wrong."

"Oh, I'm not wrong." She moved, finally, pivoted on her heel to turn to the creatures huddled together in front of the cages, the darkness beyond the bars that seemed to hold an electrified threat of danger.

She prowled the length while I stood there weaving on my feet.

"I told you these are not mine, but I do care for them, and yet you didn't ask who they belonged to. Who made them this way."

"It doesn't matter to me," I said. "I have only one interest here." My mind went to Phaedre in that trunk and my promise that I'd return for her quickly, and I realized I had more than one interest. It wasn't just about killing a king anymore and going home. It had changed the moment I made the decision for myself instead of doing what I was being exploited to do, and I amended my comment.

"I have no interests here."

She paused and looked back at me over her shoulder. The shadows behind her in those cages seemed to move. The creatures huddled together leaned away from her.

"But you have an interest somewhere," she said.

I didn't answer. As far as I was concerned, Phaedre was safe right where I'd left her, an unknown element to the equation. Anything else and this scenario went decidedly, horrifically left.

So I held my tongue and I waited her out even though her expression grew darker and more intense with each moment I refused to answer.

Finally, she sighed. "In your world you are a hunter," she said, and the change of tactic surprised me enough to reply.

"I am." No harm in admitting that.

"In your world you protect the innocent?"

"I protect the helpless from monsters, yes."

"No matter what the cost."

Air whistled out of my nostrils. "No matter the cost."

"And you are good at knowing which are monsters and which are helpless."

I gestured toward the cluster of emaciated fae. "Generally, the ones doing the attacking are the monsters. Like your playthings over there."

"The fact that you single out those poor hapless creatures indicates you are not as wise in your assessments as you think."

"If they are so helpless, then why did they attack me?" Meaning, they were the monsters here. Not me, if that was what she was implying. "They bit me. They tried to beat me into a paralyzed mess too injured to fight back while they drained my blood."

The sound of her laughter, pleased and surprised, lifted to the air and swelled around me. "Blood," she said as she laughed. "You humans think it's all about blood." She drew out another long, hard chuckle until I began to cringe at the mocking sound of it.

"Fuck you," I said and spun on my heel. I'd tired of her. I'd tired of her cloak and dagger comments and her arrogance. "I'm out of here."

The gown swirled over my ankles as I padded away. The creatures perked up, lifting their heads and peering at me as I went by. I gave them enough berth to pass unmolested, but I was pretty sure she was going to let them attack me again, anyway.

Whatever she was after, she could get it from someone else. I was done and Phaedre needed me.

"She's not there, you know," said the fae from behind me.

My mouth went dry. I halted. There was no way she could know about Phaedre and yet...

I couldn't let on the comment bothered me. I shrugged. "I don't know what you're talking about," I said over my shoulder, expecting her to have moved on me by the way my skin tingled.

But she wasn't there. Just shadows that had gained a thickness so dark it crept along the floor and rose up the walls of the cells. Something in the nearest one moved.

I needed to get out of there, I knew. The reprieve she'd given me was over. Even the air felt different. It tasted like brimstone again and the tang of cloves brushed along my palate with each inhale. My feet skimmed the surface of the flagstones, picking up more pebbles as I turned.

And at sight of her standing directly in front of me, I drew in a sharp, unexpected breath.

"You aren't leaving," she said.

My shoulders squared. My spine softened even as my feet braced. "Just fucking try to stop me," I said.

Bravado, I thought, because even as I spoke, my legs went numb. I had to look down at my feet to be sure they were still there. It took an effort of will alone just to remain standing when everything in me felt like it was breaking apart.

"Are you a coward, Ava?" she asked. "I need to know."

"What do you think?"

Her fingers swept over my chest to pluck the stone of my necklace from its place between my breasts. "I think this necklace you wear tells the true tale. You hold onto your deeds like trophies, telling yourself you are brave because of all those you've vanquished. And yet those deeds haunt you."

I lifted my chin, bringing Blade's face to mind, aching to feel his skin again, hear his voice as he liberated me from years of guilt with his embrace and his healing magic. "They do not haunt me. Not anymore."

"Because they were taken from you. You didn't face them. You let someone else remove them instead of letting them become part of the mosaic of Ava. They were yours. Your offspring. They made you what you are. Fierce and angry. But you gave them away like changeling children too awful for the mortal world."

She leaned closer. "It's not the good who die in peace, Ava. Its those who live their lives despite their flaws and rush headlong into life clinging to their imperfections like babes. You think you're unworthy because of those things, but in some realms, those very horrors are the things we foster and seek out."

My skin crawled as she watched me. I thought of the perfect sense of harmony of my liberation, of Blade's skin against mine, of the moment he'd hung that necklace over my neck and gave me back my life and I hated that she was sullying that.

"You know nothing about it."

"You've given up the best part of yourself, Ava," she said.

"You don't know me." My chest heaved. I swallowed, trying to bring some moisture to my mouth. "And you can't keep me here."

An uncharacteristic softness washed over her features. "Oh, Ava Ashe. You haven't guessed the truth even now?"

She gestured to the creatures who had inched forward, their faces hungry and attentive. Beyond them, the bars teemed with hands and claws and wings as the creatures within—cloaked in shadow before—came into the light and strained against their prisons.

Those faces, too, were hungry. The eyes manic.

And yet there was something about them all that I'd not truly noticed before. They weren't solid. Not truly spectral, but not entirely corporeal, either.

And there, in the cell closest to me, the one where I'd felt such a dread bit of tension, I recognized a familiar face.

His body was made up of black, billowing smoke, wafting up into a cloud that seemed to have its own invisible container, because it rose only so far away from his body. His eyes were dead and sunken. His mouth still carried that same condescending curve as he regarded me, this time without a stitch of sentience or intelligence.

Manic, as the others were, but there was no doubt it was Terran.

My knees buckled. But for her hand around my waist, I would have fallen. I dragged my eyes to her face.

"Sweet Jesus," I said. "What sort of fae are you?"

"Not that god, my girl, and most definitely not fae," she said with a cocky grin that made me gasp in recognition.

"Hellhound," I guessed. "My god, you're Aiofe. You're Blade's mother. The Queen of the Stygian Darkness."

"Perhaps once I was queen of the darkness," she said in a longing voice. "But not now. Now I am the darkness."

At her words, all the prisoners began slamming into their restraints over and over. The fae stopped huddling as one unit and began shuffling randomly around the area, lifting their heads back and letting loose howls that made my skin break out in goose flesh. Right down to my marrow, I felt and heard those sounds, felt the bars against my skin as though I too was in one of the cells. The fragrance of sulfur grew so strong I couldn't breathe.

Gone was her arm around me, leaving me to collapse to the flagstones. My head dropped back and sounds I'd never believed possible tore from my lungs and clawed their way around the chamber.

I felt her kneel at my side, watching me so closely I could have licked her eyelids if I had been able to do more than howl and moan. I was a puppet. No will. No backbone. I was one of those things, those wraiths, I knew now. Here in this Kumara.

And I knew there was no way out.

CHAPTER 18

I don't know how long I existed there on my knees, my face lifted skyward, mouth open, but it seemed an eternity. My throat was sore and my voice grown hoarse. I couldn't feel my fingers, my toes. The only sensation I had but for the rawness of my throat was the burning in between my shoulder blades that I'd felt immediately upon coming awake on the trunk with Phaedre atop me.

Then, Aiofe touched me once, gently, on the shoulder and mercifully, the horrible sounds emanating from my soul, the awful keening, stopped.

My jaw clicked closed so audibly one of the wraiths paused his own howling to stare at me.

I didn't know if I could speak, but for Phaedre's sake, for Blade's and Mica's and all those mortals in the veil, including Gideon, that were counting on me, I had to try.

"I'm dead," I said, my voice a flat line. "I've died somehow and passed over. That's why I'm not in the veil."

I thought of Phaedre and my heart squeezed, dread doing terrible things to its rhythm. If I was dead, then what of Phaedre? Had I killed her instead of saving her?

My mouth kept moving, and I was aware that I was saying nothing. Just. Nothing.

After a time, I felt Aiofe's hand on mine and the touch seemed to free me from the paralysis. I blinked. Feeling. Sensation. Touch. It was glorious.

"You aren't dead," she said. "But you are dying."

I didn't care about that. Not right then. I had one concern that was more important than whether I was drawing my last breath, and I asked it because risking Phaedre's life by outing her presence in the realm seemed more likely than keeping her existence a secret.

"Is she?" I said. "Is Phaedre dead? Is she dying too?"

A movement beside me. Darkness winked in and out several times, and when its flickering was done, there was a soft cushion for me to sit on.

"You mean the little goblin?" Aiofe asked as she gestured once more toward the cushion so that I had to crawl onto it finally or presume she wouldn't answer. Burgundy velvet, I thought, even though I couldn't possibly be discerning colors in the gloom. Just like Ferranus's throne seat.

"Have no fear for the little thing," she said. "The half goblin is safe and very much alive."

Only once I'd pulled my knees up, the pads of my feet tucked into the fulsome velvet, did she create a stool for herself and sit down on it with a resigned sigh.

Behind her, the wraiths stopped moving. Expectant. Alert. The prisoners went silent. But they stared. All of them. They watched me closely. I tried not to think of Terran's beady eyes holding fast to my throat the way it had done so often while he'd been alive.

Aiofe spread her legs out, long and lean, crossing the ankles neatly as she regarded me with something like matronly concern.

"You, however. That is a different issue. One that is causing me quite a bit of trouble here in Kumara."

"Phaedre," I said again. "Where is she?"

She lifted one shoulder in an offhand shrug. "If you must know in order to give me the attention I need of you, then she is in Lyonara's veil. The moment you pushed her down into the trunk and lowered the lid, she slid into that realm. I told you. She is safe."

Lyonara. A name I'd not heard and could only presume it was connected to Ferranus somehow. I stowed the information away even as I realized that the other bit of information, that Aiofe knew of our movements and conversation, meant she probably did know if Phaedre was in her realm.

If she was The Darkness, she would have seen all that. She would have heard us speaking.

"I need to get to her," I said, leaning forward on the cushion to get a better look at her face. Read her expression. "She's in danger, especially in Ferranus's veil."

She leaned forward too, giving me full view of those eyes and the way they flashed. Now, I did see serpents coiling around her irises. Same as Blade. My heart stuttered and stalled at the sight.

"You are not listening to me, hunter," she rasped. "You are causing trouble here in the Darkness."

"I thought you were the darkness."

Her eyes shuttered enough to make that gorgeous face grow hard-edged. The hellhound was easily discernible in the jawline. "Don't test me."

"I am not trying to test you. I am asking to leave. I am asking you to let me go to her. She's in danger from the king. It's why I pulled her here with me. It's why I leapt into the hagstone. I left everyone else behind."

I choked on the words, my memory feeding me unwanted images of Ferranus and his tubers reaching for Blade and striking Stone instead. I swallowed and continued before I could imagine any more. "I left anyone I cared about behind with that bastard because, of all things, your son would want me to keep her safe."

"You did not pull her here," she said. "You dove for the hagstone, yes, and you grabbed her with you, but you did not pull her here."

"I don't understand."

"You are here because of the bond and blood you share with my son. He is the reason you are here."

"Then send me back. You have the power, don't you? You, the darkness, should be able to release me?"

"There are many ways into Kumara," she said and gestured toward the wraiths watching us so silently it was eerie. "These came because the king drained them of their magic, and what was left of their spirits needed a safe place until their bodies wither and end."

She waved at the place where Terran loomed beside his cell bars. "He came because the magic from the city of the Dead possesses him even still."

"So these fae," I said, my eye trailing to the cells and hooking there on a fist wrapped around a bar so tightly the iron was bending. "These fae aren't dead?"

"These fae have had their magic depleted beyond what they can recover from. Their bodies exist somewhere in Fae and when the last of their spirits have extinguished they will be released from Kumara."

I thought of the wispy thralls Ferranus had created of his pages, and my eye returned to the wraiths in the corner. Three of them did look familiar.

"The others," I said, pushing myself to my feet. My gaze glued itself to the shadows within the cells. I knew Terran's face. But there was more darkness beyond. More darkness filled with the sort of energy I knew were other fae. Terrifying fae.

"Generations," I said in awe. "He has drained generations of fae if that darkness is filled with wraiths."

"Every one hundred years, he adds more," she said softly and my head snapped toward her.

"You mean—"

"I mean the promise of magic to one hundred fortunate fae is a lie he concocted to steal even more power from those who live in his realm."

"But the tokens." I gestured at Terran. "His men, his soldiers, they have killed to acquire them, to steal the magic grants from the king."

"A sacrifice they make willingly. And they will lose their magic to him the same as all the other lesser fae have over the generations. And they will come to Kumara and exist until their spirit is extinguished. Ferranus the Ugly doesn't grant power. He just takes it. His magic is a sleight of hand as much as it is a true power. He throws a lavish ball to distract eyes from his real intention. They are so focused on their own debauchery, that they don't ask about their lucky comrades who won their power for a year. No one wonders where they go, why they seem to disappear. They just assume they are off enjoying the use of their own magic for the first time in their lives. Those magically handicapped who give him their power presume that someday it might be them who wins a token someday and they thank their gods and goddesses for a chance to enjoy a once in a century gala."

I thought of Heuil and his hope for wings. My belly rolled over into itself and I sank back down onto the cushion.

"One hundred more fae will be added to this place," I said. "High fae and one poor half-trow."

"Kumara is already overfull. I don't know how much longer I can power it without taking back some of the magic that holds it."

"You created the veil?"

She shook her head. "Not entirely. I was one part, one small part, of its creation. The greater magic came from Lyonara herself. Kumara had always existed, like the Stygian Darkness existed. Like the river Styx, it is a river of shadow weaving in and out of our lives and creating a place, an afterlife of sorts, for the creatures of Fae.

"I was a young queen, then. Like a fool, I believed Kumara was infinite just as my mother's life seemed infinite. When Lyonara came to me, I offered her a place within Kumara, thinking it would be harmless. A small place to tuck herself into within a vast and mostly unused river of shadow. I didn't think it would be a problem to give her an anchor. I wanted her to have an anchor."

Her gaze misted over as though she were lost in memory. I held still, waiting for more, terrified that even a breath would break the spell.

She shook her head clear. "But then he warped it. And Kumara began to fill. And when my own death came, I too, came to Kumara. Except...hellhounds born of the Titan of the Stygian Darkness don't simply die. I became the darkness where Kumara existed. I became the source of the energy that held the poor hapless fae who found themselves here."

She leveled me with a hard stare. "And now that you know those secrets, Ava Ashe, it's time for me to get what I've been waiting for. It's time for me to see what you are made of."

I felt myself flinch, but she didn't make mention of it.

"Have you wondered how you came to be here in our afterlife, Ava? You who are a mortal and not fae? Have you wondered how you were able to manifest a trunk filled with magical objects when Ferranus's own thralls tossed that chest into the hagstone?"

I hadn't, but now that I knew more, I could see that those thralls on the other side were the anchoring bodies to these wraiths in Kumara. No wonder the chest came here. They'd tossed it here intentionally. To draw me here.

Without thinking, my hand moved to my back, feeling for the places where it hurt still, though there was no wound.

She saw me and nodded. She pulled her heels toward the stool and spread her legs wide, hanging down into the crevasse between her knees.

"Your body on the other side is not in good shape, Ava. The hit you took from Lilah was too much for it to withstand. You pushed Phaedre through to the veil but you never made it. My son knows this. The moment Lilah blasted you with her magic, he dove to protect you, but fast as he is, he was encumbered. He got there too late."

Encumbered. My eyes closed in recollection. Yes. He'd been running to protect Mica, thinking he was Phaedre. He must have released him to Ferranus's rage at the last second. A whimper fled my lungs at the thought that he'd abandoned his brother to save me.

"What happened to the boy?" I asked, opening my eyes and lifting my gaze to hers. "Is he dead?" My eyes scraped the cells, looking for evidence of Mica in the shadows. I thought I saw Terran shuffle sideways.

"If he was dead, Ava, he would not be here."

"Ferranus hasn't killed him? He's not draining him?"

Her voice was kind but filled with pain and grief when she spoke next. And though the news was positive the rawness of her words tore my soul into shreds of tissue.

"He is not. The king still believes the boy is the goblin and won't touch her in front of the court. He's very powerful, that one." She looked up as though a monitor of some sort claimed her attention, then said, "He's sitting unmolested even now, channeling more power into my son who is right now lying beside you on Ferranus's ballroom floor, his arm wrapping you in his embrace. His forehead is on yours. Your necklace is digging into his chest with the force of his embrace, and while it has broken the skin, he's happy to feel the pain because it tells him he's alive. He tells himself he didn't get to you in time to take Lilah's strike, but he's doing all he can to give you his magic. He's holding you here, giving you a chance at life by pumping the bond with his power. All of his power. He's giving you everything he has."

My mouth went dry. "Blade is dying."

She cocked her head sideways. "You see me here. I am not dead. He is blood and bone of my blood and bone. He is returning to the darkness that birthed him."

"You," I said through a tight throat.

"Me," she said and I could have sworn she stole a look at the cell where Terran watched us with those dead, black eyes. "He is dying so you can live. But I did not suffer the embrace of a mere fae so that my son could join the darkness. Not when he is meant to rule it."

"What are you saying?"

"I'm saying there is another way."

"Name it," I said, knowing I'd do whatever it took to keep Blade from coming here. "Tell me what I have to do to help him."

"Die."

 Chapter 19

I was about to die, and I had no regrets.

I pushed myself to my feet. Though I swayed on them, I looked down at her with unblinking eyes.

"If you were waiting to see if I had the cajones to sacrifice myself for the man I love, then you were foolish to make me sit here, listening to you rattle on about things that don't matter when your son—my mate--" I choked on the words and had to force myself to continue. "While my mate is dying."

She leaned back, taking me in with a cocky smile, infuriating me more. "I'm not afraid to die. You see what I'm made of. Your wait is over."

She stood as well, making no sound as she did so. For an instant, the hound was in her face, a challenge, I thought. But even if she planned to make my death painful, I wouldn't show her fear.

"Well?" I demanded. "What are you waiting for? Let's finish this. Tear my throat out."

The hound disappeared from her features as she lifted one eyebrow. "Permission."

"You have it already."

"It's not permission to end you that I seek," she said. "But permission to take your body."

I thought of the thralls that Ferranus had created and winced. "My body?"

She took my arm and guided me toward the cells. "You are mortal. It's the bond between you and my son that allows you to remain here. To leave, you must die, but where does a mortal go when they die?"

"Fucked if I know," I said.

"A mystery to me as well," she said with a note of humor in her voice that was not in keeping with the situation at all. "Which is why I must find a way for you to leave Kumara without sending you somewhere...unexpected while that happens."

We had arrived in front of Terran and he snarled at her, his lips curled back so viciously, I drew back out of instinct. She didn't so much as flinch.

"I took him from a young prince, once, because a king owed me a favor." She swept me with an unhurried, studying glance. "Our kind in the Stygian darkness tends toward the feminine. Sometimes we need male influence to continue our line."

She ran a palm in the air in front of Terran's face and he snarled.

"He waited centuries for his vengeance and in concocting all this, he ensnared our son to his rage. I will hold what's left of him for eternity for that, and make him suffer here for all time."

She swiveled her head to look at me. "But he knew things about Ferranus that no one else did until it was too late.

With your body, I can be the axe that severs the head from the snake. You are mortal and thus incapable of magic that will turn on you, and I am not fae so my magic cannot be held accountable by fae rules. You can leave Kumara on a technicality. You will be dead, but your body will live on."

"As you?"

She ran her hand down my back in a soothing motion. "As me. At least for a brief, gaudy hour of vengeance. With my spirit possessing your body, the bond between you and Blade will be severed. No bond, and my son can take back his magic before Ferranus drains both him and his brother's magic."

"Wait?" I said. "You said Blade can take his magic back before Ferranus drains him and his brother."

"Oh, I see I forgot that piece." She spun me around to face the stairwell I remembered from before. "Of course, Ferranus is draining him of his power while he lies there cradling you. He doesn't care. But he doesn't realize that the only reason he is still alive is that his brother, the one wearing the goblin's face, is refilling it. Like a circuit of sorts, except the one receiving the most power is the king."

"Sweet Jesus," I said.

"You see why I will do what I must stop this. My son is suffering and yet he won't give in until you are dead and gone. An impossible thing while his brother feeds him strength and he feeds yours. Eventually, even he will tire as will his brother, and he will come here."

She didn't need to say what would happen by the time he did come. That I'd be gone, and he'd be swallowed by the darkness.

I couldn't let that happen. I wouldn't.

"You say you can possess my body for a short while. What happens then? To this part of me?" I waved downward, encompassing the length of my body with a gesture. "While you have my body, where do I go?"

"You are free to enjoy the respite," she said. "This space, this setting is of your making, Ava. I can make it pleasant for you. Like a sunset field with chirping birds if you like."

My lips pursed at the thought that she believed I would have created this horrific space for myself, but I asked the more pertinent question, the one that had my mind reeling with possibilities. "And you say the veil is part of Kumara?"

"It is."

"And since my time here is my own, I may go where I like."

"Until the moment I wear down your body, finally, and you die in your world, yes. You may roam Kumara and all its pockets freely. It's not something I recommend, but that is not my decision." She peered at me intently.

I held her gaze stubbornly. "And you'll do everything in your power while you possess my body to make sure the king is dead."

"Yes. And to make sure my son lives to inherit his kingdom as the hellhound he is and not some shadow of it."

A sigh heaved out my nostrils as I gave her a nod. "How do we do this, then?" I asked.

She smiled with all her teeth showing, baring them in a feral way. "You've already done the hard part." She gave me a gentle shove toward the stairs. "But if you like, you may climb the stairs with me and see for yourself what you have been trusting my words to paint for you. Just in case you were inclined to doubt me."

I wasn't sure I wanted to see myself lying injured in front of that hagstone, with Blade beside me, doing his best to keep some shred of me viable while the king siphoned the magic from him, but I stepped aside to let her move ahead of me.

She glided like mist over the flagstones, and the movement put me in mind of Ruby's own swirling clouds. I shuddered, feeling a crisp chill in the air sweep over the back of my neck. Ruby, too, would be gone, I decided. Because that would be part of my bargain with Aiofe.

Before I followed, I cast a long look back over my shoulder, assuring myself that Blade was not already there. That Terran's eyes were the only ones I recognized. But as I peered into the shadows, they were already closing up and swallowing the wraiths and Terran and all the others in the cells beyond.

The darkness reached for me with long fingers and I pivoted sharply to follow her, the chill of the air making me shiver. I hurried after her, trailing along closely enough that I could hear the treads she took on the steps, the scuffing sound of whatever shoes she wore.

When we reached the doorway, she paused and turned around.

"This is the end of the line," she said. "You know this."

I nodded.

She laid a warm hand on my shoulder. "You may find it helpful to do some reading to pass the time."

I didn't answer, and she didn't wait for one. Instead, she lifted her hands over her head as though pulling up a magician's shroud. Billows of black shadow shuttered over her and then, in a fizzle of black beads that dropped to the floor soundlessly and disappeared, she was gone.

So, too, was the doorway between the ballroom and the stairwell. I had the feeling it was straddling a ley line of energy, that no one could see me even though I had a clear view of the ballroom and the dais and the hagstone.

I didn't want to look. I planned to spin around and descend back down those stairs, but the same sort of energy that holds a witness's eyes to a traffic accident made my gaze scan the room for the forms I knew would be there.

And even though she had prepared me, it was still a gutting thing to see myself lying on my side, my head in Blade's palms. He did, indeed, have his forehead pressed to mine, and he did indeed have a large tuber snaking into his spine. My knees went to wet bags at the sight of the two of us. A whimper fled my lungs.

I could barely tear my eyes away from Blade and I lying there, but I knew I had to. The moment I saw my body jerk, I startled right along with it. The Darkness had entered me, I realized. My body was no longer my own and was under her power.

Whatever happened now, it would be the last movements my physical self ever did.

A flash of Blade's voice ran through me, promising me he'd come for me if he had to crawl on coals in hell.

My cheeks felt cold and wet as Aiofe in my body extracted herself from Blade's embrace. Strangely enough, the tuber embedded into the bottom of his spine pulsed and recoiled as if it had tasted something foul.

It was still reeling its way back to Ferranus's throat when Aiofe stood, pulling Blade to his feet along with her.

My heart raced and skipped and ached like a hammer was beating on it too hard as I saw him stand on his own power. Alive. He was alive. He would be alright.

It took all I had in me to keep from crying out in joy. I had to stuff my hands in my mouth to keep from calling to him. But then, in those brief seconds, Blade looked Aiofe in the face. His shoulders went rigid. Hands curled into fists.

She held his gaze and said something to him. Something that made him angry. When he backed away from her, from my body, it was with a look of revulsion that made my heart ache.

I couldn't bear to see more. Dropping my gaze to the floor so I wouldn't have to witness a moment more, I felt a hand on my throat. It took a second before I realized no pulse tremored against my fingers. In fact, my skin where it touched flesh to flesh had very little sensation. No warmth. Like touching the hide of a downed deer.

It took a breath to understand what it meant. That I was nothing here. I was alone, and I was nothing. Not even a heartbeat to prove my life. I fell against the wall, my free hand catching me and propping me up. The stones had no sensation. No cold. No roughness.

I shouldn't have been surprised. I supposed this was always the way things were meant to go. Sure, I'd had a brief, but fulfilling moment with Blade, but a hunter's life and a hunter's death were all I could have expected. It was foolish to hope for more.

I tried to tell myself it was alright. That it wasn't so different from anything I'd ever expected from my life. That at least, this one thing made my death worthwhile.

I tried to smile. He was alive. Mica was out of danger.

And I had things left to do before I could finally be done.

Some reading, she'd said. The only place I knew of that had books in this realm was that trunk. And that trunk had portaled Phaedre into the veil.

The veil. Where she waited still with Gideon and God knew how many other mortals horded away like towels or blankets by the bastard fae king.

I turned around to face the stairs and the darkness beckoning me and I forced myself to move. If she kept her word,

Aiofe would be swinging for the king in moments, and if she took him out, the veil would begin to disintegrate.

And I didn't just have to get there before that happened; I also had to get there before I died.

Chapter 20

Descending the stairs was harder than I thought it would be. With my vision blurred by tears and a strange heaviness constricting my chest, I had a hard time navigating. I ended up breathing heavily and holding the wall long before I made it to the bottom.

It wasn't the only roadblock to getting to the veil. Just the first step of many and dragging in barely useful breaths was getting me nowhere. It wasn't a stretch to figure out what was making things difficult, and it wasn't just the fact that I was not whole.

I had to shut out the sight of Aiofe taking control of my body. Swallow down the ache of seeing Blade step away from me in disgust as the bond was severed. Those things. Those were the things stealing my energy.

And I needed all the spirit I could get, because getting out of the dungeons of Kumara when I didn't know the first thing about how to change my reality here would take a supreme amount of effort.

I kept telling myself that if I was making my own reality, I could decide that the end of the stairs would show me the same wooded glen that lead me to the forest where I'd left the trunk. And Phaedre.

I worked hard on that assumption. I put everything I had into the mental image of seeing that glen below me when I took that last few steps.

When the gloom below broke, I almost whooped aloud in victory. For once, things were going to go the way they needed to go. The trunk would be within easy reach. I'd pull open the lid and climb in the way I'd bade Phaedre do, and I'd yank the lid down. Easy access to the part of Kumara where the veil resided.

My steps sped up unconsciously as I hurried the last few steps and felt my feet sink into moss. The trees possessed the familiar corkscrew shapes to their branches that I'd seen upon entering Kumara with Phaedre.

But which direction would be the correct one? The forest went off in all directions. Turning around, I realized the staircase had melted into nothingness, leaving a landscape of brambles and bushes behind me.

I paused. Before I'd found the dungeon, I'd had to wade through yards and yards of trees and branches. By my recollection, I'd been drawn into the woods and away from the trunk by a very real sensation of danger and noises in the darkness.

Cocking my head to the side and closing my eyes, I listened for those sounds again, reasoning that whatever direction they came from, I could walk in the opposite direction and eventually get back to the trunk.

Like magic, they began to fill the air around me, from the whimpering cries I'd originally heard in the distance, to the growling rumble that seemed to come from everywhere and nowhere. They intensified and sharpened.

A smile moved my mouth. The relief that swam over me that this would be easy was near absolute. I felt like finally my luck was turning, and it was about time. This wasn't about me, after all. The universe had finally decided to reward that.

By the time I opened my eyes, I knew the direction I should begin walking, and it was a straight line ahead of me. The problem was that once I did open my eyes, I realized I was not alone.

How they found me didn't matter. What mattered was that they were no longer huddled together, swaying on their feet with dead pan eyes, docile monsters waiting for permission to become rabid.

Everything in their demeanor was far more manic, the way it had been the first time I'd descended into Kumara and Aiofe had let them loose on me.

They came in swarms. So many of them moved like the fae they used to be, with the speed that turned them into mere blurs, that I couldn't count or even separate them into individuals.

All I had time for was to brace my feet and lift my guard up.

I took a blow to the stomach first. It should have knocked the wind from me, but I'd already exhaled. Whether that was timing or ten thousand hours of practice, I didn't assess. I just spun on my heels and showed them my side profile, less of a target, as I grappled for whatever purchase I could.

That turned out to be an elbow, I thought, by the way it cracked as I flung my weight back and put the thrust into my grip. A yowl rent the air, then hissing and screeches. Striking out without thought, I found plenty of flesh to connect. Stillness wasn't an option. I had to keep moving. Keep fighting. Kicking. Biting at times.

Time stretched out and folded in at the same instant. There was no way the battle could take more than a few seconds, based on the sheer number of wraiths coming at me, colliding into me. And yet, I managed to toss aside at least four before I took another blow. This time to my cheek. Adrenaline kept me from feeling the contact until I tasted blood.

The smell of it must have tainted the air because, as one, they paused for a millisecond and all inhaled sharply at the same time. I took three out then, in that gap of time. An elbow backward. A donkey kick. A neatly executed flip.

But I wasn't foolish enough to believe that time would wormhole and hide me forever. I got in as many moves as I could in a frenzy of punches, kicks and head butts. Nothing neat. All of them thrown in a haphazard, panicked volley.

When teeth broke my skin, I knew time had caught up with itself. My knees threatened to buckle. I ducked and dodged and ripped at whatever had sunk its fangs into my shoulder. When that didn't work, I brought my head down hard.

Stars lit the backs of my eyelids. When I could see again, it was the taunting image of the trunk squatting a mere few yards away.

A whimper leaked from my lungs. So close. So damn close. Just not close enough.

The seething mass of bodies brought me down to my knees and the weight of them was suffocating. I tried to tell myself I wasn't dead on the outside and so I couldn't die here, but that didn't stop the sheer panic that came over me as the darkness closed in and I lost sight of the trunk.

During my younger years, when I was still innocent enough to care about school, I'd sat in one history class that made an impression. The teacher was handsome and young and ours was his first assignment. He'd been fascinated by the Salem Witch Trials and so then was I. He'd stood in front of the class and described the death of Giles Corey with such emotion and detail that I shuddered just thinking about it for weeks later.

Giles Corey's last words had a haunting effect on me. More weight. Kill me quickly, in other words, but you won't see me surrender.

I felt that way lying beneath dozens of bodies, their mouths on my bare skin, breaking the flesh as they sought—not blood, as Aiofe had explained, but some particle of magic to bring them back to their former selves.

It burned. Each one of those bites burned like a hot poker, searing into my veins like molten lead. It shouldn't have hurt when I felt so numb everywhere, but it did. But pain wasn't what bothered me most as I lay there. What hurt more than each stinging bite was knowing I'd failed.

Phaedre, Gideon, all those untold numbers of mortals in the veil would be left to die there, and I'd go to nothingness as a failure.

I should have fought harder. I should have found a way to stand my ground. Now, there wasn't even the tiniest gap of space to stick a hand through. Crawling out from beneath them was impossible. All I had left in me was to pray that Aiofe would punish the fae who did this to so many of his subjects. Because while so many fae were indeed monstrous, I'd met many who were kind. Not all monsters. Not all deserved to die.

Someone was screaming, I realized, and it took several more moments to realize it was me before I managed to clamp my mouth closed. I might be down and I might have failed, but I would not go to my end crying like a baby.

I was holding my breath, trying not to do just that, when I felt just the slightest shift in the weight pinning me flat.

A breath wheezed its way in. The barest release of pressure on one of my legs.

Something was happening around me. I wasn't sure if something was changing with the wraiths themselves, making them peel away one by one, or if I was changing somehow, but there was a definite shift in the air. I could breathe better. I could move even if it was the slightest shuffle of my legs, drawing them together as I tried to push myself up.

It took several moments to realize the wraiths were indeed disengaging and peeling away from me, but it wasn't a passive letting go. Not in the least.

It was done with much violence and pain, as with each release of weight, a searing pain razored through me. Hissing and screeching inevitably followed until I winced and cried out with every inch of relief I gained.

And it kept happening. One by one, breath by breath, scream by scream, they left me until I gained enough mobility that my lungs made a full exhale, until my spine cracked with sudden release.

Finally. Finally, I could move. An attempt at rolling over wasn't successful at first, but on a second try, I had enough energy, enough space, to dislodge the last of those holding me down.

I scrambled ungracefully onto my hands and knees. Lunged with a sprinter's lunge to my feet.

Swung around, knocking off grips that still came for me but that were mercifully less successful. I staggered backward, expecting more of the wraiths to come at me, confused. Terrified. Traumatized.

Wraiths of every shape, size, and form were being shredded as a beast the size of a small buffalo plowed through them snout and tooth first. Its head swung back and forth, bowling over what creatures it didn't seize in its massive jaws.

Paralyzed, I watched it crunch down on throats and limbs alike, spraying black and brackish blood over its shoulders and back.

"Steady," I whispered to myself. "Steady, Ava. Don't lose your shit, now."

Because losing my shit would most assuredly also lose me the unexpected ground I'd just been granted by...I had no idea. Whatever it was, it was still bowling through and chowing down on every wraith that got in the way.

And there were a lot of wraiths in the way. The beast was resolute in its advance through each one of them, its black eyes rolling back with each hard crunch of bone. A sound that made a shudder go through me every time I heard it.

A few of the wraiths dodged for me as I ducked sideways, seemingly unaware that some monster was out for their blood. Oblivious to the screams of their comrades, they lunged for me. My fists came out instinctively.

I knocked back several of them with straight force blows, and the others received roundhouse kicks or jump kicks, or anything else I could do to keep them off me.

For a time, it seemed the buffalo shape, and I were working in tandem, finding a rhythm that was almost comical. Me side kicking into bellies that sent them flying toward the monster's waiting violence. The monster crunching into throats and draining the wraith as it screeched in agony until it turned to husks of filmy flesh that disintegrated on the breeze.

But then, when there were no more than six of them remaining, and the beast raised its head from the belly of a wraith still twitching at its feet, that gaze met mine.

And I knew the creatures it was killing had indeed been in his way.

Because it had been coming for me.

CHAPTER 21

It didn't seem possible that I'd been saved only to fall beneath that massive muzzle, but I knew that's what was going to happen without that thing even having a voice to tell me. He was coming for me.

Come he might, but he wasn't going to take me without a fight.

Next time I kicked a wraith into his path, I lunged around the remaining few, skirting alongside them with the aplomb of a quarterback. Pumping my arms, I angled my feet in the direction of the trunk. It was just a few yards.

I could make it. I would make it.

Except I didn't. Something took the legs out from beneath me and I fell forward. My head bounced off the mossy carpet, slamming my nose first into a sprawling tree root. Pain sliced through my nasal cavity and down into my jaw.

The thing that had taken my legs began crawling up them to my torso. Its claws sunk into my bare calves, hooking in the skin and making me cry out in frustration.

A heartbeat and no more. Then that thing, too, was ripped from my body. I rolled over quickly, digging my elbows into the earth for purchase. Blood streamed from my nose to my mouth as I crabbed backward, digging my heels into the earth as well to push myself where my arms weren't strong enough.

Above me, the wraith was being torn limb from limb by that hulking beast. It barely made a sound until it dropped from the monster's mouth to the forest floor.

The vague awareness that I was bleeding and tasting my own blood whispered through me. In a vampire den, I'd have tried to clean it away to keep from attracting the undead to the scent, but the saltiness here was a welcome reminder that I was still alive enough to fight. If Aiofe hadn't released my body yet, then there was still time.

I was about to roll over again and lunge to my feet, head for the trunk, when a sound stopped me short.

A croak, perhaps, or the rasping clearing of a throat, as though whatever made the sound was trying to speak, but had either forgotten how or had lost the ability.

I blinked, paused. Looked over my shoulder.

There stood a shadowed form, morphing even as I caught sight of its familiar eyes into something more human. Or fae. Definitely fae. And I knew him.

"Terran," I said.

The shadow shrank and reformed. A more defined jaw took shape. The eyes flashed as the arrogant smile I knew so well slid into place.

I half expected him to speak, but of course he didn't. I knew predators well, and for all his seeming sentience, this thing before me was a predator. Whatever sound he'd made to draw my attention, it hadn't been intelligent.

I swallowed nervously, doing my best to hold my ground when everything inside me was screaming at me to run.

I held my hands out in front of me, not in surrender, but in the way you would make yourself bigger in the face of a bear.

"Aiofe," I said to the thing that was once Terran. "She's got my body. She's going to kill the king."

It was all I could think of that might appeal to the fae he'd once been to keep him from attacking me.

"I need to get to the veil," I said in a calm, very calm voice, doing my best not to look at the trunk. Not yet. No matter how badly I wanted to be sure it was still there, how badly I wanted to scrabble toward it, I did not want to draw attention to the place that might be my only salvation.

The way Terran stood there, rigid and unyielding, as if he was waiting to lunge for me at the smallest movement, kept me rooted to my spot. Kept my eyes away from the one place I might find safety if he decided to jump for me.

"Ferranus is killing your sons," I said. "If I die here, I don't know what will happen to my body. Without my body, I don't know if Aiofe can save them." Careful to phrase it in generalities, I avoided using the words, if he killed me. Just if I died. Giving him no consideration that he could even cause my death.

And I didn't mention Blade. I couldn't. If he for one second, believed this was just about the son he saw as an outcast, I wasn't sure he'd stand down.

"Flint still has a chance," I said, moving sideways. "You don't see him here, do you? That means he's still alive there. Mica is still alive."

Another sliding movement to the right. His eyes remained hooked to mine, but shifting as I shifted, minute motions that meant he knew what I was doing. I licked my lips.

"If the king gets to the veil, I need to be there to finish him," I said. It wasn't true, but I hoped he'd not read the lie in my voice. I didn't expect Ferranus to escape at all. But those mortals needed their liberation, and there was only one thing the fae he used to be cared about. "We can't let him flee there."

His chin lifted as his eyes roamed my face and settled itself on some place behind me. I so badly wanted to look over my shoulder, to see what had drawn his gaze, but I didn't dare take my eyes off him.

Not even when a rustling sound came from behind me. It took nerves of steel to stand there, holding my ground as the hair raised on the back of my neck. The knee-buckling stink of sulfur swamped me.

I held it. Held it. Held it.

There was a long moment when I thought he would turn around and leave me there. I was sure that whatever he was watching behind me was nothing of concern.

Then the inevitable happened.

He lunged for me in an explosion of movement too quick for me to react. Shadows claimed the rigid shape of his jaw and shoulders, smoothing them out into something less distinct. He was still vaguely fae-shaped but the movement alone blurred the lines of jaw and shoulder.

I lost my wind when he collided into me, and I expected to be tossed upward into the air, falling down to meet the powerful jaws of the beast he no doubt became in the seconds it took to grab for me.

Instead, I was caught up in a powerful embrace, tossed over his shoulder. He spun around, and I realized he had normal legs. Normal feet.. He was still fae. Still humanoid shaped, thank God.

I dangled awkwardly for a second before I was able to recover and lift my head to see what was happening. Where he was taking me.

More wraiths flooded my vision. So many that they sounded like a massive colony of bats echo-locating their way from a deep cavern. Terror clawed at my stomach. My hips ground into the hard bone of Terran's shoulder. I might have cursed out loud and he might have understood it because a dark sort of chuckle moved through his lungs, vibrating against my stomach.

Fast as he was, the wraiths were faster. Or more determined. One of them got close enough to grab for my arm and it yanked. Yanked so hard that if Terran hadn't had a good grip on my hips, I'd have been pulled straight off his shoulder and into the clawed hug of a magic-starved husk.

Though he ran, he could barely keep ahead of the wraiths. The one holding my wrist lost its footing and sailed behind us like a scarf. Somehow, it managed to heave its other hand onto my arm and as had begun to leverage itself higher, dragging itself closer to me, using my limb like it would a rope.

It got close enough that I saw the insides of its eyes and caught the whirlwind of dying magic in its soul.

With a grunt, I brought my forehead down hard against its skull and it yowled in pain as it lost its grip.

Another dark chuckle from Terran.

I thought of Aiofe's comment that the worst of the fae undead were housed in a prison, and I realized that without her here, that prison was open. Without her power holding them at bay, every horrible thing inside was free to roam and roar.

And that's exactly what spilled from the surrounding shadows. Terran had been one of those things. What he was now, I had no idea, but I had the sinking feeling he was saving me from the others so that he could enjoy me himself. I started to buck and fight then.

He held me fast. When I wormed myself upward, planting my hands on his back and trying to fling myself out of his hold, he shook me. I bit down hard on my tongue. Blood welled up in sour pools.

"I'm going to fucking end you," I growled. "I'm going to wait till you bite down on my throat and I'm going to cut your belly like a fish."

There was no reaction to the empty threat. We both knew I had no weapon. That he was far more powerful than I even in his undead state.

But I cursed anyway, and I fought blindly, instinctively until he yanked me off his shoulder and wrangled me onto my feet. That was when I realized the sound of my feet striking the earth was very close to the sound of feet meeting wood. The contact rustled. My soles touched down on a smooth surface.

The trunk. He'd dropped me into the trunk. By the time he shoved at my shoulders, pressing me down, forcing my knees to bend, I realized the shadows had come alive with the teeming movement of all those horrors left unseen before.

My eyes raked the darkness, meeting hundreds of pairs of eyes, flashes of teeth. His hands, both of them, planted atop my head and...a rush of images flooded my mind's eye. Words, or thoughts of words, whispered through the dark places of my mind. It took all of three seconds and it filled me to the brim like a cup, so that I thought I would tip over.

Then he pushed. I struggled against the force of it long enough to catch his eye. He blinked. A sort of sentience moved over his face before it disappeared, but in that moment, I knew what he was doing even if he couldn't speak.

I nodded. Ducked down. And by the time the lid closed down over me, he was swarmed from behind and the sides by those horrors.

I crouched inside, listening to the noises of battle, waiting for something to shift, for some magic to unwind itself from the portal long enough to take me to the veil. Nothing happened for long moments and I winced as I heard thuds on the box. Twice, I felt it roll over. Howls from outside leaked in and made my hair stand on end.

Then it was over. There wasn't a sound to be heard. Just the still, raw sensation of being completely alone.

For a moment, I thought I might still be within Kumara proper, but then a sort of electricity moved over my body, tingling as it crept with spidery pads over my skin.

I felt everything squeeze into a pressurized coil. Then it relaxed. I heard whispers and crying. Light leaked in through the crack where the lid met the trunk.

I'd done it. I'd made it to the veil.

With my hand above me, I pushed the lid off and stood. Strangely, a breeze moved over my legs and torso. I looked down almost out of confused instinct. Erachne's gown clung to me in places, but it was a gorgeous fabric with magical properties to hide and shift like water over my skin. The material stuck to me like gobs of knotted cobweb.

I was brushing a thick ball of it over my hips when a noise caught my attention.

Looking up, my heart soared. A smile broke my lips.

"Gideon," I said in relief.

Then he hit me over the head with something heavy and the darkness claimed me once again.

CHAPTER 22

Blackness swam over me for a good thirty seconds. Fortunately, I hadn't passed out, but I had crumpled to my knees at Gideon's unexpected blow, and it took several blinking, confused heartbeats before I could make out two separate voices—Gideon's one of them—talking in hushed tones, wondering if I was dead.

"You aren't lucky enough for me to be dead," I growled and tried to unfurl myself from the awkward position I'd fallen into. Before I could get my feet under me, someone manhandled me to my feet and dragged me clumsily and roughly over the edge of the chest.

I had just enough energy to throw him off once my feet touched the ground. The shadows at the edge of my vision peeled back slowly, and in the center of the bloom of light, I could just make out Gideon's eyes. Too close. They were too close.

I shoved him hard enough that he should have stumbled back onto his ass. But, being Gideon, he'd been ready for me.

"She's fine," he said in his drawling voice.

My fingers went to the top of my head, certain I was bleeding where he'd struck me because the spot was hot and sticky.

"What the fuck, Gideon?" I growled. "Why did you sucker punch me?"

I felt his fingers on my head, testing right along with my own. He found a sore spot, and I yelped.

"We thought you were Ferranus," he explained.

Grabbing his hand, I peeled it away from my skull and peered at his fingers. Clean of blood, at least. I dropped his hand and sat down on the edge of the trunk. The wood dug into my bare backside, reminding me that the gown was nothing but spider silk. A quick scan of the area proved I was in some sort of cave. The open mouth of it showed a swirl of smoke in all colors. I couldn't stop staring at it.

"How could you possibly mistake me for the king?" I demanded, adjusting myself on the edge because I was sure a splinter had come free and embedded in the back of my left thigh. "The bare boobs alone should have given me away." I ran my arm over my breasts to cover them and realized it wasn't just my boobs that were bare.

"Do you think someone can get me something to cover my bare ass?" I asked, my fingers to my forehead as I waited out the last of the pounding going on in there from the whack he'd given me.

At the comment, I felt a silky bit of material tossed over my shoulders. I pulled the edges around my shoulders, tucking it in where places needed covering.

A soft, feminine voice, vaguely familiar, wafted along with it, and I peered up at a cloud of beautiful, soft-looking blue hair.

"Phaedre?" I asked.

She turned her face to mine and nodded, eyes glistening. "I never thought I'd see you again, Ava."

I blinked. It was the goblin's voice for sure, but everything else was...different.

I eyeballed the slim, willowy figure, the lush hair falling over soft shoulders. The bulging eyes of before had softened to a sweet almond shape with lashes that would make an angel weep in envy.

She must have noticed my confusion because she took my hand in hers, turning it over so she could lay the palm on her cheek. "It's me, Ava," she said. "Am I really so different?"

My eyes stung from shame that I'd make her feel so much less than what she was. "Of course it's you, Phaedre," I whispered. "I'd know that beautiful soul anywhere."

She smiled timidly. "I feel stronger," she said and gestured toward Gideon. "He says I'm prettier too."

I glowered at him. "Did he now?" I said in an acid voice. "Did he also tell you he has a less than honorable predilection for vulnerable girls?"

Gideon swatted me on the arm. "You make me sound like a pedophile."

"How old is Shea, Gideon?"

He glowered at me. "I thought you'd be happy to see me."

I sighed through my nose. "I am. I'm really glad to see you. Honest. It's just...I'm just not myself."

He snorted. "You seem very much yourself to me with that smart ass mouth."

"Please," Phaedre said, putting a hand on my shoulder. "Please don't argue. I'm so very glad to see you, Ava. You don't have to worry about Gideon. He's been very chivalrous." She winked at me. "And besides. I'm not a child. I'm a few hundred years older than he is."

I ran my hand over the back of my neck. "Of course," I said. "It's just..." I shook my head, deciding that whatever explanation I had for my bad behavior didn't matter and opted for the truth of how I felt. "I'm so damn glad to see you safe." I looked toward Gideon. "Both of you."

He extended his hand as he shot me that charismatic half-smile of his, and I took it so he could help me to my feet and off the uncomfortable edge of the trunk.

"Thanks," I muttered. "To be honest, I don't think I have much in me to manage it by myself."

"Sorry about that," he said. "By the time I realized it was you, it was too late to haul the swing back."

"What did you hit me with?"

Phaedre propped herself beneath my arm, supporting me as Gideon guided me toward the fire. "It was a book," she said.

"Thank God he doesn't read much," I said.

With their support and aid, we made it to the small fire burning at the mouth of the cave. Two stumps and a length of tree trunk had been placed beside it. I took the log, stretching my hands out to the fire. I didn't realize how cold I was until I felt the warmth on my face.

"Where are the others?" I asked, peering out of the opening into the area beyond.

"What others?" he asked. "It's just us."

I turned a deadpan eye toward him as he settled onto the stump on the other side of the fire. "You were delivered as a blood gift along with a few other mortals."

He stretched his hand out in front of him, turning it over and over. "Is that what we were?" he mused aloud as he waggled his fingers. "I don't think I want to know what that is."

"Want to know or not, I think it best you do," I said, and explained what I knew while Phaedre took her place beside me, wrapping her slim arm around my shoulders and holding me close. I realized I was trembling.

"So why are you here, Gideon?" I asked when I was done. "How did you end up in Fae?"

He stretched his legs out. "Kit told me you were in trouble. She said you needed me. That I was to go to a specific street and a specific apartment and swing on a swing."

His expression went vacant, and I imagined he was thinking about the woman he met at Blade's apartment. "It wasn't pleasant." A scowl scraped across his features. "But I told Kit I would do it and so I did. She was very adamant I come find you."

I gawked at him. "She did?"

"Yes. She did. She told me she'd never forgive me if I let you die here."

My eyes stung at the thought that Kit still cared. My hand went to my throat, and I struggled to swallow through the thickness that overcame it. "If you did all that for her forgiveness you can forget it," I murmured. "Kit does not like you."

"No kidding," he said. "But that's not why I did it. I did it for you, Ava."

The agony in his voice made me look up at him. "She sent you to find me, and you came?" Just grappling with both of the truth was too much.

"Hell, Ava, of course I'd come." He crossed his arms over his chest, a chest he'd puffed out in indignant irritation. "You might make loving you very very difficult, but what kind of hunter would I be if I didn't try to save you?"

"I don't need saving," I grumbled.

"Says the woman who arrived naked and trembling."

I picked at the cobwebs tangled in places on my skin beneath the cloak. Blade's pick from Erachne's shop. I almost broke a sob thinking about that. Instead, I sucked in a breath.

"You came for nothing," I said. "It's too late to save me. But it's not too late to get you out of here."

"What do you mean?"

"I mean, we have to get you both out of the veil before the king does arrive."

"Listen," he said. "Phaedre told me what happened. I know you're hurting. Lilah's magic blast--"

I held up my hand. It was so much worse than being hurt by a magic blast, but this wasn't the time to get into it.

"I'm fine," I said. "The damage to my body doesn't matter right now. What does matter is getting everyone out of here." To punctuate the sense of urgency, I tried to stand and ended up collapsing back down onto the log.

"It's alright, Ava," Phaedre soothed. "You're fine. We'll take care of you."

I put my hand on hers as it lay on my shoulder. "You don't understand," I said, ignoring the lie on her breath when I knew she could feel the chill of my skin against hers. Hell. I could feel the cold seeping into my bones and if it weren't for her body heat, I'd be shaking quite violently and she had to know that. "We need to leave now. Before it's too late. Get the others. Tell them we're going."

Gideon exchanged a meaningful glance with Phaedre that made my spine itch. Something was amiss, and it wasn't just how she had changed.

"What's wrong?" I asked. "Where are the others?"

"We told you. There are no others," she said. "When you pushed me through, Gideon was the only one here."

"That can't be," I said. "I saw a line up of mortals being forced through the hagstone." I pulled up the memory, letting it replay right down to the gutted feeling that overcame me as Gideon stepped through. "They have to be here."

Gideon nodded toward the opening of the cave. "I came through the hagstone somewhere out there in the woods," he said. "Alone. Though I must admit that mist felt sentient. Creeped me the fuck out. Even felt like it was eating me alive at times, picking pieces of my skin apart. By the time I found this cave a few hours ago, I fancied I was a ghost." He shivered. "Days I was out there. Trust me. We're the only ones here."

He ran his hand over the top of his hair and I noted it trembled.

I stared at him. "But it hasn't been days. It's been hours at most." I cut a glance toward Phaedre. "How did you find each other?"

She pointed at the trunk. "When I opened the lid, he was standing in front of it."

Gideon's gaze followed. "The thing appeared out of nowhere right in that corner. I remembered those husks of fae bodies tossing it through the portal and I thought for sure you'd be inside."

"Instead it was me," Phaedre piped up with a ghostly smile. "All four feet of goggle-eyed me."

Again, I gawked at her. She wasn't four feet now. Nor was she goggle-eyed. The litheness of her body was the kind that most women worked hours in the gym to achieve.

Gideon, however, looked exactly the same. If the mist had nibbled bits of him, it was his mind, and that was all. I cocked my hip to the side.

"If you thought it was me, then why would you hit me over the head with a book?"

He shrugged. "She was sure it was the king come to get her. There wasn't much time to think things through to be honest. I just used what I already had in my hand."

"You know he's a powerful fae," I said. "A book wouldn't have bothered him in the least."

"Maybe not," he said. "But I didn't have anything else. And we weren't sure if Phaedre would keep her powers if he got here."

Something odd in the statement drew my gaze to her again. "You've changed," I said, noting the glow around the edges of her skin. "And it's not because so much time passed that you grew into a woman."

"At first, I didn't understand there was a difference," she said, giving a shake of her head that made her hair spill over her shoulders in a fetching way. "But as the hours passed, Gideon started asking me strange questions and I realized something was happening to me."

"I thought she might be using some glamor," he explained. "And I was curious to know which was the real Phaedre."

"I bet," I said, unable to keep the sarcasm from my voice, but he didn't react to it, merely watched the hybrid fae as she nodded in eager agreement.

"I was feeling different, you see," she said. "And his comments made me realize the change wasn't just in how I felt but in how I looked." She reached for something behind her back for something lying on the floor of the cave. "We realized that I was changing somehow. That's why we started reading the books, looking for answers."

When she turned back to me, she had a pile of books in her hands. All of them familiar looking. She held them out to me in a stack.

"Read one," she said. "Any of them."

With brow furrowed in confusion, I plucked the top tome from the pile and opened it. I recognized it immediately from the pictures and placement of the text. "They're in English," I said, looking up at her.

She nodded as she ran her gaze over the cloak I wore. "They've all lost whatever magic they held. Including the spells I put on them to protect Mica. Now, all of them can be read." The emphasis on the words suggested I would know exactly how interesting it was that all could be read. Because one in particular had resisted her spells altogether.

Gideon brushed his hand over the cover. "That's when we learned the truth about the veil. That it siphons magic."

I shivered beneath the cloak, and Gideon pulled off his sweatshirt and handed it to me. "That satin thing can't be warm enough." He wore a tattered t-shirt beneath, so I accepted the shirt and untied the cloak long enough to pull the sweater over my head. It smelled of tobacco and whiskey.

"I'd give anything for a pair of pants," I said as I tied the cloak back around my shoulders. Phaedre ran her gaze over the remnants of the gown so meaningfully, I finally understood what had happened to it.

"The gown," I said. "The veil took its magic. It's just...just spider webs now."

"Just like everything else," she said. "I felt a surge of energy when you tossed the lid upward and stood up. And the books still held their spells until we took them out."

"You think inside the trunk the magic remains intact?" I asked.

They both nodded.

"I'm fairly certain that's how it works," Gideon said. "When I first arrived, that smoke outside stank of magic." He cut a glance toward the cave mouth where the mist swirled about like a prowling cat, then slid his eyes back to Phaedre. "Except for that mist, she's the only thing that seems to attract magic."

I swung my attention to Phaedre. "You think the mist is the part of the veil that siphons the power? But why hasn't it taken yours?"

"It's all in the books," she said. "Gideon is right in a way. The veil siphons magic but it also gives it to someone of fae blood. Royal fae blood." She put great emphasis on this latter statement, enough that the truth hit me like a bolt.

"Ferranus," I said, testing the truth of the guess and feeling as if I was right. "He's the royal fae that receives the gift of that magic." I blinked at her, taking in the gorgeous face, the almond-shaped eyes. "Except, Ferranus is not here," I said. "He's in his own realm, waiting to come through. It's why I'm here. It's why we have to get you out. He doesn't have long to live and once he dies, this veil disintegrates."

I stood up too fast and my head spun. Phaedre was beside me in a heartbeat, wrapping her arm over my shoulders again. I swung my gaze to hers, realizing suddenly what was happening.

"You," I said. "You're the next in line for the throne." I almost swayed on my feet. "My God, he's dead. That's why you're receiving the power." I breathed out the words with excitement and relief. "He's already gone and you're siphoning the magic."

I could hardly believe this ordeal might be over. That the king was gone. That Aiofe had succeeded and now I had very little time to get her and Gideon out before the veil trapped them inside. I tried to shove her toward the trunk, but I was so weak I couldn't do more than nudge her.

She smiled sweetly as she plucked my hand from her shoulder and held it. "That's not entirely correct," Phaedre said. "I'm next in line, here," she said. "That's a fact. And it's why the magic is moving through me. But it doesn't mean my father is dead. Just that he's not...in the veil." She swept her arms out. "He must be here, in the veil, for the magic to transfer to him." She tapped the book with her finger. "The book is very clear on that."

"So I suppose since I was able to come here, that Ferranus isn't dead yet," I mused aloud. "That gives me time to get you out of here. Both of you." I turned sharply, my hand on Phaedre's arm, fully intending to guide her back to the trunk, but I missed somehow. As if I was too far away.

She tilted her head at me. "You don't look well, Ava."

I shook her off. How I felt didn't matter. I knew my time was limited by exactly how long Ferranus breathed.

"Aiofe is using my body to assassinate the king," I said, ignoring the look of alarm on both of their faces. "Thank heaven it's just the two of you. With your power, Phaedre, you should be able to travel back through the portal and take Gideon with you."

"What about you, Ava?" she said in a soft voice. "You need to return with us."

My lips pressed together as I elbowed her and Gideon toward the trunk. "I'll be there shortly," I said, not lying one bit. I had no illusions about what would happen when Aiofe left my body. I had the feeling I'd be pulled right back into it just as it took its last breath.

They were resisting, arguing, asking a bunch of questions I didn't know the answer to when a sizzle of purple light lit up the cavern.

One look at Phaedre and I knew by the way she had begun to shrink, how her hair lost it sheen, how her eyes began to bulge, that we were too late.

Her magic was being siphoned by the one true heir still left alive in the realm of smoke.

Ferranus had come for his due.

Chapter 23

The moment Ferranus slid into the cavern, everything changed. The cave itself altered to a beautiful room built of linen fold paneling. A grand fireplace roared up from the earthen floor and opened its hearth to a blazing fire that sparked and crackled and popped merrily. The smoke outside the cave crept inside and swirled around him in waves that lit up with silver sparks.

And as that mist swept in, it carried ghosts and spectres that took shape each time the mist touched the king. A swirl of fog dampened his brow and a woman dropped to the ground at his feet, naked and shaking. A brush of smoke on his fingers and two appeared on their knees in front of him.

Women of all shapes, sizes, and creed came out of the smoke, coughing and choking after that. Some had long, lush hair down to their feet, as though they'd been in the veil for decades. Some looked emaciated. All looked terrified. It didn't escape my notice that they scrabbled away from him the moment they took form and tried to huddle together in clusters. Each protecting another.

Ferranus didn't see us at first, and that was probably because even as he appeared and the scenery changed, he was looking for his first victim, scouring their faces and their bodies like a man who'd been denied food for a century. The ring on his middle finger caught the light of the fire and winked each time his fingers curled and uncurled as he swept the room with a rabid gaze.

Gideon seized on opportunity the way he always did, taking the king's distraction as a chance to sweep the cloak off my shoulders so he could cast it over Phaedre. One look at him and I knew he was as glad as I was that she was covered. The moment she was draped beneath it, he stepped between her and Ferranus, hiding her even more from view.

Now she was just one more figure in the crowd, trying to hide from his rabid view.

And because Ferranus's eyes were on the women, hungry looking, and vicious, he didn't notice the small form beneath the silk cloak, and I all but sighed in relief.

Except seeing him, something in me tightened into a knot. Aiofe had failed. Somehow, she'd lost her bid to kill him before he leaped through the hagstone. Perhaps Ruby had put up a fight, and she'd had to fend off attacks from that quarter. Maybe Blade and Flint and Mica took all her attention. Perhaps she never truly made it into my body at all or she was too late in her arrival to even attack him.

Whichever it was, it was obvious he'd taken all the remaining power he possessed and fled here to the veil to renew himself. He'd used a lot of magic in the ballroom, from saving Heuil, to punishing Terran, to his horrific display of power when he'd attacked Flint and Stone.

He was drained, no doubt. I thought of Mica, of the way too much use of his power laid him up in bed, at the mercy of blood gifts and refusing to take it from anyone but his brothers, who demanded he do so.

This fae was not the same as that benevolent youth. This fae wanted power. He was rabid for it. I was left praying he'd not had a chance to receive any gifts of power from the lesser fae before he'd plunged himself into the harem. And judging by the hungry look on his face, I thought he'd not dared steal the power from the fae holding the gilded tokens. If he had and had left, then the fae who remained were probably rioting back in the grand ballroom.

It was also clear that if he saw Phaedre here in the harem, he'd realize the fae he'd left behind wearing her glamor was not the daughter he wanted to rid himself of. I thought of those tubers he'd gagged up to steal the magic from his thralls and from Flint. Rage filled me to think he might do that to these women, to Gideon, to poor Phaedre and then return to his realm to do the same to Mica.

It was clear in that instant that while she was out of view for now, she was not safe. She wouldn't be until the king was well and truly gone.

That thought was all I needed to spur me into action. Gideon, always more aware of my thoughts than I was his, scuppered his way behind me like water chasing my footfalls on a swamped boat deck. We would do this together. Partners so fluid, we became one wave of movement without a single word passing between us.

Without registering more in my mind than the thought that the king wore a blade on his hip, I lowered my head and barreled toward him like a locomotive, giving the action all my steam.

He obviously expected to see only the helpless women he'd gathered over the years, the blood gifts the fae had gifted him with in the last hours, and not the woman who had rushed the hagstone, taking what he thought was Terran's son with him.

Surprise was an age-old tactic, and quick as he was and perfectly capable of halting me in my tracks, he didn't react at first. Good. I used that sudden rush of surprise, knowing that he wasn't immune to the same sense of startled paralysis that buckled the knees of regular humans.

It didn't matter that I had no weapon. No plan. Surprise was enough. Gideon on my heels, backing me up, was enough. It had to be.

Naked from the waist down and clothed only in that sweatshirt, I barreled those last few paces without hesitation. But I was weak and growing weaker by the moment. The last lunging jump I took fell short of the king by at least three paces.

I might have cursed, drawing the king's attention to me at last.

But then Gideon was there, his hands warm and firm on my back. He pushed me the rest of the way, using me as a battering ram, putting his entire weight into shoving me at the king so I could strike out before that attention truly registered into action.

And I was ready. Muscle memory took over, giving me the last swamp of adrenaline that remained in my body. My brain raked over the hundreds of kills I'd made, scouring for past experience in milliseconds, pulling from the ether of experience equations of attack.

In that record of time tables, I found a dozen moments when I'd used mundane objects to do what needed to be done. Whatever was at hand, to distract, attack, and finish an opponent, I took it.

My legs still carried threads of gossamer, the remnants of Erachne's gown.

That was the first value that came to mind. Spider silk was sticky and strong, and though it was devoid of magic, there was plenty of material.

The calculations formed on their own then, and the results had me scraping the silk from my hips and thighs and gathering clots of it into my fists as I kicked out at the king's shins in the hope of knocking him on his ass. Down, I could do more damage as he found himself on the defense.

Thankfully, my feet struck his shins perfectly. Too perfectly. Too much force.

A crack splintered the air. Pain shot up my heel as the damage rebounded to me instead of the king. The king refused to drop.

But I fell backward.

My arms flung out sideways of their own accord, trying their damnest to cushion the fall. The strings of gossamer cascaded over my chest in a swath of mummy linen.

I rolled to my side, pulling it into strings, rolling it into rope as I did so. Pain didn't matter. Time didn't matter. There was only attack and distract. There was only me and the king and the knowledge that Aiofe might be dead and I might at any moment be pulled back to my own dying body. There was only me and Gideon working as one the way we'd done hundreds of times.

And because Gideon and I were a fighting pair who knew each other's habits and thoughts like well-worn shoes, he came behind me in a rush. He swept in with a roundhouse elbow thrust that took the king in his throat.

A choking sound gurgled over the air, followed by a muffled curse. No reciprocal magic, though, so the king wasn't quite refueled enough to wield an attack.

But it was a temporary respite only. I didn't have to look back at Phaedre to know she was losing what power she had gained upon entering the veil. I could feel the power emanating off the king in waves as it transferred from her to him, growing stronger by the second.

He was gathering what the veil thought was his due, and if I didn't get her out of there right away, he might drain every last drop, including her natal power. I imagined her as one of those thralls in Kumara and I shouted at her.

"Get the hell out of here," I screamed at her over my shoulder. "Get in the damn trunk. Do it. Now."

Lying on the floor on my side, I clawed at those gobs of gossamer I'd coiled into a makeshift rope and fed them between Ferranus's ankles. In, out, in and around, making quick work so that when I went for that blade, he wouldn't have any wiggle room to get out of the way.

Gideon was already pummeling him in the stomach. He got in two good blows, I thought, before the king swept him aside as though he was no more than a filthy wash cloth.

Sulfur and ozone mingled in the air. Electricity tugged at the hair on my arms. Finally, the king had access to his power. Clearly, he was gaining strength minute by minute. We were going to lose if we didn't make our move, and make it fast.

My ex rolled across the floor several times, limbs flinging out and pinwheeling until he came to a stop on his face.

From my spot on the chamber floor, I took one look at the way his body lay crookedly where it landed, and I knew he wouldn't survive this battle. He would fight with me, yes. He would use everything he knew to save the humans that huddled behind us in masses. Give his all to this fight, give it all to me... and he would die here as well.

I thought of all the times he'd told me I'd get him killed with my tunnel-visioned determination to win. I thought of all the times he'd complained that I didn't know when to retreat. Shea came to mind, pliable, obedient Shea waiting for the man she loved, and I knew I couldn't let that happen.

This time, fighting was not the answer.

"Gideon," I croaked out. "Get the hell out of here. Take them all and go. Please. Now."

He didn't lift his head. No movement from his fingers or jerk of his legs indicated he heard me. No answering grunt came back with an annoyed and impatient tone.

I prayed he wasn't dead. I'd waited too long to liberate him. I'd let him come to the fight with me because of habit, because I wasn't strong enough to relieve him of the responsibility.

This wasn't his fight. It was mine. All mine. I was already dead. I wasn't going to let anyone I loved end up the same.

But there wasn't time for regret either. At the sound of my voice, the king's attention turned back to me.

His lip curled back. He reached down, agonizingly slow for all the speed he possessed.

When his fingers tangled in my hair and yanked, I let it happen because that would buy Gideon time. It would offer Phaedre and the others a chance to move. No matter that my scalp burned so impossibly in this place of magic, this realm of smoke, I let him shake me until I heard the popping sound of hairs pulling free.

I knew from experience he could easily subdue me, keep me from reacting or moving, just by exerting his magic on my blood. And judging by the look on his face, the swirl of his fingers over my shoulder, and the stink of ozone, he was fixing to do just that.

"Coward," I ground out, pulling to mind Aiofe's accusation that made me so angry. "Are you afraid of facing me on regular terms? Do you have to paralyze me so I won't cut your throat out with my teeth?"

"In the language of you mortals, 'as if'" he said. "Even withered and wasting, you don't have what it takes."

Wasting. That was what had happened to Mica. It seemed the stronger the power, the more powerful the wasting. I was surprised he'd even confess it to me.

I peered up at him through watery eyes, stinging from the burn in my scalp.

"I bet I have what it takes and then some," I told him. "But you don't dare to find out, do you? You don't dare to level the playing field because that wasting is making you weak. So weak even a human could take you."

I tried, tried very hard not to let my gaze run to his hip, to see if the blade still sat in its sheath in his sash.

He hissed and I was sure I heard the flagellating waver of a tuber in his throat. My stomach twisted but I pushed on, painfully aware that Phaedre was no where near the trunk. That Gideon was still on his face in the carpet.

"You're nothing," I said. "You had to steal power from the lesser fae to become anything at all. Tell me that's power. Tell me you're the king of the fae."

I was buying time, and that was all, but the words held a haunting truth. Goading him like he said, but not expecting any of it to pan out. He'd catch on soon enough, but would it be enough time for Gideon to herd ten women out of the portal or a dozen? Would it be enough to get all of them? I still heard nothing from the spot where he'd fallen. I still couldn't make out a single rustle of movement. I had to believe it was just because Gideon was being his usual hunter-silent self.

The grip on my shoulders tightened enough to bruise. "Bitch," he spat out. "I will break you before I bite you. You'll beg me to eat you."

"Oh please," I said. "I wouldn't beg you to eat me if you were between my wet legs with a tongue the size of a python."

Ferranus's eyes flashed. "But you'd let the Dark Enforcer eat you, is that it? A half-hound with more dog in his DNA than magic." His eyelids shuttered and something dark moved over his face and beneath his eyelids. "He's gone, you know. Gone in a whiff of smoke and shadow."

"You're lying," I said, ignoring the gutted feeling razoring through me. It was a ruse. Just as I was doing. Distraction. Distrust.

"Lie? Me? The king of the Fae?"

With an almost lazy movement, he tossed me aside in a move that I knew from experience was meant to show his power and strength...so he could show me who was boss.

And it had power. So much of it I gasped at the force.

I landed in a heap a couple of feet away. I had time to pull myself up onto my hands and knees before the adrenaline left me. I managed to lift my head, peer upward at the spot he still held just three feet away.

That was when I saw the intention on his face. He planned to close the distance between us, perhaps lean down with that lazy posture and pluck me from the floor so he could do it again.

CHAPTER 24

The king was about to tear me into strips, but he didn't realize his ankles were bound. He took a step, all fury and rage, and then...

He crashed to the floor beside me. The wind fled his lungs in a gush.

I didn't hesitate. I flew into action, scrambling to crawl atop him, to weigh him down with my body, to pin him like a bug as I aimed a fist full of gossamer for his mouth. I crammed it upward. Missed as he twisted sideways. The tendrils of silk ended up sticking to his cheek.

He wrangled my wrist into his powerful grip. The pressure opened my fingers, turning my fist into a spastic claw.

"You," he growled. He swept aside the cobwebs and a blast of power launched me across the chamber.

I collided with something hard and sharp, halting my flight so suddenly my teeth clamped down on my tongue. The edge of something wooden, I thought. Something that dug into the intercostal muscles. I counted myself lucky then that one of the ribs didn't crack.

As I caught my breath and waited out the pain, he rose with a phoenix's grace to his feet. One kick and the gossamer fled his ankles to pool on the floor as if the strings had untied themselves.

Behind him, Gideon rose too, clumsily, shakily. The look in his eye, the snarl on his lips, made it abundantly clear that he planned to attack the king again.

He wouldn't succeed. No one here was strong enough to hold against such power.

I caught my partner's eye. Just for an instant. Jerked my chin toward where Phaedre was grouping the women together. The cloak had fallen back. Her entire face was in view.

He took a step, the kind someone takes as the initial balance point to a full out run. I shook my head. Cut my eyes toward Phaedre. I needed him to understand. I needed him to put his energies in the right places.

But it wasn't just Gideon who noticed the direction of my gaze. Ferranus caught the exchange and swung around. I rolled onto my knees as his head canted to the side in confusion.

"How are you here?" he asked. "I left you weeping over Blade's body. I left you to Ruby's care."

Care. A euphemism I would make him pay for dearly if that bitch so much as touched Mica.

"Gideon," I croaked out, the wind refusing to fill my lungs completely. "Please. Take her. Go."

"Fuck you, Ava," he said. "I'm not leaving you here."

The king lifted his attention to where Gideon had gained his footing.

"Was this a trap, Ava?" he said to me in a mild voice, putting an inflection on my name that intimated he knew me the same way Gideon did, understanding the nooks and crannies of my body, the way I slept with one foot on the floor, the way I brushed my teeth with vodka if there was nothing else.

On a movement reminiscent of oil sliding across a hot griddle, the king closed the gap between us. "Were you and this human man trying to steal my magic, Ava? Were you hoping to come to the veil and try to convince it to give you its power because that's not how it works here. Is that what you're doing, Ava?"

He pulled me close enough that I could smell the copper on his breath and a deeper undertone of sulfur. I thought of those fluke-like tubers and steeled my spine.

My lip curled back. "I'm here to kill you, you bastard," I said from between gritted teeth.

He tossed his head back in a barking laugh. "You may try, oh well you may try."

His hand wound into the hair at my nape and he tugged my head back. "Aoife tried," he said. "You think I didn't know her when she took your body after Lilah felled you with that blast? When she tried to finish the job she set out to do so many generations ago?"

His gaze hardened as he yanked harder, making my eyes water. "I gave the bitch Terran to do with what she pleased in that Stygian Darkness. I thought that would mollify her, giving her a rutting bastard to sire her line. But she still came for me. Well, she failed today the same as she failed eons ago. So what makes you think you, a mere mortal, can accomplish what the daughter of the Titan of Darkness could not?"

At that, he held up his hand, and I heard Gideon behind me gag so powerfully my own stomach lurched at the noise.

When the sound of fluid splashing on the stone floor accompanied that of his choking and gagging, I knew he was vomiting whatever fluid was in his stomach.

Weaving on my feet, I forced a laugh, drawing the king's attention away from Gideon, back to me.

"Oh please," I said. "You think a little nausea will deter him? Gideon pukes like that on the daily," I drawled, pulling out my best casual tone because I knew if I acted as though I knew the pains of Gideon's suffering, the king would keep hurting him. And he didn't deserve that.

What he deserved was to get out of there in one piece. All of them did. Each and every woman lurking in the shadows. I could hear their breath, their gasps. Some of them were moaning quietly.

I tried my best to shrug. "Do you have any idea of the things we see and deal with in the run of a day? Puking is just one of the occupational hazards of hunting."

The king's eyebrow quirked up. "A hunter, you say? Now, that is unexpected. Impressive even."

I lifted my chin. "What? Did you think I was some fae's lover come here to fuck and dream of a magical future where I grow wings and flit from flower to flower?" I sucked the back of my teeth. "Monsters, all."

"I didn't think you were Terran's lover if that's what you mean," he said. "He doesn't see the pleasure in devouring mortal flesh. His sons, however." He lifted a shoulder delicately. "I've known them to pick at that odd bit of human skin. Which one of them dreamed of consuming you? Stone?" He laughed. "Though his want for you was a stink that offended my nostrils, he wouldn't have peeled that flesh from your bones before he took it another way. Not Flint, either, surely. I tasted his desire for another on his blood when I drained him."

My mouth went dry. I recalled Stone's comment that fae like him hadn't eaten human flesh in generations. I didn't want to think of Stone hunting and devouring human flesh. I tried not to think about Blade that way. Tried not to think of Blade at all.

But the king cocked his head sideways at the whisper of threat of Blade's image trekking through my mind.

"It's the other, isn't it?" he said. "The half-fae hellhound bastard I lured into the Days by proclaiming I needed guarding." He sniffed. "He might have wished to possess your flesh, but you're mine."

A possessive flash went through his eyes just as I heard Gideon finally getting his stomach under control. "I left him lying on the floor beside his mother, that half-goblin bastard of mine sobbing over his body."

I tried, really tried, not to envision that. I marshaled the fortitude to remain calm.

"Get out of here, Gideon," I said in a low voice, aiming the words over my shoulder.

"Ava—"

"I said leave. You know what you have to do. Do it now. Please."

I'd never begged Gideon in all my days with him, but I begged now. I wanted him to know that what he did in saving the others meant more than coming to my aid. I didn't need him anymore. I was already a lost cause. I'd been a lost cause for so many years, and yet this time I was surrendering to the truth of it.

I wouldn't need anyone soon, and in my last moments, I wanted him to understand I did this of my own free will.

I'd never told him I loved him. Never showed him an inch of softness. Maybe that was what he saw in Shea. Maybe she had a softer side that he could bed down with at night and curl up against, where I'd been all hard angles and unyielding flesh. Shea was that moment of respite he needed from the hardness of hunting.

I almost sobbed at the thought of what might have been now that Blade had helped soften my own edges. But I bit that back too.

"Tell Kit I love her. That I'm sorry for everything I did to her. I've always been sorry. I just didn't know how to show it."

"Tell her yourself," he said in a soft voice that had the king furrowing his brow at the exchange.

Tears stung the backs of my eyelids. I couldn't tell him that wasn't going to happen. I made peace with the fact that I wouldn't be traveling back through the veil except to slip into my body and sigh my last.

But if I thought my mentor would just give up, I was mistaken. He was already on the way, and not in the right direction. His arms pumping. His mouth opened wide to drag in every draft of air he could.

The king straightened his spine with an almost leisurely slowness, squared his shoulders.

Before Gideon made it within a yard, the king made a sweeping gesture with his arm, circling the air in a graceful gesture reminiscent of a ballerina's dance.

Gideon's feet left the ground instantly. The women huddled in masses behind him, Phaedre, the trunk, all of it whipped upward in a funnel of energy that didn't just hold them aloft but spun them in manic circles.

Even though every woman's mouth opened in a scream, silence dropped over the chamber. The horror on their faces as the sound was pulled from their voice boxes was more frightening than seeing the cuts that sliced into their faces and arms and legs and torsos, wounds committed by an invisible blade.

Their blood beaded on their skin and began to stream from them into one single river that twirled in the funnel like a ribbon. It sparkled, that blood, as though magic was weaving its way through the fluid and sparking the hemoglobin and flaring it with a phosphorescent sizzle.

I had to do something and yet, I was as powerless here as everyone else. I had no magic. I had no weapon. I had no energy, for pity's sake. I'd come to this realm with an arrogant belief that I could do the impossible, and I knew in that moment, the one truth I'd been avoiding all along.

I was never going to go home, even to claim my body.

CHAPTER 25

Some monsters require brute force. Some, shock and awe. And some monsters require cunning. I'd never been crafty. I was a strike and kill sort of hunter. Gideon was the brains. Gideon, who was swirling around, trying in vain to grapple Phaedre into his embrace and hold on to her.

All while I just lay there, gawking at the spectacle and sensing the doom of its final moments.

That was about to change, and I knew the only way it could change would cost me that trip back home to my body. I'd not have a chance to look into Blade's eyes as I expired. I wouldn't see Kit ever again.

I closed my eyes. One moment. That was all I needed to brace myself for what I needed to do. Save the innocent at all costs.

And then I breathed through my nose and pinned my gaze on the king. Cleared my throat. When the words came, they were barely audible at first, but hearing them gave me the courage to say them again. Louder.

"Terran isn't dead."

Ferranus whipped around to glare at me.

"What did you say?"

I propped myself up on my elbows. "Terran isn't dead. I've seen him. Spoken to him. I know where he is."

He pivoted sharply on his heel. Dragged a hand over the back of his neck. I'd got him.

"Tell me," he demanded.

I planted a cocky grin on my face because I knew he'd hate it. I needed him enraged. Needed all that fury aimed at me. Away from Gideon and Phaedre and the other women who I heard whimpering and crying and rushing along behind me.

"Who do you think I am? Scheherazade?" I asked sweetly. "I'm not the sort to tell stories to save my hide. But I do have stories. So many of them."

An echo of my own mocking smile smeared his face as he peered down at me. "No. You're the pathetic human with the Dark Enforcer's protection."

"I don't need protection," I said. "Not from a coward."

He glowered at me for a moment, then, without a word, flicked his arm toward the funnel. A woman with long red hair and a sickly pallor jerked free of the whirlwind and dropped to the floor of the chamber. She got up in a herky jerky movement and zombie-walked toward the king.

My mouth went dry. "Don't," I said, but he ignored me.

With a flash of movement, he grabbed the woman by the hair and yanked her close.

"You don't have to do this," I said. "I'll tell you where he is. Just let them go."

He looked at me over his head before dipping his mouth to her throat. There was no violent shake. No rage-filled frenzy. Just cool and calculated, intentional killing. Like a true monster.

Her sobs drowned in the sound of her flesh being torn. I dropped my head back onto the wall, unable to hold it aloft at the sight. But I didn't close my eyes from the violence. I chose to take it all in. To give the woman the dignity of a witness.

He dropped her to the floor in a heap and turned to me, his mouth covered in blood. "Cowards don't have the stomach for that," he said.

I blinked away the sight of his teeth coated in the woman's life-giving fluids and said, "It isn't an inability to kill with merciless cruelty that a coward shows himself. It's in attacking someone more helpless, knowing they can't fight back that reveals the yellow streak in his spine."

I had the feeling he very much wanted to storm the few feet to where I sat, but was resisting the urge because that would make him look weak. And he was right. The moment he showed emotion, I'd know I'd won.

But I didn't expect it. Not yet.

"You'll tell me where that bastard is or I'll devour every single one of these gifts and make you watch."

I shook my head with a casual shrug. "You'll kill them anyway," I said. "Each and every one will die beneath your teeth, but your real enemy will be waiting for you, for the moment he can exact his revenge."

Pushing my back into the wall, I used it to leverage myself to my feet. Slowly at first, a bit shakily, but my legs held beneath me. I trained my gaze on his face, the pulse in his neck. The blade at his side and the way his fingers curled into fists as the ring on his hand glinted in the firelight. Anything except that dizzying tornado of silent victims bleeding slowly into the eye of the cyclone.

"I know your secret," I rasped, letting the words vibrate in a hushed whisper.

"You know nothing."

With a resolve that came from somewhere outside me, I forced my legs to move. My foot lifted, stepped down purposely one step more. "Don't I?"

A growl ripped free of his throat as he turned away from me to face the cyclone. With a violent jerk, his magic tore another woman free. She didn't drop to the floor, this one. Instead, she looked as if she were being dragged by her belly with such force her head fell back and her spine cracked as it bowed backward in a sharp curve.

Her death was more brutal. It made me gag and bow my shoulders as I fought the heaving of my stomach. When he was done, after the crunch of bone and the slurping of fluids too grisly to name, he turned that feral smile back on me.

I swallowed down the nausea so hard I could feel my throat bob on it. I couldn't let that woman's death be for nothing. I had to press on, no matter how sick it made me.

I took another step. "I spoke to him, you see," I said. "He told me everything."

"He couldn't," Ferranus said.

"No? How else do you think I found this place? Not through the hagstone, surely. I didn't even make it into the circle before Lilah hit me."

He paled, and visibly. "I'm going to drain you the old fashioned way," he said in a throaty voice, one filled with suppressed rage and, I thought, a little fear. "And I'm going to take my time with it so I can enjoy every morsel of flesh, every ounce of fluid, every damn crunch of your bones."

"Do it," I said. "I've been told I'm prone to causing heartburn."

"Tell me what you know," he said. "And maybe I'll show you mercy. Maybe I'll make your death quick."

I shrugged. "I'm already dying. The trouble for you is, when I do, I'm going to return to my body. And with my last breath, I'll reveal all I know to Mica."

"A boy," he said with a snuff.

"A boy who can project the truth into every fae there." I lifted my chin in defiance. "I would think that would make returning home and using them very difficult. No fae will give you want you want ever again."

"Impossible," he said. "You'll be dead by the time you return." He advanced on me.

"Not impossible. Improbable," I corrected. "But are you willing to take that risk? Something pulled me into Kumara, something allowed Terran to help me find this place. What do you think that something...someone will do to enable me to spread the truth."

His lips pressed together as he considered exactly what that something might be. The ring on his finger flashed. I tried not to let it distract me.

"Let them go," I said in a calm voice. "Phaedre first."

"No."

I wouldn't relent. "Let half go and I'll tell you where Terran is. Let them all go and I'll keep your secret."

At my words, both Phaedre and Gideon started shouting at me. I held my hand up to silence them. "Let them go. I give you my word."

The cyclone halted with a waft of hurricane-force winds, making me stagger to keep my footing. Every single woman, as well as Gideon and Phaedre, fell to the floor. Some of them fell atop each other. Some groaned as they landed. Others shrieked in pain. I imagined bones broke and skin bruised. But they were free. Almost.

I took a step toward the king, who was watching me carefully. I thought for a moment he might give in. I tried one more time. "Give the order," I said, letting him see just how much I was shaking with effort. "But you best be quick or there won't be anything left of me to keep my bargain."

He cursed and gestured angrily toward the door to the chamber that had once been the mouth of a cave. Etched in light just in front, the shape of a square showed itself.

"This will take them to a stairwell beneath my throne room," he said, and my mind drew out an image of a seam in front of that horrible throne. "The iron latch requires royal blood." At that, his lips curled in Phaedre's direction, and I knew by the way he eyeballed her that he fully expected to kill her himself when he returned to the ballroom. After he'd made certain I died at his feet in that same chamber without divulging his secrets.

"Go on," he said, jerking his chin at Gideon. "Take them with you."

I tried not to collapse from relief as Gideon nudged Phaedre toward the portal. It flared as she drew near, the outline turning blood red. She looked back at me and I offered her a wan smile. "Give Mica my best," I said.

I thought she might break down and cry. Her eyes were shining with tears, but she lifted her chin bravely. Nodded.

Then, in a flash of white, her teeth bit down on her wrist and she held it out over the iron cover in front of her. A whoosh of air and a sigh not unlike a woman crying and the portal opened. Stairs rose up out of the chamber floor with a wrought iron railing covered in blood.

She swallowed and looked back at me. I schooled my features into a mask of control. I couldn't, wouldn't, let her see what this was costing me. Because while I might know it was worth it, she might not feel the same.

Then Gideon put his hand on her shoulder and she turned away. Her steps sounded throughout the chamber, drawing the other woman along too. They moved swiftly, with Gideon urging them on. One by one, then two by two, they went like prisoners terrified of freedom but eager to face it.

But they went.

The king stood rigidly beside me, watching them ascend the staircase. When at last it was Gideon's turn, he pivoted sharply to face me, a sheen of tears in his eyes. He knew. He knew the toll this would take.

"I'll tell Kit what a hero her sister was," he said in a hoarse rasp. "I'll make sure she understands."

That almost broke me. I had to turn away as he took the first step and I kept my eyes averted until I knew he had reached the top of the staircase.

I swallowed hard enough that I felt the knot in my throat plunging and sticking at the bottom beneath the force. Terran had failed. Aoife had failed. It was my turn now.

I would not fail.

He swung his gaze to me. "Now for our unfinished business. Time for you to tell me where Terran is."

I held that gaze with a coy smile. My legs grew weaker. My breathing was short. Time was counting down. I inhaled deeply. Bring it, I thought. Let it come.

"You thought you left Phaedre behind sobbing over Blade's body," I said. "But you had no idea she was here. You haven't asked who wore her face back in your ballroom. You worry about Terran, yet you have no idea of the power you left behind in his youngest."

"None of that matters," he said. "I see the way you shake. I can smell the death on you. It won't be long now."

He flicked his hand with such grace, it was almost unexpected to feel myself moving toward him, my feet dragging across the chamber floor, stumbling, unable to truly move. On numb soles that felt thick and awkward. Each step was a slap against the surface that had no rhythm, no pacing. Each step broadened his smile.

He had won. He was about to take his spoils.

"Where is he?" he demanded in a low, threatening voice. "Tell me now so you can die with those secrets clinging to your tongue."

I smirked, plastering the callous expression over the neutral one so expertly that even I felt the change in my posture. My grin felt tight and pained, but I flashed it just the same.

"He's in Hell," I croaked out. "Feel free to follow him there."

I saw the realization move across his face as he understood exactly where Terran was, and what it meant. "Kumara," he muttered. "He's in the Stygian Darkness. A place I can't go unless I'm dead or wasted."

His hand closed over my throat, fingers splayed, palm resting over the tender curve of my neck. "You think you've tricked me," he said in a throaty voice. "You think I can't do anything to harm you because you're already dying."

He laughed then, a nasty rasping sound that reminded me of fingernails dragging down ragged stone. "I'm going to kill you now," he said. "And it's not going to be pleasant."

His magic thrummed over my skin, lighting up every cell, turning each hair on my body into a lightning rod. I was a steak sizzling on a low flame.

Tears blurred my vision, yet I wasn't sad. I'd not known happiness or peace since the days before my parents died. Long before I'd watched Kit step into a dilapidated gymnasium and fall to her knees in front of a repulsive drug dealer.

But I knew elation now. I knew the wash of ecstasy that made me feel as though I was rising above it all. Above my guilt and shame. Above my rage and fury. Above the desperation of trying to be something I wasn't.

And I knew absolution. What happened next, no matter how vicious his attack was, no matter how badly he tore at my soul, it was impenetrable at the core.

I felt a sharp tug first. One that quickly turned into a searing pain that shattered my calm. It dragged me back to the present, to the look on his face, the tiny pinpricks of hundreds of teeth on the tip of his tongue. It lashed out again, striking with a serpent's speed into my shoulder. And again on my breast. It clamped down on my nipple and buried deep.

I gasped. My lungs refused to expand. Fire spread through my veins.

Not a magnificently grotesque death, after all. Just death by a thousand tiny bites, each more painful than the last until he decided he'd had enough and wanted to hear me scream.

I watched his mouth move around those teeth as he spoke. "Did you know I can keep you alive while I forage through your entrails? I can hold your heart in my hands and feel the pulse of it, use the rhythm to mark each strike. I can make sure you feel each agonizing moment to its fullest and yet keep you numb enough you can't resist."

I couldn't speak, and I didn't think he expected me to. It didn't matter. The ordeal was almost over. Patience was never my long suit. Gideon. Gideon had often complained about it, but I was patient now. A humorless chuckle moved through my throat.

He paused, pulling back. "You laugh?" he asked. "You're insane, hunter. Am I not giving you enough pain?"

I swallowed hard, trying to wrestle my tongue, my voice-box, into action. When I spoke, my voice sounded as if it had been scoured with sand paper.

"It's funny, is all," I said.

"Funny?" He sounded upset. "What is funny about your death?"

I nodded. "Just that you think I would keep my word. Me. A mortal with no blood oath to keep me honest."

He blinked stupidly as the statement crept through his mind. I could see him trying to work through the thought that he wasn't the only one who had decided a vow was nothing here in Fae.

And that moment, when he paused, when his brain was busy with his angry sense of indignation, that was the moment of happenstance I'd been waiting for.

Like Gideon, I used the opportunity.

That was when my hand flashed out, not reaching for the blade on his hip, but for the ring on his finger, the one currently embedded in my hair.

And I pulled it free.

CHAPTER 26

No matter how many kills I'd made in my career, how many evil things I'd removed from the world, there was always a hole within that couldn't be caulked or mended by the violence, even if it was to save an innocent life. I suppose that was why I took trophies. Why I hid them in the back part of a closet. They were a sort of proof that I'd done something worthwhile, that my life wasn't a waste. Each time I staked a vamp or took out a golem or a witch, I needed that physical token to remind myself I'd done SOMETHING. I'd ran the length of the prison on the right side. I was the vengeance not the harm that required it.

I didn't take trophies to relive the violence. They weren't spoils to parade in front of those I wanted to impress. They were laurels that taunted me to never sit still, to never begin to believe I'd done enough that I could finally rest. Because I didn't deserve to rest. I didn't deserve a celebration of victory.

I might have considered the taking of Ferranus's ring as a gathering of laurels there in Fae, a place that had cost me so much, except I knew differently. Stealing that ring had nothing to do with me. Not one bit. What did have to do with me right at the moment I pulled the ring free, was the roar of fury the moment it left his finger. The sound was better than any ecstasy of absolution.

I'd seen that ring flash but hadn't paid it much heed until Terran had gripped me by the shoulder in the moments before he'd shoved me into the trunk. Not until he sent me to the harem with the secrets he'd been keeping for generations whispering in my ear.

The cursed objects were not Lilah made at all. They were much, much older. That's what the book was trying to tell me. What Mica's visions were all about. It was about the Iron Dynasty and Ferranus's history. And Terran's.

And Lyonara's.

She who made the veil with Aiofe's help to escape the brother who had compelled her to bond with him so he could have the throne. It was about a gem of compulsion that had a partner, the same way the coins had a partner.

And it was about what he'd done with them.

The moment the ring came free, the veil began to collapse around us. The fireplace disappeared. The linen-fold paneling warped into stone. The cave bled back into vision and the loud mournful cry of children rose around us.

Somehow, I found the strength to wrench free of his grip. Maybe because he was surprised. Maybe because without the ring, he couldn't hold on to all that stolen power.

And in that second, I took one more opportunity, the way Gideon would, and I pivoted with the last of my grace and muscle memory. Sweeping around in an arc, the hand holding the ring stretched out and away, pulling his gaze, pulling his reach even as my free hand went for that blade, finally.

Blade. It was ironic, almost, that the fae I loved would be part of this end, even if he wasn't there. I felt the spectral smile curve my mouth.

But then the cold handle was in my grip and I was still spinning. My feet shuffled in place just the right amount, just the right way. My shoulders twisted. My head turned. One complete rotation, blade edge held just the right way, and I felt the telltale tug of metal on skin. I sliced. Deep. Long. Danced away. Spun again.

This time, the knife moved with my magic, that synergistic flow of hunter to weapon. My energy controlled the movement. I took the king in the throat next. His blood sprayed over me in thick, coppery waves. It sizzled as it left his body.

Surprise. That was the opportunity I had to grab like a brass ring. I held onto it with every ounce of energy I had left. And surprise was exactly what was written all over his face, his posture.

I was still spinning, still slicing, still ducking and cutting. A dervish couldn't have moved so fluidly. The ecstasy carried me on its velvet wings until the moment the king dropped to his knees and I stood over him, gasping for each breath.

I was covered in his blood, the same as he was. The veil possessed the dying energy of a fae queen, but the ability to control it was in that ring clasped in my hand. I stood there, looking down at him, watching the king of the iron realm bleed over the floor of the cave without doing a damn thing to stop it, and yet, something told me it wasn't the wounds I'd inflicted that hurt him.

Something else was happening that I didn't understand. Something that caused him pain and confusion.

But I knew I couldn't kill him. He was fae and immortal. He was the last of the line here in the veil, the recipient of whatever magic Lyonara had given it with her last breath.

With a deep breath, I foraged for the last of my strength and tossed the ring over-handed into the darkness of the veil beyond the cave's mouth.

"It's gone," I said, although it was clear he had seen me throw it. "It's over. She's free."

He hung his head.

"You didn't just kill your get from mortals and goblins," I said. "You took her children too. Each time she got with child, you took it from her and stole its magic. You transferred it to that ring. The ring she gave you. Then you had your own children killed so you would never have an heir, so the fae would empower you for eternity. Who did that for you?" I asked. "Was it Terran? Was that what drove him to leave the Sentinels and take his soldiers with him?"

Nothing. Not even a look upward. Instead, he fell onto his haunches, broken in some way I didn't understand. His silence unnerved me, galled me even. I wanted him to fight, dammit. I wanted him to argue, defend himself, tear at his clothes. Something. Anything. I goaded him further, trying to get him to confess at last, even though I knew the truth.

"But she broke free of the compulsion, didn't she? And she built this place to save the last of her children. To keep you from murdering more of them. She might have done it if you'd not found her here and threatened to murder even that last poor child until she'd taken her own life to protect it. Used her own blood and spirit to power the veil. Except it wasn't yours, was it? That child was fully fae but it was of her blood. And Terran's."

I could barely stand to look at him as the words freed themselves. Centuries of compulsion and murder, only to continue the horrors in the disguise of a gift to his subjects. It was beyond evil. And he deserved to die.

But I'd waited too long. The battle had cost too much. I was swaying on my feet by then. My breathing was shallow. The blade I'd stolen from the king dropped from numb fingers to clatter to the floor of the cave.

I expected Ferranus to reach for it, but he didn't. He seemed...more frail than a moment earlier. The incandescent glow of his skin lost its luster.

My knees buckled beneath me finally, and a whimper fled my lungs as I realized my vision was starting to go. I could barely see him anymore through the blur. I had nothing in me to finish him. I couldn't lift my arm. My voice was nothing but a whisper.

"I can't finish you," I said. "But I can make sure you are trapped here. I can make sure you meet your maker as I take my last breath."

That last breath wasn't far away, but the veil was breaking apart too. With each heaving, grasping breath he took, it was starting to fray.

That was when I heard footsteps coming from the mouth of the cave. Someone spoke, and something in me cracked at the familiar sound of that voice.

"If that last breath is coming, Ponytail," Blade said in a gruff, throaty voice. "Then you best let me be his maker."

A gentle but powerful hand cupped my chin and lifted my face upward. He stood there looking like such a shining thing, haloed by crimson light, that I gasped.

"I'm dreaming," I murmured, and it didn't matter. If sight of him, my beloved, my mate...was the last thing I saw in this world or any other, I could go happy.

I drank in his face. A weak smile moved my lips. "What a dream."

His own, emotive smile took possession of his face as he shook his head. "Not a dream, Alathir. I told you I would crawl through hell to find you and till my last breath, I will keep that vow."

"You're dying too," I said, my throat so tight the words barely rasped free. He was dead and come to Kumara. My eyes stung as I squeezed out the tears to see him. I didn't want to go to my hereafter without a clear image to take with me.

"No, Ava," he said. "My last breath is not today. I need you to hold on. But if you go without me, before I can finish this, I'll follow you there, too. There is no life, no sense to immortality, without you."

I thought of Phaedre's words, so similar, when she spoke of Mica. My heart squeezed. My chest felt so tight I thought my ribs had shrunk.

He was crouching beside me. The king behind him had slumped sideways onto the cave floor. His frail looking form seemed dull and shrived. He blinked slowly as he watched us.

"You've done magnificently," Blade said, holding my gaze. I was sure he glowed with power. The serpents in his gaze circled his irises, making them flare with light. Not red this time. Gold. He fiddled with something, then lifted my hand and slid a cold circle over my finger.

"Your trophy," he said. "You've done everything you are able. But what needs to be done is not something a human can do. The rest is mine to finish. We don't have much time."

I nodded. He touched me lightly on the chin, brushing his thumb up toward my lip. It pained me to see such gentleness in such a powerful being, as if he, too, was broken by emotion.

Then his eyes went black. His face and all the liveliness that I knew and loved, from the potential for cold rage, to the softness of passion, all that grew wooden and flat.

Something spectral wavered over his body as he rose, a sort of liquid darkness that both consumed and revealed. I shivered, the ice in my bones racking the muscles and tissue surrounding them, and I wasn't sure if it was from a chill or from a sense of reverence. All I knew was that I couldn't hug myself tight enough to ward off the shuddering.

Without another word, he closed the short distance between himself and Ferranus with a silent step. As he looked down, a shadow claimed him, large and hulking. Reminiscent of the hound he was, and I knew that beneath it all, he wasn't half-fae, half-hellhound. He was the son of the queen of the Stygian Darkness, the grandson of the Darkness's Titan, and there was no true form but the shape of shadow.

"His magic is mine," he murmured as he knelt on one knee. "The last of what you are belongs to me, do you understand?"

Ferranus peered up at him. Nodded. I thought I saw the great iron king shudder.

And then, for an instant, the hellhound was not Blade but Aiofe. I saw her in the tilt of his head, the angle of his jaw. She/he lowered a massive muzzle to the king's throat. Thrashed once. Twice. A crumpling sound, as the noise of paper being balled up and shredded, buckled the air.

There was no sound in the chamber after that except that of the hound consuming all that the king was and though it was a disquieting noise, it possessed a certain victory too.

Then, a blast of purple, sizzling light burst from the king's body in all the places where I'd cut him. A thousand or more beams of light shining through the cavern, lighting the shadows.

I saw children lurking there, hands stuffed in their mouths as if to hold back sobs or screams. Dozens of them, all lustrous and beautiful, watching silently. Their shoulders sagged with each passing second, as relief and release took them. Till at last, they disappeared into nothingness and all that remained was one willowy, silver-haired female in a golden raiment standing in the shadows.

"At last," she murmured. And then she, too, was gone.

A sigh moved through the veil. Blade turned to me, reached out his hand. He was all Blade then. The fae I knew and recognized except he was more.

His thumb found my thrumming pulse, lingering there as if taking the measure of ten seconds. Twenty. I felt the shift in the rhythm long before his smile suggested it had begun to pound in a frenzy the moment he touched me.

"You're the next in line," I said, realization striking me like a hammer. "Not Ferranus. You were meant to be king."

He nodded. "The ancient king wanted to broaden his reach and his power, and so he bedded a titan of the Stygian Darkness."

"Your grandmother."

He nodded. "Aiofe has as much claim to the Iron Realm as the Stygian Darkness, but being half hellhound, she was better suited to the latter."

"How long have you known?"

He ran a finger over my forearm, raising the hairs and making me feel alive at his touch, and not the spectral thing I was in Kumara. "An hour. Maybe two." His eyes gleamed.

"Maybe a century. Who knows. But I won't take the throne. And not just because doing so would mean you'd have to stay here in Fae with me forever, and I can't ask that of you." His finger halted its path up my arm as he caught my gaze with his heated one. "I love you, Ava. All of you. I love the rasp in your voice when you're angry, the way your fingers dig into your palms when you want to hit something. I love the soft, near whimper in the back of your throat when you think no one can tell they've hurt you, when you're holding back, a sound I don't even think you can hear. But I hear it. I hear it and I love you all the more for it. And I love that you think I can wear the crown and rule a land of monsters."

"But there is another, far more worthy fae than Ferranus or me who should fill that chair."

I inclined my head in agreement. Phaedre. Not fully fae, but powerful, someone who would rule with a kind heart and not an iron fist. Who would nurture the fae and not exploit them.

Kneeling in front of me, he scooped me into his arms. "Does it hurt so much, Alathir?" he asked quietly.

"Not anymore," I said and laid my head against his chest. His heart thrummed and vibrated against my cheek, reassuring me. I could go now, I thought. With his arms around me. I was home.

CHAPTER 27

Someone wheezed with each breath they took, and it took several heartbeats to realize it was me. My eyelids fluttered open to see I wasn't in the veil anymore. Not Kumara either. I lay cradled in someone's arms.

Blade's, I realized once I understood that the worried face looking into mine belonged to the Dark Enforcer.

"Alathir," he said as he crouched above me. "You're alive."

I sucked in another breath. Pain splintered over my spine, making me jerk in surprise.

"Don't move," he said. "You took a terrible blast of black magic."

I went still as the last hours or days came rushing in. This was my moment, I realized. The one where I returned to my body for that last breath. I wasn't sad about it. All that had happened, all that it had cost, was worth it.

And yet, it seemed I'd been granted more than one last inhale. Somehow, the gods had given me the chance to feel my mate's arms around me, to see the crimson flare of his irises once more, and know it was him...the real him and not the shadow he'd been in the veil.

My vision was tunneled into a pinprick that let just the briefest of light and shape through. I took whatever sight I had to roam his face, drinking in each feature before my lungs failed me.

A terrible blast of magic hadn't been all my body had endured, apparently. I felt an ache in my bones that came from something more. As if rigor mortis had set in and someone had forced my body to move, anyway. Every muscle burned.

But I drank him in just the same and as I did so, two other faces popped into view over his shoulder. Phaedre. Mica. A tear formed in my eye at the sight of them. That I could see them, too, was a gift.

"You're home," she said, and even as she spoke, I realized her features had changed from the goblin I'd met weeks before to the beautiful half-fae I'd seen in the veil.

I tried to speak, to tell her I was happy to see her, but my mouth wouldn't obey. She seemed to understand and brushed my forehead with the backs of her fingers.

"You're going to be fine, Ava," she said, and though there was a strange thickness to her tone, I heard the relief in it as well. She slid her gaze to Mica. "It's working." She said to him.

He nodded from his spot next to her. "She's getting stronger."

Stronger? I blinked. Realized that my vision had expanded. It was clearing a bit, enough to see the two of them hovering over me. I tested my lungs. They did seem to expand more fully. What was this magic?

Phaedre's gaze cut to Blade. "Are you sure this is what he wants?" She looked worried.

"Yes," Mica said and his voice was so tight with emotion that I understood it was the only word he could get out.

My gaze roamed my surroundings. The hagstone stood several yards away, inert and dead-looking. Above me, the ceiling twinkled with fairy lights. If I swept my gaze to the side, I caught sight of a thousand or more fae clustered silently in one large mass. I was sure Pan stood in a huddle with several nymphs, looking on with a worried expression. The nymphs merely looked intrigued.

Gideon and Heuil stood beside one another, but while Heuil was openly sobbing, Gideon had his hand covering the bottom half of his face as though he was trying his best to stifle any sign of emotion.

Egotistical as it was to take heart in that, it was good to see I would be mourned. It made it worthwhile, somehow. I thought of those tokens I'd hoarded from each of my kills and suddenly the image of them, the taking of them felt ridiculous.

Except, I didn't feel like I was dying. At least not right away. I slid my gaze to Blade's face, thinking to smile for him now that I felt stronger, affect him with the same hope now fluttering in my chest. I might live. Sweet Jesus I might live long enough to tell him how I felt.

But something didn't look right. His eyes, pinned to mine, didn't have the same luster. The skin around the corners looked gray and crepey.

"Blade?" I asked through a parched throat that raked over his name in an unfamiliar sound.

A small movement from him that corresponded with a bobbing of my own body. So I was on his lap. My mind quickly readjusted to the new information and fed me a dozen touchpoints of muscle and skin.

"Blade." I said again, this time more urgently.

A wan smile moved his lips. "It's alright, Alathir."

I blinked. Hard. Something wasn't right. By the time my eyes opened again, my mind felt less fogged. I could see better. I could even feel where both of his arms were wrapped around my body, holding me close.

Except his embrace was getting slacker.

And I knew right then what was happening.

"No," I rasped and fought for the strength to tear myself from his embrace. It didn't take much. I slid to the floor onto my knees, my hands still on his thighs. He looked like he'd fallen back onto the throne, his legs flung out in front of him.

Over his shoulder, both Phaedre and Gideon hovered, trying not to look at me. Beyond them, Ruby was lashed by ropes of her own entrails to a thick, glowing white pillar of light. Smoke rose around her. Gone were the clouds of shadow that usually engulfed her. The wings she'd sported before, bright, powerful outreaches of feathers and shadow were wilted, frayed bits of darkness.

Gods knew what had gone on in this chamber while I'd been in Kumara, but it hadn't been pretty. The result of it was slumped over the throne in front of me.

My eyes razored to Blade again. He was sagging more now, tossing me a look that was half cocky dark enforcer, half weary lover. My mate. The fae I would die for and not look back. The fae who was dying to heal me so I could live.

It hurt to inhale.

My hands scrabbled up his legs to find his face. I cupped his jaw. "No, no, no." I pulled myself up, feeling stronger now, so that I was level with his face. Eye to eye. Heart to heart.

"No," I croaked.

His lips pressed together. His throat worked over the words he was struggling to let free.

"You can't do this," I said. "Stop. Take it back."

He was using too much power. After whatever battle he'd fought in this ballroom, after holding back Ferranus, healing me was taking too much.

I flicked my attention to Mica. "Fix it," I said. "Heal him. Make him stop."

His face lifted, a flare of hurt anger in his expression. "You don't think I tried? He begged me, Ava. Begged me to let him do this for you." His hand found Phaedre's as it lay on his shoulder and he held it tight. "This is a mate's choice. I can't deny him of it."

I choked on a breath, dragged my eyes from his to Blade's face. "You damned foolish beast. Why would you risk yourself like that?"

A blink, then an inhale through his nostrils. But no answer. Stubborn. Gorgeous. Foolish male.

"There is no life without you," I said, doing my best not to break down. The sob in my voice galled me. I needed to show him strength here. He needed me to be hard and firm. "I'm no damsel, Blade. I'm no soft, yielding woman who needs protection. I made my choice. You have no right to take it away from me."

"Too late," he croaked. "It's done."

Even my knees felt stronger. The pain in my back subsided. If I couldn't remember what it felt like to be eighteen again without the scars of battle, my body did. It straightened and it strengthened to something even better than it had been.

"Mica, do something."

"You don't understand, Ava," Mica said. "I don't know if I can. I might kill him. I don't have that sort of control."

"He's already dying," I countered. "What are you risking by trying?"

Mica shook his head. "I'm risking letting him die in agony, and I won't do that, Ava. Not even for you. Not even for Blade. This is what he wanted. He wants you to live."

A sob broke free of my throat. "Even if it takes everything he has?" I growled. "I won't let that happen. I can't."

I thought Mica was going to argue but Phaedre put a hand on his shoulder, making him drop his eyes to the floor. His hands trembled. It was clear this was more than he could take. Yet I didn't feel guilty demanding it of him.

A movement from the corner of my eye caught my attention. Someone stepped out of the crowd and onto the dais. My eyes caught on his clothing, the blur of his face. Tutor, my mind whispered. This was Mica's tutor.

It all took a mere heartbeat, but I saw the tutor smile as he threw me a meaningful glance. Put a pulse in my throat that tasted like copper.

A membrane ticked down over his eyes. Small tattoos flashed on his fingers as they moved. As if he'd peeled away a bit of nylon stocking from his face, it came into view at last.

And I knew him.

Finally.

Castor. The fae from the catacombs who had spoken to me before I'd been put on the auction block. I saw him the way I saw him then, as if he'd peeled away the glamor for me that made him blurry and hard to make out. *I suppose now that you have the power of my true name, you might use it against me.*

The words rang out through my mind, and I reeled back with the sterling brightness of it. At last, a thread to grasp onto. I almost said his name out loud for everyone to hear.

Castor. I almost divulged his secret name and only at the last minute did I manage to clamp down on the syllables and keep them from being uttered aloud, giving everyone in the room the power of his name.

He must have realized how close I was to doing that, because he lifted his hand to the air in defense, palm out.

"There is something you don't understand, warrior," he said to me. "Something that makes all the difference, the reason Mica can't do this work."

"I hear you yapping but I don't hear you doing," I said, glaring at him to infer I would, if I had to, scream his name to the heavens.

"He's only half-fae," Castor said.

"No shit," I fairly screamed. "The hellhound has his other side."

He cleared his throat. "I mean, he has given up the other half."

"I don't understand." I noticed Castor looked from me to Mica and the look that exchanged between the two of the them chilled my marrow.

"Mica?" I prompted, but Mica only dropped his gaze. Ashamed? Guilty? Terrified? I wasn't sure.

It was Castor who answered, and he did so after he cozied up closer to me without me so much as hearing him move.

"He is only half a fae now," he said. "The part that made up the other half, the hellhound, Prince of the Stygian Darkness is gone," he said.

"Gone where?"

He only canted his head at me as if I should know.

I looked at Blade, feeling the last of his magic moving through me and I choked on the sob that dislodged itself from my throat. All I could do was shake my head in misery because

I didn't know. And if I didn't figure it out, I had a feeling I would feel the last of his spirit slip through my fingers as well.

I tapped Blade's cheek. It was cold and clammy. His eyes were the only thing that had any life in them. I thought he was trying to speak but it was clear he was losing the last of the control he had.

Control. The word crept with a mouse's padded feet through my mind. I'd given Aiofe control of my body. I'd assumed she'd lost her battle with the king, but what if she'd taken control of Blade's instead?

I looked into his face. What if he'd convinced her to take it?

"Aiofe," I said, and Blade's eyes lit up from within. "Did you let her take your body, Blade? Did she do all this work?"

Castor leaned over us, his shadow casting an even greyer pall over the Dark Enforcer's face.

"Aiofe did not rend the chamber with violence and blood. That was the Dark Enforcer. His rage was magnificent as he stole the life from those who hurt you. But she did agree to relinquish your form when he asked." He paused, as though what he had to say next was painful. "For a price."

"Blade," I guessed.

"Not just Blade. Not just his body. He gave control of the half of him that was darkness so she could return to Kumara."

"So he could enter it with her," I murmured, thinking of the ways a fae might crawl on his hands and knees over hellfire coals if he had to. And he had.

He'd given himself to the queen of the darkness so he could enter her lands and pull me through like a camel through the eye of a needle.

By then, the tears ran freely down my face. It was too high a price. I cupped his face in my palms, kissed the cold lips and didn't move my mouth from his for so long I felt a tap on my shoulder.

"Mica may be able to heal that part of him that is fae, but he can't replace the darkness. But the right fae might be able to replace it with something else. If he had enough magic to do the transfer."

Hope. Dear sweet gods. Hope. I grasped for it like a brass ring. "Tell me what to do."

Castor shrugged. "Only a warrior who knows my true name can ask such a thing of my power, and they may do it only once. But there still remains the problem of finding enough magic to complete the swap."

"You don't have it," I guessed, feeling that hope dash like a wave on hard shale. "And neither does Mica."

He didn't answer. He didn't have to. The look on Mica's face was enough to give me all the truth I needed. Blade had given all he could of himself to his mother so he could find me in the veil the way he'd promised, and he'd used the last of his magic to heal me.

The one thing I'd learned more than anything else in Fae was that Magic wasn't an eternal well. It ebbed and flowed. It had a cost.

Blade had paid everything he possessed for me.

I crawled onto his lap and wrapped my arms around his neck. The necklace he'd given me pressed between us, digging into my skin and I relished the pain it brought. I'd never been a damsel in distress and I'd never given myself so wholly as I'd done with Blade. And now, I just didn't want to live.

My face buried in his neck, feeling for the last thrum of his heartbeat. Tears greased the place where our skin met and magnified the thready vibration. He was still there, still holding on.

"Ava," someone said, Phaedre, I thought. I didn't want to look up. I wanted, needed, to feel the last of his heart's vibration stop.

"Ava."

This time Gideon. And again, with Mica saying my name. I refused to look up until someone touched the back of my head.

"Ava," he said, wonder filling his voice. "Ava, look. Oh my God, you have to see."

CHAPTER 28

Whatever Gideon wanted me to see, it couldn't compare to watching the light dull in my lover's eyes. Nothing could pull me away from that. And yet...when Heuil spoke, it was filled with such pain and urgency, that the hunter in me perked up. Someone needed me. Someone was in trouble. Without thinking, my head snapped up. The little half-trow stood there on the dais in front of the throne, hands wringing together, the gilded token woven between his fingers. And then...

He held it out. To Mica.

"If this fae has the natal magics to take what is given," he said in a loud, booming voice that somehow lifted to the ceiling and echoed around the chamber. "Then I give whatever magic lies within me to Mica of my own free will to use as he sees fit. I ask nothing in return."

A gasp took possession of the entire room, and then others holding tokens came forward. They, too, passed their stolen tokens to Mica. One by one, they spoke the same words.

Others came after that, lining up neatly at first, and then in a rush of bodies that pressed so closely together that the air grew suffocating. Each of them spoke the same words. Each of them knelt after, submitting themselves and the power in their marrow that they could not access.

My gaze flew to Mica, whose confusion was evident. He was shaking his head in astonishment. Phaedre was coaxing him forward.

"I need help," he said in a soft voice. "I can't do it alone." It was clear he was terrified as he scanned his tutor's face for permission.

"You may not ask it of me," Castor said. "Only a warrior may do that, young one, and you are not a warrior."

No, I thought. Mica wasn't a warrior at heart. But I was. Hope, that bastard thing, flared in my chest again.

I scraped myself off Blade's lap, loathe to abandon him in what might be his last moments, but knowing one heartbeat might be too late to give him one more.

And Castor was there to meet me. He leaned down, ear toward me and I whispered his name, asking him to guide Mica in safely accepting the fae's magic so that it could be transferred to Blade. I was very careful to phrase it as one ask and not two. One sentence, both parts dependent on the other.

With a brief inclination of his head, Castor went to Mica and put his hands over the youth's heart. A glow began there, at first with a hint of red, then orange, yellow, green. It changed softly to a beautiful blue and then violet.

At last, the colors evaporated, leaving behind the brightest white light imaginable. It hurt to look at it. I had to turn away.

And as I did, I saw Erachne in her true form, spinning a web that blotted out the twinkling lights in the ceiling, that covered over the sconces and the gorgeous tapestries. Her web enclosed the entire chamber in a gauzy film.

Like Lilah, she was warping time, giving Mica and Blade and Castor and all the fae host the duration they needed to transfer the magic. And though I wasn't sure, I had the feeling that the cocoon she spun might be able to warp that time into a moment of time outside the web. Maybe a day would pass, but no more. The same as it had when she'd healed me.

I fell to my knees because hope came on thief's feet to steal all my strength..

That was the moment the fae all over the ballroom lifted to the air. In clusters of them, in all shapes, and creeds, and species, they arched backward, their spines curving so gracefully they looked like dancers. Auras edged their bodies in all colors. And then the energy merged, and separated and and streamed toward Mica, slamming into him so hard, so fast, he staggered backward.

But Phaedre had his hand. Castor held his body within his power. And Mica held fast to both of them, using them as anchors while each bolt of magical lightning entered his body.

It was a magnificent, terrifying sight, and one that made him glow like a god, brighter each time a hit of magic saturated his body. Euphoria rode his features. Sometimes he winced in pain, and at others, he merely moaned softly.

The high fae stood back, giving them all room. Pan and his nymphs applauded, cheered, and laughed with pleasure at the spectacle they were fortunate enough to witness.

I was paralyzed with fear and hope. My hands wrung together, and I sought out Gideon's face in the crowd. For a time, his eyes locked with mine was the only thing that kept me breathing. I couldn't look at Blade. I was terrified of what I might see. Coward. That's what I was, really. A frightened rabbit too afraid to look for the hawk, knowing it would be there and all would be lost.

An eternity passed and yet it felt like a breath, and then Mica stepped over to Blade at last. I sucked in a draft of air. Held it. My heart pounded in my ears.

Castor nodded at him, and Mica, too, sucked in a breath. He swallowed.

And then he laid his hands on Blade's heart and while I expected to see a steam of light travel between them, all that was visible was a soft white glow.

At first, nothing happened. I heard someone sobbing softly and only realized it was me when my hands, held against my chin, grew wet and warm.

Then Blade's foot jerked. A small, spastic movement, but movement.

I didn't wait a moment longer. I was up on my feet and racing toward him. I had him in my arms before Mica could even take his hands away from his chest.

I didn't trust my voice. The only thing I could count on was my hands and my mouth, my body, as it pressed against him, as I roamed his face with my fingers.

And when I felt him gather my hands into his and lower them to his heart, I caught my breath.

"Alathir," he murmured.

"Sweet Jesus," I said, and he chuckled. Darkly. Throatily.

"Not that god," he said and his mouth descended to mine.

He claimed me once more, this time with a softness that felt almost human. As he kissed me thoroughly, and if the entire room exploded in cheers and applause, I was oblivious to anything but his kiss.

When he pulled away, I searched his gaze. The kundalini serpent had gone, but the silver of his eyes was still there, clouding out the rest of his iris. There was nothing there but a glint of silver.

"You damn fool," I said. "I should have killed you myself for trying such a ridiculous trick. I should have boiled your balls in oil. I should have—"

"I love you too," he whispered, and that broke me. I fell against him in a sobbing mess and he enfolded me in his arms. I felt the wetness of his tears on my neck as he burrowed his face in. I clung to him without care for who saw me, what they thought. I just needed to feel his heart hammering against mine.

At last, it was time to acknowledge the others. I felt them standing around us, waiting for the reunion to wane. Mica's energy was the strongest. It felt like an itch over my skin. Loathe as I was to let Blade go, his brother had the right to celebrate his victory.

The brothers embraced. Phaedre flew to them both, putting her arms around them and squeezing until someone inside the melee began to laugh. I laughed. Castor laughed.

The relief was palpable.

It was a moan from behind the dais that cut the celebration short. Blade disengaged himself from the arms encircling him wherever they could, and he stood from the throne. He reached out his hand to me and I took it, reveling in the warmth in his touch.

"Ruby," he said, directing the word to Phaedre.

She nodded. "And Lilah."

She squared her shoulders and pulled a breath in through her nose, lifted her chin. She looked decidedly regal, and I realized with a start that she was queen now. Something she seemed to realize at about the same time, because she made a graceful flourish with her hands.

Immediately, a circlet of iron, with pointed tops and jewels crushed into the metal appeared. She held out her hand, and the crown rose upward. It hovered in the air for a long moment before she spoke and when she did, the crown glowed bright red, as though it were sitting in the heart of a smelting furnace.

"Dearest fae of the Iron Realm," she said in a voice that gained confidence. "The king is dead."

Silence fell over the assembly. Not from shock, I realized, but from reverence. Blade hugged me close, tucking me in beneath his arm, and I pressed even closer.

"Only the next in line may conjure the Iron Crown," she said.

"Long live the queen," Blade shouted.

"Long live the queen," Castor repeated.

Mica shouted it the loudest, his voice raising over the others, ringing like the Liberty Bell.

With a long look at me, she smiled. My heart swelled with pride for her. The little half-goblin who was going to rule a nation of high fae. I couldn't help the grin that stole my face.

Then she stepped beneath the crown. The moment she did, it went slate grey and a crack rent the air, as though the circlet of iron had been quenched far too quickly and split the metal.

It lowered itself onto her head. It glowed brightly again, this time with white light. Each point sparked and shot up into the air, tearing holes in the cobweb that contained the room. Erachne's carefully spun gossamer melted away and disappeared.

The room broke out in cheers that seemed to go on until my legs grew tired of standing. Then she lifted her hand above her head, silencing them once more.

"Mine is the head that wears the crown," she said in a booming voice, then turned to Mica. "But yours is the head of power. Both should be in one fae, not two." She reached for his hand and he took it. "Both shall be one," she said, this time in a whisper, and she lifted the crown from her head to place it on his. "Long live the Iron King."

And the cacophony of noise that ricocheted through the chamber then was enough to split my ear drums.

"She knows the truth of Fae," Blade whispered in my ear. "She may be the true queen, but Mica has their hearts."

"He'll be a good king," I said.

"Indeed. He'll be the best the realm has known."

I turned to him, drinking in each feature. "And what of you?" I asked. "What are you now that you are not half hellhound, half fae?"

He tightened his embrace. "That's easy, Ponytail," he said. "I'm yours and you are mine. Nothing else matters." His smile tugged something deep inside me and I would have kissed him again whole-heartedly and unashamed, but he directed my gaze away from his with a movement of his. "Look," he said. "Mica's addressing the crowd."

I turned to see Mica striding to the edge of the dais. Phaedre came along at his side, at exactly the same pace. Both were beaming.

"My mate has honored me," Mica began and had to hold up his hand to quell the next round of raucous cheering. "And now I honor you. All of you who gave of yourself so selflessly so I might save the warrior who won your magic back from the bastard who used it all these centuries."

At that, he gestured toward the crowd and, as one, they gasped as though struck. Magic bloomed in the chamber like a heat wave. Beside me, Blade grunted.

"What is it?" I asked. "What's happening?"

"He's showing them the truth," he said. "What Ferranus has done with their magic."

"No fae will ever have to grant their magic again," Mica said once he was sure his message had been received. "But I will honor the tradition. Once per century, those with the gilded tokens will receive their year of access. But no fae will have to feed me their power to do so." He turned toward the place where Heuil still stood.

"Starting with this one," Mica said. And with a sweep of his arm, he released a stream of light that enveloped the half trow, lifting him from the floor.

Heuil spun in place a half dozen turns, and then...

He disappeared

"Sweet Jesus," I said. "Did he just—"

But my words were cut off as a tall, gorgeous creature stood in the place where the trow had once been. Wings of silver spread out to six feet on either side. They closed onto his back with a click that reminded me of a knife being snapped closed. A sword almost as big as the little trow he had been jutted out from between the space where the wings closed.

"Behold the Sword of Justice," Mica said and Blade gasped.

"That creature has been extinct for generations," he said in a soft tone.

Heuil looked my way and smiled broadly. I returned it. Tipped my invisible hat. He had his wings and then some, and the pleasure written all over his body could have lighted the belly of the darkest cave. With a reverent step, Heuil approached Mica. When he knelt before the new king, his head was bowed, the wings clicked audibly as if saluting him.

With a regal movement, Mica slid the sword from between Heuil's wings. It whispered in metallic notes as it slid free.

It hummed as Mica lifted it heavenward and it sang in soft, lullaby notes as he drew it along his throat.

Blood welled in a crooked smile along his neck and spilled onto the blade. For a moment, I feared Mica might bleed out and collapse, but then his wound sealed, and healed, and no scar remained to mar his perfectly smooth skin.

He held the sword out a hair's breadth away from Heuil's neck.

"Your magic is bound to mine. For as long as I live, you will have access to your magic so you may be what you were meant to be. Do you accept this charge?"

Heuil looked up at the new king and nodded solemnly. With barely a grunt, he rose to stand before Mica, his fingers to his brow in deference. A click of his heels and accepted the proffered sword. With lifted chin, the sort that intimated he was accepting a great honor that might take a great chunk of his soul, he spun on his heels. The Sword of Justice hung at his side, somehow deathly ominous and small at the same time. His wings retracted tightly to his back, looking for all the world like two more blades to partner the one in his grip.

With squared shoulders, he headed toward where Ruby stood lashed to the pillar. He said nothing to her. She raised her lolling head so she could look at him. There was no fear in her face. Only resignation.

With a single swing, he cut her head from her body. A shriek echoed through the chamber. The shadows evaporated. All that was left of the Morvannon was the smoking entrails that had bound her.

These, he lifted with the tip of his sword and tossed them into the air.

His wings flashed out, and he rose, circling over the entrails twice before he pointed the sword at them. Flame shot from the point of the blade and consumed the viscera. The smell of roasting meat and sulfur wafted through the air.

Then he flew to where Lilah was hanging from a cross of silver and he did the same, this time, slicing through her belly first to let them spill onto her feet as she watched. No one spoke as he did this. No one cheered. It was the execution of justice, and they all sensed the reverence of it.

The fact that they made no sound in response, offered no protest, was a sign that maybe, just maybe things would be OK.

CHAPTER 29

Our journey to the Velvet Boar was quiet for the first several miles. Both Blade and I sat atop Nutkin's back, me with my backside tucked against Blade's hips, relishing the way we swayed together. We fit. Perfectly.

Gideon rode beside us on a dapple colored mare a few hands shorter than Nutkin. I wasn't entirely sure the mare wasn't giving Nutkin the side eye every few paces, and when Blade let him have his rein, testing, because the great horse plodded sideways as much as forward, the great horse let his flanks brush against her.

I was grateful for the silence, as I imagined the other two were. Lots had happened over the last forty-eight hours—or whatever time had actually passed in the Iron Court's ballroom. I had a lot to work through, as did Blade.

I felt bad for him. We still didn't know exactly what effects he would deal with now that his darkness was gone. I was just thankful he was alive and breathing. It didn't matter if it would be an hour or a century. Every moment with him was a blessing.

He'd changed, though. In subtle ways. His face was the same. His hands felt the same on my body, as he'd proved that night after the Days ended. But while he was still the arrogant, rough fae I loved, there were shadows collecting around him that had nothing to do with the Stygian Darkness that had borne him.

Melancholy, I thought. I knew the emotion, the signs well. It wasn't easy to adjust to a new sense of being, a new sense of self when you didn't recognize the spirit within. It had taken me decades to come to terms with who I was, and he had been a major part of that development. If I had to go to war to retrieve his sense of self, then I would.

He hadn't spoken much since he'd made his bald and raw admission to me. I understood. He wasn't the same. Not after the things he'd gone through. But it didn't mean he was less than he was. Just that he needed to figure out where he fit. And I'd be there as he worked through it. Laying cool wet cloths on his psyche whenever he needed it.

He'd taken me to bed after Mica's ascension to the throne. In a small room that smelled of earth and herbs, a chamber one of the servants gave us so they could continue their own celebration into the early morning. He'd made love to me in the most caring and gentle way I'd ever been touched. And though I wasn't a sweet and gentle lover, I'd let him.

We both needed tenderness after what we'd gone through.

After peeling Gideon's over-sized sweatshirt from me, he roamed my skin with awed, heated fingers and lips. He didn't leave one inch of my body without his searing touch. It was as if he was seeing me for the first time, and I him. And perhaps it was our first time. We were both different. Both of us needing to find ourselves in each other.

When it was my turn, I did the same. We drew out the love-making into an almost unendurable yearning that echoed the pain we'd felt thinking the other dead. That was the purpose, I thought, to stretch our spirits like elastic bands, seeing how much they could take, filling the cellular spaces with energy so that when we let go, it wasn't just a release but a rebound.

And when we'd finally exhausted ourselves in delaying the gratification, he took me gently, reverently and he drew out that pleasure too, until I clasped him to me in sweat-soaked need. When he was sure I'd taken my fill, he let go with a howl that sent chills down my spine. It was the keening of a hound in the dark wilderness, bereft but not broken. Never broken. Not the Dark Enforcer.

Thinking about it now, and the things he'd whispered into my throat and hair and breasts as he took his release, I felt my skin heat, but I wasn't ashamed. Not even with Gideon riding beside us, sneaking looks my way now and then.

What Blade and I experienced together was sacred, and I had the feeling Gideon would be doing the same with Shea when he returned. At least, I hoped for his sake he did. The haunted look dogging his eyes was an eerie echo of the one that had been in Blade's.

We weren't just bringing Gideon home to the earthen realm, and I wasn't just going home to Kit. A third rider plodded on along behind us several paces back. That fae hadn't spoken three words since we'd found him surrounded by a host of Terran's soldiers, drained and nearly turned thrall the way Ferranus's page had been.

Flint had survived Ferranus's attack because Mica had been able to feed him power while Blade ravaged the dais and forced the king to flee. Later, Mica healed him and hugged him tightly, telling him he needed to find respite where he could.

So we were bringing him to Kit because that was the only word he spoke to Mica when asked. Turned out the fae I hated had fallen for her soft ways, and done everything he could to protect her, even bringing her to Fae so he could watch over her. Knowing it now, I felt slightly guilty for hating him so much. Slightly.

But while Flint survived, Stone did not. I'd not seen him in Kumara and hoped he'd been spared, but he was gone. Truly gone. There wasn't even a husk of remains to mourn.

When I'd told Blade I hadn't seen Stone in his mother's realm, he'd quietly suggested Stone had gone on to the elements, as all fae who truly died found. Their magic dispersed to the leaves and grass and essence of Fae.

Then he'd gone quiet again, pulling me so close that even the sweat from our bodies had no space. We'd made love again, this time rougher, with an almost violent determination.

I let him have everything I had then, just as I'd done the first time. When you love someone, I thought, you don't judge why they need your touch. You just give it.

The trunk had never returned to the Iron Realm. Whatever Ferranus had glimpsed inside was gone along with it. The cursed objects had been lost again, too. I secretly wondered if they were sentient the way the veil and the book were, that they allowed themselves to be found periodically to remind the fae-folk that they existed.

And I wondered if perhaps Lyonara or her spirit or her children had made sure they'd not traveled with the trunk to the veil, ensuring their magic did not give the king any extra power. Wherever they were, I was also sure they wouldn't end up in the earthen realm.

Ferranus's ring did not disappear, though. It remained on the chain of the necklace Blade had given me until I held it out to Phaedre. It was her family's ring, after all. When it settled onto her finger, it had flickered to white and then black again.

Whether it was Lyonara's essence offering her blessing, I couldn't know. If the spirits of her long-gone siblings were with her in that ring, then there could be no more fitting vengeance for those poor souls, but the goblin queen ran a finger over the surface in reverence before tucking her hand back into Mica's.

Now, the road to the Velvet Boar seemed brighter than it had on my first journey. By the time the tavern came into view, my backside was aching and I was thirsty enough to drink an entire keg of ale. The light in the sky had waned to a strip of crimson on the horizon that reminded me of Blade's eyes. I laid my hand on his where it held the reins.

"I'm looking forward to seeing Seamus," I said.

He made a sound in the back of his throat. "That's not what I'm looking forward to. You're damned lucky your bastard lover and my bastard brother aren't following along or I'd have carried you off into the woods long ago and taken you against a tree." His palm pressed against my belly. "I might just throw you into the nearest stall when we get inside."

"What, right in front of Nutkin?" I hadn't forgotten that the horse chose his form and could shift into something akin to a very large human man when he wanted.

"Nutkin will be busy enough with his own filly to ignore all the things I'd be doing to you in the stall next door."

I squirmed on the saddle, feeling how sore I already was after such a long ride. "I doubt this ass will be open for business for a good long while," I complained. "You forget I'm not a rider."

He chuckled. "That's not how it seemed last night."

I was glad to hear his humor had returned. "Last night I was sore in other spots," I said.

He murmured his agreement, and I was surprised to hear him confess, "My soul was aching, too, Ponytail. But I'm glad I had you to balm the rawest wounds in me."

He laid a kiss on my ear and I thought he planned to nip the lobe but was interrupted by Gideon, who had surprised me with his horsemanship. I'd always thought him a city boy from his belly button to his backbone.

"How long before we reach the portal?" he asked.

Blade cast a sidelong glance at him without pulling his mouth from my ear. "You both can take the portal right away," he said.

Gideon twisted in the saddle. "Ava?"

"Ava is with me," Blade said. "We have some final business to attend to before I send her through."

He reined in Nutkin at the paddock gate. He jumped off the horse's back to land on light feet beside the tethering post before holding out his arms for me.

"I don't need any help, thanks," I said with a raised eyebrow.

Gideon snorted. "No change there," he grumbled, and I cut a look his way.

"The day that changes," I quipped. "You'll know the person wearing my skin is not me."

Blade stepped away. "Don't even joke about that," he said.

I hopped down, not as neatly and lightly as him, but with enough grace that I didn't feel awkward when Gideon did the same, suggesting he did more with his spare time than sit in front of a dozen monitors, watching Slow Smoke.

Watching Blade tack Nutkin, back turned away from me, I finally had the courage to ask.

"What happened then?" I asked. "You know, when Aiofe took my body?"

"She offered him the crown," Flint said. The first words I'd heard him utter since he'd said Kit's name. "Of course, he didn't take it."

This said with a hint of sarcasm. So the bastard fae hadn't changed much after all.

I ignored him, but not the comment. The image ran through my mind that Ferranus had painted for me, of Aiofe reaching for Blade and him turning away in disgust.

"You knew it wasn't me," I said to Blade's back.

"Of course I knew," he said, hefting the massive saddle and angling it so he could drop it onto the waiting fence post. "Even if she hadn't spoken, I'd have known it wasn't you, Ponytail." He sent me a side-eye. "You carry your body a certain way. Cocky, sure, but with a subtle rounding of the shoulders that speaks to a hint of fear...not a lack of courage, but a fear of being rejected."

I pressed my lips together at the bald assessment as he continued. "My mother carries herself as though everything belongs to her, and I suppose it does in the end. Most fae go to her for a short time. Seeing her there in your stead did something to me. I can't explain it. But then, even before she told me what was happening, she wanted me to take her place as king."

I hadn't known that.

Gideon snuck over. "Ask him what happened then, Ava."

My gaze darted to the way Blade's hands trembled ever so slightly as he peeled the blanket from Nutkins' back.

"Blade," I said. "What happened then?"

He sighed. "I knew you were gone," he said. "The moment I saw her in your body. I knew what it meant. I...I lost myself for a time."

I laid my hand on his arm. "I know. I saw you there in the veil. You weren't lost."

"I don't think that's what he means," Gideon interjected. "You weren't there, Ava. What happened in between the king's escape and your reanimation..." he let the words trail off as he exchanged a glance with Flint.

Flint, who had already tacked both his and Gideon's mounts, took the blanket from Blade, who was standing with it in his idle grip. "It's best we not bring all that up," he said.

Blade took the blanket from him and strode with it to the stable, leaving us to stand there alone, watching the usual fluid grace turn rigid in his movements. Finally, Gideon closed the distance between us.

"Aiofe gave him a choice to accept his rightful place as king. He told her he wasn't king material." He leaned in close, conspiratorially. But whatever he was going to say next, it was cut off as Blade came back out into the sunshine.

"Let's get you two home," he said in a brusque voice.

We trooped to the tavern. Seamus rushed over to us as with a tray of tankards the moment he caught sight of us crossing the threshold. Nothing escaped his notice, it seemed. No doubt, he'd seen us enter the paddock and had drawn mugs of ale in preparation.

Of course, I waited until Flint and Blade downed theirs before taking a drink, and I felt a little like Terran as I did so.

But I noted Gideon did as well, and didn't feel so foolish. Even if we trusted the two of them, we'd both learned that Fae was not a place for the naive and complacent. Maybe now with Mica and Phaedre ruling the realm, things could be different. Perhaps Fae could be safe for the unwary mortal who found themselves unintentionally in the land of magic. It was a nice thought.

A look around the tavern bowed my shoulders. The mortal women who lived in bondage were still there, plying their trade, wearing the fairy paint and offering themselves to the fae who ogled them. Change might come, I realized, but it wouldn't be swift. That might be a good thing. Sudden change could be difficult and not always in a positive way. Slow but constant evolution might be a better way to steal the horrors of the realm, something so subtle, so quiet, no fae would complain. I sighed for the notion that these women might not get to enjoy their mortal freedom again. Yet, for some, coming to Fae might be a choice instead of a trap. That might be all I could ask for under the circumstances.

It was a disconcerting thing, to think that all the violence I'd endured and enacted might not be as sudden a thing as staking a vamp and saving a kid. The thought took some of the stuffing out of my ego. It dropped my gaze thoughtfully to my drink. There on the glassy surface of the meady murk, glistening against the lights of the tavern, I caught sight of my face. I looked strangely serene. An oddity on my usually tense facade. A blink, and it was gone. The crumple between my eyebrows returning and reminding me that I was who I was at the end of it all. I might be at peace, but I was also a warrior. And warriors didn't stay still for long.

The moments of quiet contemplation that settled over us all was brief. Even before Gideon was swiping the foam from his mouth with his sleeve, Blade was herding us to the bathroom. I dropped my tankard on a table on the way by, and Gideon placed his fastidiously upon Seamus's tray. I felt my mentor's eagerness like the vibration of a tuning fork, but I couldn't say I felt the same. A certain dread dogged my steps as we pushed through the ladys' room door.

Blade pointed to a stall. The familiar wooden door hung askew and half ajar, dissuading any would-be users from entering.

"My brother will help you," he said to Gideon, and Flint nodded in response.

A flash of movement from the silent fae, and he was holding his arm out and pulling a knife from a sheath on his hip. "We've done this before," he said as the edge cut into his palm. Blood welled, purple and viscous, against his skin. With a nod toward Gideon, he stepped into the stall backward.

Gideon started to follow, but paused long enough to turn to me. "I'll wait for you on the other side."

"No need," Blade snapped. "She'll be safe with me. Go to your woman. Leave me to mine."

Duly chastised or merely too eager to return home, Gideon nodded and pulled the door closed behind him. Some muttering went on behind the door and then a light flashed and all was silent.

I looked to Blade.

"Yes," he said. "That's it. Jasmine will take care of them when they arrive at my apartment."

I nodded, not trusting my voice.

"You will stay for a while?" he said in a plaintive voice.

"You're sending me away," is how I answered. The words sounded like they'd been scraped over rough cement.

His throat bobbed as he swallowed. "You didn't accept Mica's offer."

Mica's offer. I gave it thought now. The youth I knew had changed, transforming from a gangly fae to a man of wisdom. But as wise as he'd grown in a short time, he didn't understand me the way Blade did. And though he and Phaedre had created a new dynasty, blending the old bloodline with a new, gentler one, their monarchy was one of a magical realm. Not human. Not mortal.

And as the reigning monarch of a magical realm, he'd offered me what he could as a thanks. A trophy I could keep in my heart instead of in a trunk hidden in a closet.

"He named you Saviour of the Fae," Blade said, his voice sounding strangely hollow for all the pride in it.

"Indeed, a lovely sentiment."

"And you refused the posting that came with it. Captain of the Sentinels. A high honor for any fae let alone a human."

I nodded. "I'm sure it is."

The post came with a long life. Not immortality, but a magically induced extension similar to the way Lilah had lengthened her own—except with the help of Mica's pure magic, not the fae sorceress's black powers.

I'd given it a moment's thought back then, but I'd noted at the same time that Blade had shuffled his feet beside me as I'd gawked at the king and queen at that proclamation. Both of them smiled with the joy of being able to gift me such a thing, and it was clear they expected me to accept.

But that one look at Blade, had shown me I couldn't, and it wasn't just because we had no idea if he was fully fae now or if exactly how long of a life he had waiting for him. No one knew. What was a hellhound fae shifter without the hellhound half? No one knew except possibly Aiofe, and she was back in Kumara, caring for those fae who were waiting in vain for their magic to return.

But I did know one thing, and that was an eternity would be useless without him. I had no wish to live that long if he didn't. And there was one more thing. Something more critical. Something I'd discovered about myself that I'd once thought was a bandaid when all along it had been the flesh it sealed.

"I'm a hunter," I said to Blade as we stood in the bathroom beside the sink he and Jasmine had christened so many weeks ago. "Fae will be fine without me. I'm no powerhouse of magic. But my world...that has need of people like me."

"Yes," he said as he ran the backs of his fingers along my jaw. "My brave beloved. My Alathir. Your kind need you. I can't keep you from that. You were made to be a protector. Mica had it right, he just didn't understand that while Fae may well become gentler under his rule, it is still filled with monsters."

"And I kill monsters," I said.

His mouth curved in a sad smile. "I know this about you, Alathir," he said in a gruff voice. "Perhaps more than you understand about me. There's a ribbon of of power running through you to me, blurring the line of where you begin and I end. It aches sometimes. Like the moment you chose me over the gift Mica gave you." He inched close enough that I could smell the cinnamon swirl around me. At least he hadn't lost that. "So believe me when I say I count myself blessed you haven't killed this monster."

I harumphed, uncomfortable with the emotion in his confession. His response was to slide his hands beneath my thighs and hoist me onto the sink. "However," he said in gruff, throaty voice. "There's still time to thrash me within an inch of my near-immortal life before you go."

Before I go. He was sending me away. I tried to protest because I didn't want to leave him even if I knew in my marrow that he was sending me away. That whatever he had to face, he had to do it alone. He shushed my protests with a smothering kiss that didn't change my mind, but that distracted me enough to reach for the back of his neck, pulling him closer. He nuzzled my throat with his lips, spreading my legs and sliding between them, and I let them part, eager for his touch. A sort of sadness clinging to me like sweet molasses.

"What if someone comes in?" I said. A weak attempt at protest for dignity's sake, the echo of another woman on this sink, giving him ease. And that too, made my throat ache.

His teeth nipped at my throat, making me gasp as he said, "Then I'll tell them to get the fuck out."

He took me then, with a desperation that reverberated through my entire body, and I tried not to think about what my life would be like without him.

CHAPTER 30

I left Fae alone, and I arrived home alone. When the portal tossed me into Blade's bedroom, the lights were low and the bed unmade. Someone had slept in it recently and not bothered to pull the sheets up. The thready tang of copper mingled with that of a woman's perfume, suggesting a wound had been opened in the room and bled for a while before being sealed. I had to close my eyes for a moment to push away the images of Blade that crept to my mind at the scent, threatening to overcome me, force me to spin around and hop back through the portal.

Because I couldn't do that. I'd made my choice back in Fae, and I'd made it consciously. I didn't have to wonder if he understood. I knew he did. I thought of his comment when we'd seen the tavern come into view and he told Gideon he was sending them through right away. That he would send me through later.... and I realized he'd probably understood it long before I had. He'd known the night we'd lain together in that servant's bedroom that he wouldn't be returning to the earthen realm.

It had slipped my notice then, maybe because I'd foolishly believed he would travel the portal with me, the fae who declared he'd come to me no matter the cost. But he hadn't.

Whatever held him in Fae was as strong as the thing that made me leave, I supposed. He needed to be there. Who was I to question his conviction when I knew so intimately the ache of feeling out of place, of feeling like you were in someone else's skin, a victim of circumstance and your own choices that turned you inside out until you didn't recognize yourself anymore.

I'd turned to drugs and violence to scaffold the Ava that remained after the traumas of my youth. But as defenses, those things were rickety structures at best. The moment I'd refused Mica's gift, I'd understood, finally, that my life as a hunter was the one authentic thing in my life. It wasn't an existence thrust upon me by circumstance, but a calling. The night my parents died was a quenching of the sword I'd become. It was the real me.

But Blade had literally lost himself, and I knew better than most just how difficult the journey back to self could be. He thought he needed to do it alone. I'd protested. Refused, at first, to leave without him. But in the end, I had to respect his choice the way he respected mine. We were, what we were.

I called out to Jasmine, but no answer came back. A quick survey of the room showed that someone, probably she, had left a calendar out on the bureau with a date circled. A newspaper sat next to it with the date highlighted. A thin blade lay beside it stained with red.

The day's date, I guessed when I scanned the calendar. Six weeks from the day I'd rode the portal with Stone to the fae realm.

I sighed. Six weeks wasn't a lot of time to miss, and I'd lived it surely enough. Survived and thrived and returned home. Gideon was safely home with his lover, Shea. All was as well as it could be in the Iron Realm.

I looked at my hands. They looked the same. A check in the mirror above the newspaper and calendar showed my features remained youthful. My hair was swept back in its usual ponytail and though a few strands had escaped to frame my face, they weren't grey. A bit of puffiness around the eyes and the scar was gone from my throat, but I was the same Ava physically.

Except I wasn't the same, and I knew it. I felt hollowed out like a pumpkin three days after Halloween. My fingers toyed with the necklace around my neck. The stone was smooth. I found myself imagining the tooth embedded within, the trophy that now seemed impotent as a token.

I sat on the bed for a long while, considering, measuring and weighing how I felt. That was a new thing, surely, but it wasn't the root cause of the ache. I didn't think it was because I missed Blade, though I did with an ache that made my stomach hurt. Maybe I was giving my body time to adjust to the earthen realm, and the knowledge that I had survived. Perhaps I just needed to let myself rest, let my mind gather the threads of memories into a tapestry I could hang in the closet where I stuffed things I didn't want to examine. But neither of those things felt right.

Everything felt like it did after every damn monster hunt. Victory, survival, salvation of the innocent, those things didn't fill the gouged out spaces inside, and as I gave that thought some area to stretch out in, I understood what was missing.

With a sigh, I shoved myself off the bed and strode from the apartment, a resigned and almost sinking dread clotting my stomach. Traffic hummed along the streets as I stepped outside, carrying home those who worked the day shift. The streetlights started to blink on. Though filled with the exhaust of all those cars, the air was also brisk and satisfying. This wasn't Fae. This was home. Blade-less, yes, but home.

I found my motorcycle where I'd parked it, covered in bird shit, but more or less as I'd left it. A gruff chuckle fled my throat. Some things didn't change.

Once I'd pulled on my helmet and clipped it locked beneath my chin, I straddled the bike. It started instantly, purring to life with a soft roar. After engaging the clutch, I let the bike have its head.

It found the shortcut to Kit's house without hesitation. I supposed I'd always known that's where I'd go. A tingle moved over the back of my neck in a deja vu that was not welcome but familiar. Like a compulsive tic that's impossible to give up. Flowers lined the walkway in all colors and nestled into a bedding of catnip. Kit's spoiled cat, Ashes, rolled around in a euphoric daze.

That was the moment I realized what was missing. The reason I'd let my bike wind through the streets to a familiar abode that cut through my viscera as much as it tugged on it with an insatiable urge.

The truth was, I'd come for the same reason I pulled out my cellphone after every kill and tapped in her number. It was the reason I listened to her breath and invited her righteous anger to filter through my ears into my heart. The act was like picking at a scab, like poking a sore tooth with your tongue.

Now, standing in that driveway was very much like pressing a cell phone to my ear. All the memories swept over me so fast, so hard, I thought I would buckle under the torrent and be ripped out to sea along with them. This was why I'd come. Self-flagellation. Punishing myself for all those things I'd done to her. I deserved it all. No matter how many monsters I killed. No matter how many poor addicts I saved from their dealers. No matter how many nights I took a lover and refused to let myself feel intimate and whole beneath their bodies.

It was all for Kit. And my parents. And a life I'd robbed myself of all those years ago when I paused at the brink of choice and still hurried on ahead.

In my mind, I saw myself sitting on my bike's seat in the cul de sac of Lilah's property. The engine purred beneath me, a soft, grumbling roar of victory after a hard fight. I felt again the hollowness of that victory, the sense that something wasn't quite right no matter how many baddies I killed, no matter how brutal the battle that left me standing after it all. Kit had abandoned me, the same as my parents had. And both of those were my own damn fault.

I remembered tapping her number into my cell and listening to her breath for the few seconds she let me hear it. My eyes squeezed closed at the curse she'd spat into the wires. The empty click of her ending the call. Just like she always did.

The breath I dragged in recalling it and the images of her on her knees begging for my life...that breath felt too tight. It whistled in through a clogged straw, trying in vain to fill my lungs. I let it sweep over me and remind me why this was such a mistake. Like it always was.

And then the cat yowled at my feet. Her soft body curled around my ankles. Ashes. A perfect name, now that I thought about it, and not just because she was the color of soot. She was the feline me. The Ashe Kit could love who would always come home to her. Distant as all cats could be, but one she who came home every night.

I stooped to ran a palm over Ashes grey coat, but before I could scratch the soot-colored spot behind her ears, a door fly open behind me with a bang, halting my hand.

My head snapped up. I'd lingered too long. I caught my breath. Took a step back. If I gave any thought to swinging around and fleeing, the inclination was slammed out of me as Kit struck me full on, chest to chest, belly to belly. She threw her arms around me in a hug so tight the wind fled my lungs.

"Ava," she said in a husky voice. "Oh, Ava, Ava, Ava."

For a second, I didn't know what to do. I was frozen there in her embrace. Shock, I realized. I'd not hugged my sister for more than a decade. I wasn't sure if I would even remember how.

Then, my arms crept around her waist and she was squeezing me even tighter. I didn't bother to fight the sting that burned the backs of my eyelids. I fought and failed to find words and ease them through a tight tight.

"You're home," she said in a rush, filling the silence expertly. "We have so much to talk about. I have so many apologies to make."

She pulled away and searched my face, her own lit by the glow of the streetlamps and her porch light. I thought I saw hesitation there, worry.

"You have to forgive me, Ava," she said. "I've been a fool."

I caught sight of Flint behind her, arms crossed as he stood on the porch watching us. He didn't glower, but he was examining me, probably waiting for me to find some way to hurt her, the way I always did.

But that wasn't going to happen. I dragged my eyes from his face to hers and found the words, finally. "I'm the one who needs forgiveness," I said in a hoarse voice, my throat so tight I could barely squeeze the words through. "All these years, the things I've done—"

"Stop," she said in that older sister, matronly tone she had. "If ever there was a time you need to listen to me, it's now. The things you've done? Don't even." She sliced the air with her hand. "I know what they are and what it makes you. Not an addict. Not a shitty sister. You're a hero, Ava." She caught on her lip with her teeth as her breath hitched. "You're a goddamned bonafide hero."

She dragged me into the house, then, fed me. We laughed. We drank. We reconnected, at first, clumsily, sticking to topics that were safe. But then, it grew easier. She smiled when she looked at me. She told me things about her life. I felt a weight lift.

And when at last, the night crept on us and I began to feel the new weight of exhaustion, I begged my leave and gained a promise of weekly dinner dates and shopping excursions. We'd plant flowers together and talk of our love lives.

I knew most of it would never happen, but I let her indulge herself. It felt good to see her smile. It felt good to be included. Then I left. I was more than ready to fall into my bed and a comatose sleep that I prayed would not feed me images of the fae I'd left behind.

The drive to my own apartment felt like I was flying, and I realized that magic did exist in the human realm. If you knew where to look. If you knew how to recognize it.

And yet, light as I felt, with a renewed sense of purpose and peace, I knew there was one hole I wouldn't be able to fill. I thought of Blade as I parked the cycle and took off my helmet.

I tried to convince myself that he'd come for me some time in the future, like he'd come for me in the catacombs. Like he'd come for me in the veil. But one thought nagged me, a tic burrowing into tender flesh. The question of time. While it passed in his realm, how much would pass in mine? When he came for me, would I still be the same Ava? Would I still be young enough to be his match in every way?

I couldn't know the answer to those things, and I couldn't do anything about the answers even if I did work it through. So with a heaving sigh, I trod the steps to the front entrance and buzzed myself in. I lived on the third floor and took the steps as a matter of habit. This time, I was too exhausted to do so. The elevator was it for this chick. Then a bath. Then I'd fall naked between the sheets and sleep till the apocalypse...which with my luck would no doubt fire off in the next twenty-four hours.

Understandably, the foyer was empty. My neighbors weren't night owls and the clock in the foyer read two AM. My feet were dragging as I hit the elevator button. I sagged against the wall of the cabin until it dinged my floor.

Shuffling out into the hallway, I aimed my feet toward the lock box at the door and typed in my code. Because I never knew when or what state I'd be in when I returned home from a hunt, I didn't carry my key with me. I found it inside with the shot of tequila I usually left there for the times I'd had a really rough day.

It was full, of course. My mouth watered at the sight of it, and I had to plant my palm against the wall as the distinct tang of memory carried with it the taste of BloodMist. I sighed as I looked the shot glass over. Examined how I felt.

To my surprise, I didn't feel the craving for the drug at all. A smile tugged at my mouth, a tired one, but one that felt good. I'd helped take out a powerful fae. I'd survived the catacombs. I'd gathered the bonds of sisterhood. I didn't need the BloodMist.

I would be ok.

So, with a steady hand, I pulled the glass from the box and shot it back. It tasted smoky and caramelized. The heat of it spread to the back of my throat, catching my wind for an instant, and I let my lungs stutter before relaxing and taking a long gust of air through pursed lips.

I was about to put the glass back when a sound from beyond the door made my spine go rigid. Unlike Kit, I didn't have a cat to keep me company. The only thing I owned that purred was my motorcycle. That noise meant someone was inside my apartment.

Canting my head to the side to listen better, I slid the glass as silently as I could back into the box and extracted the key. Fitting it into the lock was going to be difficult. It was a rattling thing that required a good shake at just the right moment to free the mechanism.

An action that would have to be timed just right if I was going to be able to either overpower the intruder or avoid him. An action that had to happen now or never.

It took precision and speed, but the door flew open like a boss, leaving me with the realization that it had been forced so slickly I'd not noticed the mechanism was broken. I stood inside with my feet hip width apart, bracing for impact, my hands ready to strike or defend, key a spike between my fingers that I could stab out with if I had to.

The heady waft of floral perfume breezed back at me with the backdraft. I blinked stupidly at the sight of an apartment filled with flowers, all of them standing alone, in full bloom without support or a vase or water of any kind. So many that they took up most of the living room. Petals of every sort dusted the floor, leading my eye to the shadow moving ever so slightly at the corner of the room. A person sized shadow, hulking and broad.

As the shade bled over the nearest stand of roses, I ducked fast. Instinct and training overwhelming everything except the brief notice that the roses that succumbed to the darkness were yellow.

In a habitual, long-engrained defensive maneuver, I rolled out of my crouch and into the same position behind the sofa. Time ticked off in stuttered heartbeats as I tried to assess the threat by breath and sound alone.

"Mica wanted you to have them," a familiar voice said.

I froze. Blinked twice as I floundered through the confusion. My chest squeezed. My heart pounded.

Then I wasn't crouched behind my sofa. I was leaping over it, pin-wheeling to catch my balance as I bolted through the flowers, brushing them aside, to where that shadow waited.

Blade caught me as though he was wrangling a hurricane, and maybe he was. He gathered me into his arms without losing an inch of ground, even though I struck him full force.

"You're here," I said.

His hand ran over my hair, tugging at the very bottom. "I'm here, Ponytail" he said in a soft voice. "I told you. As long as I have breath, I'll find you. This wasn't the coals of hell but getting here might as well have been." His smile was mournful even though his eyes sparked with humor.

I ran worried fingers over his face, his shoulders, his back. "Are you alright?"

He kissed the tip of my nose. "I'm fine. Tested, trialed, and tuned."

"Fae?" I asked. "Or a piano keyboard?"

His sigh-like chuckle moved my hair. "High fae, apparently. The hellhound shifter is no more. But Mica's magic, and that of the fae was able to fill me and salvage what was there into something akin to whole." A playful smirk curved his lips. "Are you disappointed? Will you miss the beast?"

I shook my head. "I wouldn't care if you were human," I said. "So long as you breathed."

"Well, that I do," he said.

I tilted my head at him, remembering the things I knew, things I couldn't forget.

"You could have taken the Iron Throne," I said. "You could have taken the Stygian Darkness. You are a king, twice over." My fingers began roaming his chest, testing to be sure he was really there. "But you didn't."

His answer was to scoop me into his arms. "I'm not king material, Alathir. I'm a terrible, violent fae who would reign with a terrible, violent command."

My arms found anchor around his neck. I nuzzled into his chest, his scent enfolding me as tightly as his arms. "But Mica won't."

He shook his head, dropping his mouth to the corner of mine as he strode toward my bedroom as though he knew exactly where it was. "Mica will not. And Fae needs that."

He lowered me onto the bed, for he had indeed known the path to my bedroom, had probably scanned my entire apartment while he waited for me. His straddling of my waist with his powerful thighs felt like scaffolding.

I squirmed beneath him, my hands moving over his neck and back, trying to scrape aside the shirt he wore. With a gentle movement, he held my wrists aside, his eyebrows arched.

"I have something else for you," he said in rasp. "But if you keep doing that I'm not going to be able to show you what it is."

"Unless it's your naked body pressed against mine," I said, running my palm down his bare chest to his belly button where it lingered long enough to feel the thrum of his heartbeat, "then it can wait."

He curled down over my hand to nip my neck with his teeth. He chuckled against my skin. "Oh, don't worry, Ponytail," he said in a throaty voice. "I'll be doing more than pressing my naked body against yours." He inhaled deeply, shuddered, and his desire was so palpable it scored the air with prickly heat. "The things I'm going to do to you will be from one monster to another, testing ourselves. Testing this link between us that tugs on the deepest part of my soul and makes it ache like the devil's own balls. Those things I do to you will make you want to belong to me and now one else."

He lifted his head to look deeply into my face. I thought for a second, he could see beyond my eyes to the brash teen who hesitated just one moment before pressing forward, and all I could think in the face of that nakedness was that he was here. With me. I hardly dared hope it meant he would be staying.

"I am yours, Alathir. For as long as I draw breath and beyond when I go to my own mossy forest, nothing more than a whisper on the wind."

He reached behind his back to hook my hands and then laid them flat against the mattress, pinning my wrists with his knees to the bed. Then he dragged his palm along my skin from the base of my earlobe to the middle of my sternum, braising the edges of my breasts with the broad touch of his hand as it scraped away my shirt. The buttons popped free as if by magic with each inch he gained toward my belly. The panels sagged to the sides as my belly exposed itself to the air, to his gaze, his touch. Hunger crested his expression and held itself there, poised like a deer about to bolt. My belly quivered beneath his fingers.

"Do it," I said, not sure what I expected of him, just wanted something to crack through the electricity in the room that lifted each hair. His smile was slow and knowing. Then, with a flourish, he pulled something from the air at his shoulder. A filmy thing that looked like it was unraveling from a spool, slid into view from an invisible slit.

I gasped. Erachne's gown.

"But how?" I asked, my fingers unable to resist whispering along the material as I pulled it from the air to drape over my chest. "It was lost in the veil."

"It's not the same one," he rasped. "This one is different."

"Different how?" I asked, but even as I spoke, the differences became evident. This one was white, as though the silver of the gossamer had been bleached. Small pearls studded it, giving it a weight that made it hang in perfect folds between us.

He gave it a shake and the dress became a pair of soft-looking leather pants, the pearls turned to embroidery that seemed to give the supple hide shadows that moved with each waver of the garment. He shook it again and it became a soft-looking sweater with pockets both inside and out. Another shake and it was the leather pants again.

A moan of awe escaped me. I reached out to touch the embroidery and he chuckled. "You see the difference," he said. "Not a wedding gown like the other. But just as special. It's made for one woman. The only one who has the courage and grit to mate with the likes of a hellhound turned high fae, a vicious bastard with no real home. Those pearls will offer you protection when you hunt, when I can't be there to be your blade in the thick of danger. Made for someone who protects the innocent..."

"Someone who kills monsters," I breathed.

"But not this monster," he said as he lowered his mouth to mine.

And if there was a protest about what sort of creature or monster he might be, it was lost in his delirious kiss. And the ache that had been inside me since the moment I'd come home, dissolved along with it.

-the end-

Dearest Reader:

I can't thank you enough for going on this journey with me. At times, I felt like I couldn't nail down all the threads weaving their way through my head. I had notebooks filled with plot points and thoughts and even with them all, the story somehow went where it wanted.

I hope it was a good ride for you, though, and that you'll keep Ava and Blade in your thoughts. I'm sure they'll be fine, but you never know. wink.

It's Stone and Ruby that have my mind right now. And the things Blade did in that ballroom when Ava was dying haunts me in the most delicious ways. Maybe I'll pen a scene to exorcise that storyline from my psyche. I wonder if you'd enjoy that. I'll be polling my readers' group to see if it's a nice little exclusive bonus they might enjoy reading.

You can get in on that when you **join us**

While you wait for that exclusive goodie, you might want to slip into the skin of another strong-willed chick. Stone Magic introduces you to Brie Duncan, a fraud psychic medium who just discovered a black magic coven is killing witches in her area and she might be next.

And if you're wondering more about Maddox and the Shadow Bazaar that you heard about at the start of the journey, you can **slip into that world with Rune Thief.** He's an immortal warrior and she's strong-willed but the story is very different.

AUTHOR THANKS

A very special thanks goes out to Julie Pederick for all the insights to Fae and the individual fae-folk that helped me shape the storyline. Her excitement as she read and the notes she sent me will be in my file of cherished messages that I read every now and then to keep reminding me to never give up. Thanks, Julie. Ruby Morvannon of the Nocturnes hopes her death pleased you.

Other readers simply cannot be replaced. Debra L Martin, a fellow author of fantasy always alpha reads for me and keeps me honest. Caroline Jenkins, Evelyn Dotson, Kerry Taylor-Gorman, and Denise Sherman find all the oopsies that creep in. You ladies save my 'face' each book launch.

Then there's readers like Crystal Amason, the first real reader I gained in this journey, who has been with me since Witches of Etlantium, and who I am so grateful still reads me. I always reserve a special thanks for her because she believed in me first.

To those patrons who prefer to remain anonymous, I thank you. You know who you are.

I really appreciate you all.

-thea-

MORE BY THEA

What are you missing?

By Series

THE IRON KING'S ASSASSIN

ISABELLA HUSH SERIES

COUNTERFEIT PSYCHIC

WITCHES OF ETLANTUM

VAMPIRE ADDICTIONS

REAPERS REDEMPTION

GRAVES FILES

ROGUE HUNTRESS

THETA WAVES

QUEEN OF SKY AND SHADOW

Hale Saint

Mainstream and Stand-alones

One Insular Tahiti

Anomaly

Secret Language of Crows

Throwing Clay Shadows